LAND OF FRIGHT™

Collection VII

JACK O'DONNELL

Welcome to Land of Fright™!

Land of Fright™ is a world of spine-tingling short horror stories filled with the strange, the eerie, and the weird. The **Land of Fright**™ tales encompass the vast expanse of time and space. In the **Land of Fright**™ series of books you will visit the world of the Past in Ancient Rome, Medieval England, the old West, World War II, and other eras yet to be explored. You will find many tales that exist right here in the Present, tales filled with modern lives that have taken a turn down a darker path. You will travel into the Future to tour strange new worlds and interact with alien societies, or to just take a disturbing peek at what tomorrow may bring.

Each **Land of Fright**™ story exists in its own territory (which we like to call a **terrorstory**.) Some of the story realms you visit will intrigue you. Some of them may unsettle you. Some of them may even titillate and amuse you. We hope many of them will give you delicious chills along your journey as you enter a haunted castle, visit an eerie wax museum, shop at a strange garage sale, take a tour of an Indian slum, and visit many more odd places.

First, we need to check your ID. **Land of Fright**™ is intended for mature audiences. You will experience adult language, graphic violence, and some explicit sex. Ready to enter? Good. We'll take that ticket now. **Land of Fright**™ awaits. You can pass through the dark gates and—Step Into Fear!

Readers Love Land of Fright™!

"This is the first story I've read by this author and it blew me away! A gripping tale that kept me wondering until the end. Images from this will, I fear, haunt me at unexpected moments for many months to come. Readers, be warned! :)" – Amazon review for **Dung Beetles (Land of Fright™ #27 – in Collection III)**

"Some truly original stories. At last, a great collection of unique and different stories. Whilst this is billed as horror, the author managed to steer away from senseless violence and gratuitous gore and instead with artful story telling inspires you to use your own imagination. A great collection. Already looking for other collections… especially loved Kill the Queen (God Save the Queen)." – Amazon UK review for **Land of Fright™ Collection I**

"This was a great story. Even though it was short I still connected with the main character and was rooting for her. Once I read the twist I cheered her on. This was an enjoyable short story." – Amazon review for **Snowflakes (Land of Fright™ #3 – in Collection I)**

"Love the freaky tales from the Land of Fright. This one is particularly nasty and dark. A tale of double revenge unfolds in a graveyard where a perceived business betrayal causes the perceiver to enact an insidious plan to impose the ultimate suffering on his partner. The suffering takes an unexpected turn that I did not see coming." – Amazon review for **Cemetery Dance (Land of Fright™ #49 – in Collection V)**

"I absolutely loved the heck out of this story. The whole story was bizarre, and the end? Well, it was perfect!" – Amazon review for **The Throw-Aways (Land of Fright™ #31 – in Collection IV)**

"Perfect bite size weirdness. Land of Fright does it again with this Zone like short that has two creative plot twists that really caught me off guard. I know comparing this type of work to the Twilight Zone is overdone but it really is a high compliment that denotes original, well conceived and delightfully weird short fiction. Recommended." – Amazon review for **Flipbook (Land of Fright™ #19 – in Collection II)**

"An enjoyable story; refreshingly told from the point of view of the cat...definitely good suspense." – Amazon review for **Pharaoh's Cat (Land of Fright™ #30 – in Collection III)**

"A fun thrill-ride into the Mexican jungle, and another great Land of Fright tale. Not enough people have written horror stories or novels about Aztec sacrifices." -Amazon review for **Virgin Sacrifice (Land of Fright™ #42 – in Collection V)**

"This short has a cool premise and was very effective at quickly transporting me to the sands of the coliseum in ancient Rome. The images of dead and dying gladiators are detailed and vivid. There is a malevolent force that very much likes its job and is not about to give it up, ever. Recommended." – Amazon review for **Hammer of Charon (Land of Fright™ #29 - in Collection III)**

"The thing I like about the Land of Fright series of short stories is that they are so diverse yet share a common weird, unusual and original vibe. From horror to science fiction they are all powerful despite of their brevity. Another great addition to the Land of Fright festival of the odd." - Amazon review for **Snowflakes (Land of Fright™ #3 – in Collection I)**

DEDICATION

To everyone who still likes adventuring into the weird world of Land of Fright™ with me!

LAND OF FRIGHT^{TM}
COLLECTION VII
CONTENTS

TERRORSTORY #61
GARAGE SALE SECRETS

It was a copy of True Life Detective Tales magazine. Mike Klint didn't know why he felt the sudden urge to buy it, but he did. No one he knew even read physical books anymore, let alone magazines. Everything they read came from the web, and most of what they read came from their phones or their little tablets. Maybe it was the salacious photographs on the cover of the magazine that drew his gaze. One of the photos in particular demanded his attention. There was a woman dressed in ripped lingerie, her large breasts just about to fall out of the fabric, her nipples just barely hidden beneath the gauzy clothing. He read the title that was emblazoned across her breasts. *"I Stripped Her and Made Love to Her - After I Killed Her."*

"That's a good one," the old lady said. She was sitting behind a rickety folding table in the back of her garage, lording over her garage sale. She had thinning gray hair, her face entirely coated in layers of wrinkles that only seven or eight decades could have painted onto her flesh. The garage was full of old clothes piled in heaps, ancient plates, thick fake crystal goblets, cracked and chipped angel statues, old beat-up toys, leftover electronics that absolutely no one would have any use for, cardboard boxes full of old paperbacks and hardcover books, plastic bins full of old VHS tapes. The old woman glanced at the magazine Mike held in his hand. "Lots of good stories in that one. All true. Twenty-five cents."

Mike glanced down at the magazine. Hell, it was only a quarter. What the hell could you even get for a quarter these days? One piece of caramel, maybe? Not even. The magazine itself was in pretty decent shape despite its age; the edges were a bit worn and the pages a bit wrinkled, but the cover was still vibrant and glossy. He gave the coin he tugged out of the pocket of his jeans to the old lady sitting behind the folding table.

She took the quarter and plopped it into the old beat-up tackle box she was using for her till. "Good stories," she repeated, nodding her head. "All true."

Mike grunted at her. He rolled up the magazine into a tight cylinder and shoved it into the back pocket of his jeans. It would make good toilet reading at the very least. A little titillation while dropping a turd never hurt anybody, right? He continued rummaging through the garage sale, fingering knick-knacks, picking up trinkets, glancing at old audio cassette tapes, scanning the titles of well-worn books, but he didn't find anything else that interested him.

"Have a nice life," the old woman said as he left the garage.

Mike hesitated, then turned back to glance at her. "You too," he said reflexively.

She nodded. "I already have. I already have." Her body rocked slightly back and forth in the metal folding chair she sat in, moving as if she was sitting in a rocking chair, but she wasn't.

Mike turned away and headed back to his car, the rolled up magazine that was about to change his life forever jutting out from the back pocket of his jeans.

Mike cracked open a beer, took a drink, and settled into his oversized chair. The brown fabric on the chair was starting to get a little worn, but he was nowhere close to feeling the need to replace it with a new one. It was way too comfortable just the way it was; over a decade of use had molded it perfectly to his body. Several bookshelves lined the walls near his chair, reaching from the floor to just a few feet below the ceiling, every shelf completely filled with books of all types, fiction, non-fiction, history, biographies, books of all manner of sizes and bindings. "Alexa, turn my reading light on."

"Okay," Alexa replied in her mechanical, but still somewhat sexy, female voice, and the pale smart bulb situated in a standing floor lamp illuminated the small side table, casting just enough light for him to be able to read comfortably.

His dog, Ranger, padded over to him and nuzzled his hand affectionately. "Hey, buddy," Mike said, his voice full of as much affection as the dog's snout demanding some love and attention showed in its snuggling motion. He scratched Ranger behind the ears and patted his head. He had picked up Ranger at a shelter five years ago after his wife left him. He wasn't sure what kind of dog Ranger was, some mix of collie and shepherd he supposed, but it didn't matter to him one whit. All it took was one look at the dog's excited face as he approached the cage, one frantic wave of tail wagging, and that was it. He knew he had found a friend.

Satisfied with his master's reaction, Ranger curled up at Mike's feet and sat quietly.

Mike glanced over at the copy of True Life Detective Tales magazine and read the cover blurbs on the front of the magazine. *"Evil Stepfather Abuses Possessed Stepdaughter." "Killer Confesses: I'll Show You Where I Buried The Bodies."* The next one made him smile. *"She Saw Her Mother and Brother Mutilated by Sex Aliens."* He always loved shit about aliens. And sex aliens? What the fuck was a sex alien? He would definitely need to read that one. *"Why I Chopped My Husband's Head Off."* He finished reading the titles then brought his gaze back to the terrified woman pictured for the main story *"I Stripped Her and Made Love to Her - After I Killed Her."* Behind her screaming mouth and the agony-contorted features on her face, she was really quite a pretty blonde.

Then he noticed a smaller inset on the bottom right of the cover. The text was much smaller than the main headlines. It was a pretty innocuous caption, even a bit boring. But when he read the caption again and saw the picture that accompanied it, he felt a chill shooting up his spine. Not just racing, but shooting up along the ridges of his vertebrae with the velocity of a bullet bursting out of the barrel of a gun. It was really the small picture that accompanied this small headline that set off the sudden and powerful sense of fear and dread that rushed over his flesh. The picture was a bit grainy, but he still recognized the woman in the picture. He read the caption again. *"Body of lost woman found."*

He snatched the magazine off the side table and flipped to the table of contents. He was going to save the magazine for a bathroom read, but the quickening beat of his heart and the tightening of every muscle in his body was impossible to ignore or deny. He quickly found the story of the lost woman's body being found listed in the table of contents, then flipped through the pages. His fingers were trembling so badly that it took him a few tries of fumbling through the pages to find page thirty-five. He didn't stop reading until he finished the entire story, never stopping to even take the second drink from the can of beer he had opened earlier.

Ranger shifted his position, looking up curiously at Mike, but the dog remained curled down at his master's feet. He lowered his head back down, resting it on his paws.

Mike read the story again, going slower this time,

absorbing the entire thing.

It was a story about him. About what he had done twenty five years ago. His hands shook. Who could possibly know all this? There were things in the story only he knew about. He glanced up, his face filled with fear of the imminent arrival of law enforcement, dreading the wailing sound of a police siren as its screeching scream raced closer, expecting the thumping sound of clenched fists pounding incessantly at his door at any moment.

Ranger raised his head back up and barked at Mike. Startled by his dog's cry of alarm, Mike nearly wet himself.

The last twenty-five years of Mike's life vanished in an instant. In his mind, he was thirty years old again. And he was scared to death.

Mike shook the rolled up magazine at the old woman, waving it like a cop's night stick as he stormed into the garage and approached her. His sneakered feet made loud slapping noises as he pounded across the cement garage floor. "Where the fuck did you get this?"

The old woman frowned deeply at him, shaking her head disapprovingly. "I don't tolerate that kind of language on my property, young man."

"Young man?" He laughed. He reached the edge of the table she sat behind and thrust his face closer to her. "Do I look like a young man to you?"

She cocked her head at him, making an exaggerated emphasis of studying his face. "Yes. Yes, you do." She was sitting behind her folding table in the back of her garage, looking as if she had not moved from that spot since the last time he had seen her. She was still wearing the same plain white dress he had seen her clothed in earlier.

Mike wondered if she was actually part of the chair. Did she even have legs? He couldn't see them because an old tablecloth covered the table, the faded green fabric dangling down over the front to pool up in a pile of folds on the garage floor, keeping whatever was under and behind the table hidden from view. His jaw clenched tighter. He thrust the rolled up magazine towards the old woman. "Where did you get this?"

The old woman shrugged her dainty shoulders. "Here and there. Things just come to me and I put them up for sale."

Mike frowned. "Things just come to you? What the hell does that mean?"

She remained silent.

He squeezed his left hand into a fist, then slowly unclenched his fingers. "What does that mean?"

"They just... show up." She waved her hand around, indicating the interior of her garage. "They just show up." She pointed to a plastic bin filled with DVDs on a small table nearby, several DVD discs resting askew beside it. "See that? That wasn't here yesterday. Now it is. It just showed up." She gave another slight shrug.

He looked at the table, at the bin filled with DVDs, staring at the scattered pile of silver discs for a moment. He turned back to the old woman. "Those just showed up?"

She nodded. "They weren't here yesterday."

Mike frowned at her. "You realize that doesn't

make any sense, right?"

She laughed. "Oh, I know. I stopped trying to figure it out years ago. It just happens." She rocked back and forth ever so slightly in her chair that wasn't a rocking chair.

He turned back to look at the DVDs. Were those there yesterday? Hell, he couldn't remember. The old woman had so much shit laying around in her cluttered garage that it was impossible to recall all of it.

"Don't worry, someone will come round to buy them," the old woman said with an air of increasing boredom in her tone. "They always do." The old woman glanced away from him. "Now, if you'll excuse me, I have another customer."

Mike frowned at the old woman. He looked over his shoulder to see a figure entering the shadowed garage. For a moment, he couldn't make out who the person was because the bright sun burning hotly behind this new visitor made it impossible to discern any features. But in a matter of seconds he could make out the shape of a woman as she exited the bright sunlight and entered the murky depths of the much dimmer garage. She looked to be in her forties, maybe early fifties, but he knew he sucked at guessing people's ages so he didn't give it much effort. She was overweight by a good twenty pounds, her midsection bulging under her blouse. She had a decent enough face, her cheeks a little chubby with fat. She wore plastic-rimmed tortoise shell glasses. There was a curious look on her face, as if she was looking for something, but not sure exactly what she wanted.

Mike moved away from the old woman, pretending to be interested in a box of old plastic toy soldiers that was sitting on a table nearby filled with various old toys and items for kids, but kept the corner of his eye on the new visitor.

"You like movies? You look like you like to curl up by yourself on the couch and watch movies." The old woman grinned slyly at her. "Well, not all the time by yourself, right?"

Shannon Donnelly looked curiously at the old woman.

The old woman pointed to a plastic bin filled with DVDs. "Ten bucks for the whole lot," she said. "I'll bet you get ten times the entertainment value for that." She opened and closed her wrinkled hand twice, splaying out her aged digits as she did so.

Shannon eased her way over to the bin and glanced inside. There were movies from the 80s, the 90s, some TV shows, and even some more current hits from the 2000s and up, plus a select few from the past decade. She fingered a few of the DVD cases. They appeared to be in decent condition. She looked at the old woman. "How many movies are in here?"

"Oh, I'm not sure. I never counted them." She pointed to the scattered pile of loose DVD discs near the bin. "Those, too. They're all included."

Shannon glanced into the bin again. It looked like there were at least forty or fifty DVDs in the bin. "Hell," she said. "I don't know if my DVD player even works anymore. I usually just binge something on Netflix or Hulu. I haven't bought a DVD in years. Heck, I haven't even rented one."

"Oh, it works," the old woman said. She rocked

gently back and forth.

Shannon squinted her eyes at the old woman, eyeing her curiously, then just dismissed her odd statement. The woman clearly just wanted to get rid of them all. She would say anything to sell them. Ten bucks for about fifty movies and TV shows. That was a sweet deal. Even if she only watched a few of them, it would be worth it. She fished ten bucks out of her purse and handed the bill to the old woman.

Mike watched the woman leave the garage with a bin full of DVDs. He turned to look back over at the old woman. She rocked gently in her chair, paying him no heed.

"What happens now?" Mike asked, waving the magazine he still clutched in his hand at the old woman.

She shrugged.

Mike frowned. "Nothing? That's it?"

She shrugged again. "It's for you. What you do with it, is up to you."

Mike's frown deepened. "What am I supposed to do? Turn myself in?"

She frowned at him, cocking her head ever so slightly. "Turn yourself in for what? You do something wrong?"

He waved the magazine again at her. "You didn't read it? You don't know what's in here?"

She shook her head. "I just sell the stuff." She glanced around the garage. "You think I have time to go through all this shit?"

He paused for just a second at her use of vulgarity,

but he had no intention of calling her out on it. "You really don't know what's in here?" He again waved the magazine at her.

She shook her head. "I really don't."

He looked back out of the garage to see the woman putting the bin of DVDs into the trunk of her car. He looked back to the old woman sitting behind the folding table and saw the hint of a smile, just the barest of hints, just the barest of upturning lips quirking up into what he could only describe as a devilishly sly grin.

He gripped the rolled up magazine tightly in his hand and moved quickly out of the garage, hurrying towards his car.

Shannon rummaged through the bin of DVDs, looking for something that struck her fancy, but nothing was leaping out at her. There were a few old Tom Cruise movies, some vampire movies, some romantic comedies, a few TV shows from the 70's, some Adam Sandler movies. What the hell had she bought them for? She was already having buyer's remorse. She would probably never even watch any of them.

She noticed one DVD case that didn't have a cover insert in place. It was just a blank black DVD case. She looked at it curiously. She grabbed the blank DVD case and lifted it out of the box. She opened it up to find a DVD inside. And then dropped the case as if it had suddenly turned into a lit match, raising her hands up high to get her fingers as quickly away from the case as possible. The disc popped out of the case as the hard plastic hit the floor, and the shiny silver DVD rolled along the tile for a moment, before wobbling and then falling flat, face-up on the floor. She stared with horror at the words scribbled onto the disk in black permanent marker. It was just two words. Two words. A first name and a last name. But they filled her with such fear that she could only stare motionless at them with her hand over her mouth. Two simple words. Thomas Cavendish. One of her former students. Tommy.

She stared at the disc for a long moment, not sure what to do. Memories of Tommy came flooding into her head. His sweetly innocent, but knowingly crafty smile. His piercing blue eyes. That strong handsome face. It was so long ago. A lifetime ago. Over twenty years now. Where had the disc come from? What could possibly be on it? She didn't remember recording any of their... encounters. Had someone secretly taped them?

She knew she should just smash the disc or burn it or shred it, but she also knew that she had to see what was on it. Her heart pounded in her chest. She just had to know. She frowned deeply at the disc. Where the hell had it come from?

Outside Shannon's home, keenly observant eyes watched her through a crack in the window blinds as she picked the DVD up of the floor with trembling fingers. She moved towards the big screen TV that dominated the living room.

The first thing Shannon noticed was that she was about forty pounds lighter in the DVD. Damn, she used to have a tight, lithe body. She glanced down at her chubby midsection, then back up at the screen. The second thing she noticed was Tommy undressing in front of her. He had only been sixteen at the time, but he had been wise beyond his years. There had been a maturity about him that had drawn her to him. He made her feel less alone than any other man ever had before. Or since.

From the angle of the activity being filmed, she surmised the camera was positioned on a dresser to the side of the bed, looking slightly up from the bottom corner area of the bed. She didn't recall them ever taping their... She paused to think of a polite word, as if someone was listening in on her thoughts. Trysts. Love-making. She mentally derided herself. Their fuck fests. That's what they really were. Fuck fests. They spent hours fucking. Tommy had the stamina of a stallion in heat. She remembered him staying hard for hours, making her come again and again and again.

She stood in front of the big TV, too mesmerized to even move. Tommy was naked on the screen now, his cock long and hard. He was always so damn hard, she remembered. She felt a familiar stirring within her. God, she missed him. She missed his smile, his hands touching her, his body pressed tight against hers. She glanced down at her own body, startled but not surprised to find one of her hands pressing against her skirt, pushing the fabric of her panties up tight against her womanhood. Womanhood, hah. She was touching her pussy. She was fingering her own goddamned cunt. She was staring with lust at

Tommy's rock-hard cock and fingering her fucking cunt.

Outside, the keenly observant eyes continued to watch Shannon through the crack in the window blinds, the eyes growing slightly wider as Shannon continued to touch herself with greater and greater enthusiasm.

But then Shannon remembered what happened to Tommy and she felt a bitter wave of disgust surge up in her throat. She was disgusted by her own wanton behavior. She took her hand away from her crotch and looked away from the screen. A hot flood of tears seemed to come out of nowhere and the warm, salty liquid stained her cheeks with rivulets of an old sadness.

A loud pounding at the door jarred her.

Who the fuck was that? She quickly composed herself, angrily wiping at the tears on her cheeks, pushing the salty residue away from her lips. She fumbled with the TV remote and turned the power off.

The pounding at the door continued.

For a brief moment, she thought of just ignoring it. Who the hell would be pounding at her door on a Sunday afternoon? Jehovah's Witnesses? Girl Scouts? No, they wouldn't be so insistent. But then a voice called out and she knew she couldn't ignore this intrusion any longer.

"Hey, open up," a male voice said. "I need to talk

to you. I saw you at that garage sale. I need to talk to you."

She moved hesitantly closer to the door.

The voice was insistent, and there was a tone of desperation clearly apparent in the man's voice. The pounding at the door intensified. "Open up! I need to talk to you!"

"Go away!" Shannon shouted back. "I'll call the police."

"No, you won't," the man said immediately. "I saw you get that bin of DVDs from the garage sale. I know there's something on there, something from your past that you're hoping no one ever finds out about."

Shannon felt a tightness in her chest, felt her throat clamping shut. She moved to the door and started to reach for the lock, but hesitated. What the hell was she doing? Unlocking the door for a strange man who was demanding to talk to her? Was she crazy? She felt her heart pounding against her chest.

"I know you did something..." the man said from behind the door. His voice trailed off, but then he continued with one more word. "Bad," he said. "Didn't you? You did something bad in your past." He paused, but only for a short moment. "I did, too. We need to talk."

Shannon reached for the lock.

"How do you know that old woman?" Mike asked. He was sitting on a chair near the couch where Shannon was now sitting. The big TV screen was dark behind them, its rectangular screen reflecting their images back at them.

"I don't," Shannon said, giving a soft shake of her head. "I don't know her."

"Why did you go to her garage sale?"

She shrugged. "I was just driving around and saw it."

"It pulled you to it," Mike said.

Shannon frowned at him.

"It drew you there. It pulled you in like a magnet." It had been like a siren call for him. He remembered what he had felt driving when he had first seen the sign. He felt an almost irresistible urge to go to the address scribbled on the crude handmade garage sale sign. Almost? Hell, not almost. It *was* irresistible. It had compelled him to visit that old woman and her insane garage sale.

"No, it didn't," Shannon said.

Mike waved his hand. She was lying, but he wasn't going to press it. "Okay, never mind." He pointed to the big dark TV screen. "What else is on that DVD?"

Her answer came quick, short and curt. "None of your damn business."

He pulled out the magazine and showed her the copy of True Life Detective Tales. "I bought this from her yesterday. It has a story in it. A story about me." He paused. "About what... I did... a long time ago. I bought it for a goddamned quarter and it's fucking with my head a million ways to Sunday."

Shannon looked at him with a noticeable increase in her nervousness. "What did you do?"

He waved his hand. "It doesn't matter. It was a long time ago. I've paid my penance." He looked at Shannon. "What matters is how that fucking old woman had a magazine with a story in it about me.

And how she had a DVD that had something about you on it. How the fuck is that even possible?"

Just then, the TV screen flickered back on and Shannon realized with a sickening lurch in her chest that the DVD had still been playing even though she had turned the TV off.

They both stared at the screen in silence, watching Tommy Cavendish swing from a noose that was tied around a rafter, his bloated blue face emptied of his youthful vigor, his open eyes emptied of life.

"Fuck," Mike whispered. "Did you do that to him?"

Shannon didn't answer. She turned away from the TV screen and buried her face in her hands.

"We have to destroy them," Shannon said. She knew she couldn't let anybody see what was on the DVD. The school would fire her in a second. Her career, her life, would be over. She imagined the scandal that would erupt if it became known that she had an affair with an underage student. It didn't matter if it happened over two decades ago. It didn't matter that she was a changed person who learned from her mistakes. Not in this day and age.

Besides, she hadn't actually killed Tommy. He had put the noose around his own neck. But the guilt still festered inside her because she hadn't tried to stop him, either; she was supposed to have joined him.

There had been two nooses hanging from the rafters that day. They were going to go out together. But then she got scared and she couldn't go through with it. Right at the last second, right as Tommy kicked the stool out from under himself, she felt an intense wave of panic rushing through her mind that she couldn't fight off. She kept her feet on the stool, feeling the noose chafing against her throat. She just watched Tommy, listened to him choke and sputter, watched him dangle, watched his body spasm grotesquely as he died.

Mike nodded. "I'm with you on that," he replied in response to her call to destroy the evidence. "But these scientist fuckers these days can recreate just about anything. We have to really destroy them, spread the shit around. I need to burn the magazine and spread the ashes in half a dozen different places. You need to smash that DVD to bits and do the same thing. Flush some down the toilet, bury some pieces in the park, throw some in the trash disposal, scatter them in the wind. Whatever. I need to do the same."

Shannon nodded.

They set about the task at hand, working together to destroy the residual vestiges of their dark pasts.

Mike and Shannon made love that night. It wasn't great, but it wasn't terrible. They were just two scared, lonely people looking for some comfort in each other's arms and they found it. At least for a few hours.

Shannon shook her head. "I don't want to go back there. She probably already took it down. Garage sales are usually just on the weekends. She probably won't even be there."

"Let's just go see," Mike said. He reached out and squeezed her hand.

They were sitting at Shannon's kitchen table, both already dressed for the day.

"I have to go to work," Shannon said.

Mike nodded. So did he. He took his hand away from hers. "Saturday then," he said. "We'll go back on Saturday. Saturday morning."

Shannon hesitated, then nodded softly. "Does that mean I won't see you again until then?"

Mike was quiet for a moment. "Does that mean you want to see me again before then?"

Shannon demurely bit at her lower lip and shrugged softly, glancing at him through lidded eyes.

They made love on the kitchen floor.

<hr />

The crudely hand-drawn garage sale sign was stuck in the grass, just as it had been a week ago. Mike felt a quickening of his breath as he stared at it.

"Why are we even doing this?" Shannon asked. She was sitting in the passenger seat next to Mike as he drove. Outside, the sky was grey and dreary, foreshadowing the rain that the forecasters had predicted would arrive later in the afternoon.

"I don't know. I just have to know," Mike said.

"Have to know what?"

"If that crazy old bitty has more shit about me," Mike said.

Shannon was quiet for a moment. "Is there more... shit about you to find?"

Mike glanced over at her. He shook his head. "No, there isn't. There's just that one thing. I swear. And that was an accident, really. I didn't mean to do it." He paused. "It just happened." He lowered his head and looked away from her.

"Why didn't you go to the police?" Shannon asked after a long moment of silence.

"Why didn't you?"

That quieted her.

"There it is," Mike said.

Shannon followed his gaze, seeing the open garage but unable to see the old woman from their current vantage point. "Looks busy," Shannon said. There were at least half a dozen cars parked along the street, and more than that number of people milling about the driveway, moving in and out of the garage.

Mike parked the car behind an old minivan. He rested his forearms on the steering wheel for a moment, staring out the window of his car at the bustling garage sale activity going on a few hundred feet away.

"My heart is pounding in my chest," Shannon said. "Never thought I'd be this goddamned scared of a garage sale."

Mike nodded in agreement. "Let's go."

<hr />

"Oh, shit," Shannon said as they approached the driveway.

Mike glanced at her. "What?"

"That's Vince Dormer," Shannon said. "He's another teacher in my wing. Teaches algebra."

"Okay, just be calm, be calm," Mike said. "What do you teach, by the way?"

"English Lit and a few History classes sometimes."

Mike nodded. "I love books. I'm a big reader myself."

They moved onto the driveway, heading towards the garage. The table in the back of the garage was hidden from their view, blocked by a few patrons rummaging through the various apparel offerings filling up a nearby clothing rack, so they couldn't see if the old woman was present or not.

Suddenly, Mike whirled, nearly knocking Shannon over her as he turned abruptly to face her. "Oh, shit," he said, but his oh shit moment had a much greater emphasis than hers had, a much more pronounced level of dread.

"What is it?" Shannon asked, instinctively feeling the need to keep her voice down. "What's wrong?" Mike's nervousness was contagious and she felt a snaking chill squirm its way up her spine.

"It's Bill Callahan. He investigated..." Mike's voice trailed off. "He knows who I am."

Shannon looked at Mike, then glanced over his shoulder to see a grizzled old man who looked to be in his eighties hunched over a table. His grey hair was thinning, and had gone nearly completely white, but he still had a decent amount atop his head for a man his age. His left hand seemed to shake slightly as he moved, old age clearly taking a toll on his fine motor skills. She looked back to Mike. "That old man? Do you think he would even recognize you anymore?"

"I don't know," Mike said.

"Maybe we should just leave," Shannon said.

"No!" Mike said sharply, hissing the word but keeping his voice down. He clenched his lips tight. "No," he repeated, putting a calmness into his tone. He glanced down and to his right, but didn't turn enough to get an actual look at the old man. "What's he doing?"

Shannon gently shifted her gaze, looking over Mike's shoulder. "He's just looking at all this junk."

"Is the old woman here?" Mike asked. He was facing the garage door opening, so his line of eyesight was looking back out towards the driveway and the neighborhood beyond.

Shannon again gently shifted her gaze, looking over Mike's opposite shoulder, seeking out the back of the garage. And there she was; the old woman was sitting in her chair, her body rocking ever so gently back and forth. "Yes," she said. "She's here."

"What is she doing?" Mike asked.

"What do you think she's doing?" Shannon's voice rose in agitation. "She's just sitting in that fucking chair, swaying in some invisible fucking wind."

"Okay, okay," Mike said. "Keep your voice down. What's he doing?"

Shannon shifted her gaze to the right, but before she could answer her heart lurched into her throat. Vince Dormer was staring at a bin full of DVDs. It was a bin that looked identical to the one she had purchased a week ago.

"Damn it, Shannon," Mike said, keeping his teeth clenched tight. "What's he doing?"

Shannon didn't answer. She kept her gaze riveted on Vince Dormer.

Mike glanced up at Shannon to see that she was clearly preoccupied with something else happening behind him. He chanced a quick glance in the direction Shannon was looking and saw her fellow teacher fingering a black DVD case as he plucked it out of a plastic bin filled with DVDs of old movies and old TV shows.

Shannon walked up to Vince Dormer. "Be careful with those, Vince," Shannon said.

"Oh, hi, Shannon," Vince said.

"I bought some last week and they were all scratched," Shannon said, indicating the DVDs with a toss of her head in their direction. "None of them played."

"Don't listen to her," the old woman's voice called out.

Shannon looked up to see the old woman sitting motionless behind her folding table, staring at them.

"They're not scratched. They'll play just fine," the old woman said, not kowtowing to the venomous glare that Shannon had just shot in her direction. "Ten bucks for the whole lot."

There was a veil of hostility hanging in the air between the two women that almost had a physical, tangible feeling.

Vince dropped the black DVD case back into the bin. "I'm just browsing," he said, neither directly to the old woman, nor to Shannon.

Mike watched Shannon's teacher friend leave the garage sale empty-handed. The man shuffled out of the garage awkwardly, bumping into a table as he exited. He seemed in an awful hurry to leave.

Mike turned back to see Shannon lifting a black DVD case from the bin. She slowly cracked open the case and eased the two sides apart, revealing the silver disc within. She quickly snapped the case shut, nearly pinching the flesh on her fingers. She looked over to Mike and he saw true genuine fear in her eyes.

Something was wrong. Something was very wrong. Mike quickly looked over at old man Callahan to see him fingering an old magazine. He could clearly read the cover. It was a copy of True Life Detective Tales. But he couldn't see anything else. Callahan's body was blocking the rest of the magazine. A feeling of dread creeped up Mike's spine. He had to know.

Mike moved closer, not trying to be so blatant with his movement, but knowing he had to get closer to Callahan in a hurry. The photographs on the cover looked exactly the same as those on the magazine he had burned to a pile of ash a week ago. Was it the same issue? Did the woman have multiple copies of the same issue? It was possible. He used to collect comics when he was young and sometimes he would buy multiple copies of the same issue to sell later.

Callahan shifted his body, revealing more of the cover. *"I Stripped Her and Made Love to Her - After I Killed Her."* Mike could hear the words on the magazine cover echoing in his head, as if the headline itself was shouting out to him. His chest constricted and his throat tightened. It was the same issue. It was the same goddamn issue. His story was in there! All of it. All the details. There was enough to put him away for the rest of his life in that stapled-together pile of pages printed on shitty pulp paper.

Just then, Shannon stepped up to Mike, slapping the black DVD case against his chest, startling him, nearly making him shout out in alarm. He bit back the cry that was in his throat.

"It's the same DVD," Shannon said, her words

coming out in a scared, angry hiss. "It's the same fucking DVD."

Mike glanced down to where she was pushing the black DVD case against his chest. He looked up to her distraught face.

"Look at it," she said. She pushed the DVD case against his chest again. "Look at it," she hissed.

Mike looked back down at the DVD case, then took it from Shannon. He clicked open the case and stared at its contents. The name Thomas Cavendish was written on the silver disc in black indelible ink.

"How can that be?" Shannon asked, her words still coming out in tight, angry hisses. "We destroyed it."

"She must have made copies," Mike said. He clicked the case closed. He motioned for Shannon to look over her shoulder. "That old cop Callahan has the same issue that I shredded up and burned."

Shannon looked over her shoulder to see the old man Mike was referring to skimming through the magazine he held in his Parkinson's-induced trembling hands. She looked back at Mike. "What the fuck, Mike? What do we do now?"

Mike shook his head. "I don't know. I don't know." He looked over to Callahan. "I can't let him get that magazine." He looked back to Shannon.

"Too late," she said.

Mike's eyes went wide and he looked up to see Callahan shuffling over to the old woman sitting behind the folding table, the magazine gripped in his hand. He dug some change out of his pocket and handed it to the old woman. She took the coins and dropped them into her old tackle-box till. "Some real good stories in there, I hear," she said to the old cop, then turned to stare directly at Mike. She had the same devilish smile on her face she had given him when he had purchase the magazine.

Callahan shuffled out of the garage, heading towards his car.

"We have to follow him," Mike said. He headed out of the garage and Shannon followed closely behind.

"Hey!" The old woman's voice rang out loud behind them, her shout echoing in the garage. "You didn't pay for that!"

Mike stopped and turned to see the old woman pointing a bony finger at him. Only then did he realize he was still clutching the DVD case that Shannon had handed to him. He felt eyes on him and looked opposite the old woman to see Callahan in the distance staring directly at him over the roof of his car from the street beyond. Was that a flash of recognition in the old cop's face? Mike didn't know if he imagined it or not, but it didn't matter. He knew he couldn't let him read that magazine. He looked back to the old woman, doing his best to avoid all the other accusatory stares stabbing at him from all sides from the other garage sale patrons. He looked at Shannon. "Go pay her for this. Hurry up."

Shannon hesitated, then move towards the old woman.

Mike looked back to Callahan to see him lowering himself into his vehicle. He looked back into the garage to see Shannon paying the old woman with numerous bills. She quickly returned to his side, a disgruntled frown tugging her lips sharply down. "Damn old bitty charged me twenty bucks for that DVD."

Mike squinted at her.

"Said it was a rare collectible," Shannon said.

"Shit, whatever, just come on. We'll deal with her later." He grabbed Shannon's arm and hurried her along. "We have to follow him."

"She said something else, too," Shannon added.

Mike glanced at her as they hurried towards his car.

"She said the past can never be destroyed."

Mike sat in the driver's seat of his car, staring out the window at the small house that belonged to retired police officer William Callahan. It was situated in a remote section of town, the nearest house a good distance away.

Shannon sat in the passenger seat, absently fingering the DVD case. "Now what?" she asked.

"Shit, I don't know," Mike said. He twisted his fingers around the steering wheel. "I need to get that fucking magazine away from him."

"What if he's reading it now?"

"That's not helping."

"Well, he could be," Shannon said.

"I know he could be. Fuck." He turned to Shannon. "Go knock on the door."

"And say what?"

"I don't know. Anything. Be a Jehovah's Witness. Praise Jesus. Say anything. Just get him to open the door."

"Then what?" Shannon asked.

"Shit, I don't know. I'll knock him out or something."

"You'll knock him out? With what? Your mighty

fists?" Shannon frowned at him.

"Get my flashlight out of the glove compartment. I'll use that," Mike said.

Shannon didn't move.

"Damn it," Mike grunted. He reached over her, flipped down the glove compartment lid, and angrily snatched at the small plastic yellow flashlight that was resting inside.

Shannon glanced at the flashlight. "You're going to knock him out with that?"

"If I have to, yeah," Mike said.

"So I go knock on the door, get him to open it, then you knock him out, rush inside and steal the magazine," Shannon stated.

Mike expelled an exasperated breath. "Yes."

"Then when he comes to, he calls his police buddies, gives them a description of me, and they lock me up as being some kind of accessory to breaking and entering and assault." Shannon shook her head. "I don't think so."

"Shit," Mike said. "I don't have any masks handy. I must have left them at home on my night stand. You got a better idea?"

Shannon was silent.

"Look, for better or for worse, we're in this together. To the end." Mike paused. "Whatever that end might be."

Shannon remained silent.

Mike's hand shook, the cheap flashlight glass rattling in its casing. "Jesus, we need to do this. I can't let him read that fucking story. We need to do this now."

⸻⸱⸱⸱⸺

Shannon reached up and rang the doorbell.

Mike stood off to the side of the door, just out of sight, pressing himself into the gray siding that lined the house. He clutched the flashlight to his chest.

After a moment, they could hear movement inside. A pair of old, tired eyes peered out from behind a small curtain that covered the tiny window next to the door.

"Package for Bill Callahan. I need a signature," Shannon said.

The door lock clicked. The door handle turned.

And the business end of a snub-nosed .38 police revolver stuck its head out. "Come in. Both of you."

⸻⸱⸱⸱⸺

Bill Callahan squinted at Mike. "Do I know you?" The old man stood near his kitchen table, dressed in an old green University of Michigan sweatshirt and faded jeans.

Mike glanced at the gun Callahan clutched in his trembling hand. "Is that necessary?"

"With you two following me?" Callahan nodded. "I think so. What the hell do you want? I don't have any money in the house." Callahan shook his head. "Nothing worth stealing." The hand clutching the gun continued to shake.

Mike glanced down at the kitchen table to see the copy of True Life Detective Tales magazine sitting right there next to a heavily stained cup that the old man clearly used for his tea. A moist tea bag sat plopped in the saucer upon which the stained cup rested, the cup more than half empty of its dark brew.

Callahan continued to squint as he studied Mike. "I know you from somewhere. I put you away? That why you're here? You just get out of the joint?"

Mike shook his head. "No."

Callahan looked to Shannon. "I don't have any drugs, if that's what you're looking for. Unless you're running really low on Tylenol. I got some of that on the counter over there." Callahan pointed to the counter area next to the softly humming refrigerator.

"Do I look like a drug addict to you?" Shannon asked, trying not to show an insulted face to the old man but not succeeding very well.

Callahan shrugged. "They come in all shapes and sizes."

"We're not here to steal your drugs," Shannon said.

"But you are here to steal something." Callahan studied her. "You've got thief written all over your face. Them darting eyes give you away."

Shannon said nothing. She looked over at Mike.

Callahan kept the gun pointed at Mike, his trembling fingers causing the weapon to shake ever so slightly. "You two are the worst thieves I've ever seen."

"We just want the magazine," Shannon blurted out. "We don't want to hurt anyone."

Callahan squinted heavily, his brow furrowing deeply. "The magazine? What the hell are you talking about?"

Shannon pointed to the copy of True Life Detective Tales sitting on the kitchen table. "That magazine."

Callahan looked away from her, glancing down at

the kitchen table.

That's when Mike struck, surging towards Callahan, reaching for the gun. He caught Callahan off guard, striking down hard on his wrist, the sharp blow causing the old retired cop to drop the gun.

Shannon surged forward, dropping down to scoop the gun up off the floor. She quickly moved back away from the brawling men, clutching the gun, gripping it tightly with both hands. Her hands shook even more than Callahan's hand had been shaking as she raised the gun, aiming the weapon in the direction of the two men.

Mike and Callahan were on the floor now, punching and kicking and flailing their arms and legs, each man desperate to get the upper hand on the other. The men huffed and grunted as they battled each other.

One of the kitchen chairs toppled over as they collided with it, forcing Shannon to take a little leap back away from it.

A butter knife had fallen to the floor amidst the men's scuffle and Callahan was the first to see the blade. A hint of yellow butter still smeared the silver blade. With one fast motion, Callahan reached out his hand and grabbed the knife and swung it towards Mike, sinking the blade into the upper part of Mike's right shoulder. Mike jerked back, grimacing in pain, instinctively kicking his shoes on the floor tiles, pushing himself back away from Callahan to clutch at his bleeding shoulder.

Callahan still clutched the butter knife, his fingers and the back of his hand now red with Mike's blood. The old cop panted heavily, struggling for a breath. Despite his obvious discomfort, Callahan managed to get on his knees and keep coming after Mike. The old cop drew the knife back and started a thrusting motion forward, obviously intent on sinking the blade into Mike's chest.

Shannon fired, her startled cry mixing in with the cracking sound of the bullet exploding out of the barrel.

The bullet slammed into Callahan, striking him in the center of his chest, puncturing his heart, killing him instantly. He didn't make a sound. He just keeled over and lay unmoving, his eyes open, blood oozing out of his chest and pouring out of the hole in his back where the bullet had exited.

"I didn't mean it," Shannon sputtered. "I didn't mean it. I didn't mean it. The gun just went off. I didn't mean it." She dropped the gun like it was a hot chunk of metal scalding her hands and the weapon clattered on the kitchen floor tiles.

From his position on the floor, Mike stared at Callahan for a long moment. The old man didn't move, didn't take a breath, didn't blink. The fetid stench of his released bowels filled the kitchen.

"I didn't mean it, I didn't mean it," Shannon said, muttering the same phrase over and over and over.

Mike rose shakily to his feet. He moved slowly towards Shannon, still clutching at his bleeding shoulder.

Shannon slowly looked up at him. Her eyes were rimmed with red, her cheeks wet with tears.

Mike felt a welling of anguish rise up in his chest for her. "It's okay, you didn't mean it," he said to her, his voice soft, trying to be reassuring. He saw her glance down and his gaze followed hers to the fallen gun.

"My fingerprints are all over that," she said.

"It's okay," he said. "You didn't mean it."

"He was going to kill you," Shannon said.

Mike looked at Shannon, saw her entire body trembling. He moved to the fallen gun and picked it up. He purposefully rubbed his hand all over the dark metal of the gun, smearing his fingers across the barrel, across the body of the gun, across the grip, over the trigger. He wasn't really sure why he had felt compelled to do that; he just thought it was the right thing to do at the time. "It's okay. Look, now my fingerprints are all over it." He laid the gun in his palm and displayed it for Shannon to see. "We're in this together."

She glanced at the gun, then looked over her shoulder towards the front door of the house. "Do you think somebody heard it?"

Mike was quiet for a moment. "I don't know. His house is pretty isolated."

They stood quietly for a moment, listening, waiting for the screaming sound of a siren to fill up the silence.

"Jesus," Mike heard Shannon mutter. He looked over to her and saw her staring at Callahan's corpse. "He's dead. He's really fucking dead," she said. And then he saw a tremor of emotion working its way across her entire body until she was shaking from head to toe. He set the gun down on the kitchen table and went to her. He grabbed her arm, firmly but still gently, and guided her out of the kitchen, leading her away from the blood-stained body lying on the floor just a few feet away.

Shannon turned and leaned into him, wrapping her arms around him, shuddering against his body, clinging desperately to him. He hugged her back, holding her tight, ignoring the pain in his shoulder. She was wearing the same lavender perfume she had been wearing the first time they had made love and the scent of it, of her, brought back a flood of erotic memories and he felt himself getting hard despite, or perhaps because of, the extreme horror of the moment. He nuzzled his face against her neck, taking in the sweet scent of her. He felt ashamed at his growing hardness and waited for her to pull away in disgust.

But Shannon didn't pull away. She turned to face him and their lips hovered inches away from each other. Neither one of them spoke. Their lips met, drawn together by an undeniable attraction.

A thin rivulet of blood oozed into view on the kitchen floor behind them.

The garage sale was open. Mike moved out of his car and headed towards the dark opening. Shannon and his dog Ranger waited in the car; Shannon gently stroked Ranger's head as they sat quietly.

The old woman was seated in her chair behind her folding table, the green tablecloth in its usual place over the top of the table, shielding whatever was beneath the table from any prying eyes. She rocked ever so slightly back and forth in an unseen wind.

Mike moved over to a table on the old woman's right, eyeing the smattering pile of magazines that littered the table's surface in a haphazard array. The glossy covers on various issues of True Life Detective Tales magazine flashed at him as the afternoon's sunlight hit their surfaces. One issue in particular had particularly vibrant colors, as if perhaps it might have been printed just recently. One headline immediately drew his attention: *"Murderers Make Love After Making Death!"*

Mike grabbed the magazine and examined the cover. A picture of a dead body lying on a kitchen floor was in full focus in the foreground, and in the background was a hazy blur of a man and a woman clearly in the throes of making love. He thought about what the old woman had told Shannon earlier. The past can never be destroyed. But that didn't mean you couldn't have some fun making it. A morbid smile slid up into place on Mike's lips and a strangely keen eagerness surfaced in his expression.

He moved over to the old woman. He dug into his pocket to pull out a quarter, setting it down on the table before her. "See you next week," Mike said cheerfully and waved the copy of True Life Detective Tales magazine over his head as he headed out of the garage.

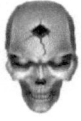

TERRORSTORY #62
THIEF'S REWARD

Gino the thief tried not to think about his cursed cock as he surveyed the room. He was of medium height for the men in his village, with brown hair and golden brown eyes. A slight paunch gave a rounded look to his belly. He glanced to his right, noticing there was a rusty old dagger resting on a small table near the right side wall. Who leaves a weapon like that out in the open? Don't they know someone might come along and steal it? Gino grinned at his own thoughts. He didn't really need the extra dagger because he already had two daggers of his own, but he took it anyway. He still had room in his burlap sack for more stuff. Half a sack is a sack half empty. He knew he could probably sell the dagger in town, or least barter for some food or drink with it.

Or maybe he could cut Werko's throat with it. He envisioned the rusty blade slicing through the wizard's fat neck, drawing a spray of blood that showered Werko's corpulent blubber with his own fluids. It was a disgusting image, but it still made Gino smile.

You really think you can even get close to that wizard before he cuts you down with a spell? You've never been able to get closer than a hundred feet before he gives you that evil eye of his. Maybe you'll wet yourself again. But that might not be so bad since you only have about half a cock now anyway.

Gino tried to push away the belittling voice, but it refused to go unheard.

He already took two inches off your cock. Maybe he'll take a few more. Maybe he'll turn you from a Gino into a Gina.

He felt his rage growing at the thought of the fat wizard. That fat fuck. Humiliating him. Gino was only twenty years old and once had a full life of sexual adventures ahead of him, but that spiteful wizard Werko had felt the need to curse his cock. Gino had no idea how to counter the spell, had no idea how to get his lost inches back, but word on the streets was that if you killed a vampire, all those under his control were released and his spells were reversed.

He's not a vampire, you stupid ass. He's a wizard.

I know, I know. But maybe if a wizard is killed then all his spells die off too, or get reversed, or fade away, or something.

Right, you're gonna kill a wizard. You're gonna kill a wizard with a rusty blade.

Maybe.

No, you're not. You ain't got the balls for that.

Maybe I can kidnap him. Make him reverse the spell.

How do you think you are going to do that? You ever hear of a wizard being kidnapped? You ever hear of a wizard being forced to do something he doesn't want to do?

No.

Stop being stupid then. Think of something else.

What about another wizard?

What?

Another wizard. I can find another wizard and, I don't know, pay him or something. Pay him to go after Werko. Get him to kidnap Werko. Get him to make Werko reverse the spell.

The other voice was quiet for a long moment.

Go on.

All wizards are all high and mighty and prideful, right?

Yes.

Then we need to praise Werko far and wide. Spread tales of his might and power. Sow the seeds of his legendary strength and his magic prowess.

What the hell are you talking about? You want to praise Werko after what he did to you?

Yes. Call him the greatest wizard in all the lands. The other wizards won't like that. They won't like that at all. I know some of them will come see what all the fuss is about. Their egos won't let them leave it alone. They'll need to see who this Werko is and why he is so powerful. Gino nodded to himself. See, we

43

don't need to find any wizards. They'll come out of the woodwork like flies coming to feast on shit.

You know what? Most of the time you're just a drunken dumbass thief. But this time, not as much. That's actually a great fucking idea. Almost brilliant.

Gino grinned a face-splitting grin.

And so the legend of Werko the Wondrous began to grow, the tales of his wondrous deeds spreading across the lands far and wide.

"Who is this Werko the Wondrous?" Malandrake the Magnificent stared down at his inner council from his seated position on his throne. He was a tall man, slender but obviously of great physical strength. He refused to hide behind a cumbersome robe, preferring to wear tight fitting leggings and tight fitting tunics that clearly displayed his corded muscles. His face was clean shaven, his black hair cut short.

"Werko the Wacko is more appropriate, don't you think?" Zinnia said. She was a pretty blonde with a pert nose and a sensual mouth. She was an excellent researcher, somehow having the innate skill to know exactly which ancient tome to look through to find just the right combination of ingredients to create very powerful spells and potions.

"I hear he can make the skies rain with frogs," Malandrake said.

"Nonsense," Grifik snorted. He was a portly man, piggish in body, piggish in face. His crude, abrupt manner was occasionally annoying to Malandrake but the fat man had counseled him with sage words of wisdom more often than not, so Malandrake considered him a valuable part of his inner council.

"I also hear he doubled the production of corn of an entire acre with just a thimble full of a new potion he concocted," Malandrake added.

"Ridiculous," Grifik snorted. "Even you can't do that."

Zinnia froze where she stood, holding her breath in. She glared at Grifik, then slowly cast a hesitant eye in Malandrake's direction.

The dark cloud shadowing Malandrake's unhappy expression was an obvious indicator of what was about to happen next.

⚜

"Who the fuck is this Werko the Wondrous?" Sebastian the Spectacular pounded his wooden staff into the chamber floor with such force that the tiles cracked beneath the blow. To be fair, several other tiles were already cracked on the floor nearby, but Sebastian was even more pissed now than he was when he had cracked those.

Sebastian had long flowing brunette hair, a long hooked nose, a pointed chin, and a thin mouth lined with what can only be described as cruel lips. His oily hair gleamed in the torchlight and his oily skin glimmered. He was dressed in a long crimson robe that reached down to the tops of his feet. He used to wear a much longer robe but he kept tripping over the ends of it and had actually fallen flat on his face in public once because of it. He was still pissed off about it to this day, the mere memory of the incident putting him in a perpetual state of high agitation.

"He is from Lucor," Prater said. Prater was a tall man, his body long and thin. He was dressed in a dull off-white robe that befitted his station of trusted adviser to the wizard. He bowed to the wizard, his hands tucked into the wide sleeves of his robe as he tilted his upper body forward and down in Sebastian's direction.

Sebastian frowned. "Lucor?"

"It is a small village west of here."

"I know where the fuck Lucor is," Sebastian growled. "What the fuck is a wizard with that kind of power doing in some fucking farming village?"

"Powers accompanied by exaggerations and amplifications and embellishments, to be sure," Prater said. "As is often the case with tales of wizards."

Sebastian frowned. "Are you telling me the stories that circulate about *my* powers may be false and misleading, Prater?"

"Of course not," Prater answered quickly, but with just a hint of nervousness in his voice that he couldn't hide.

Sebastian pursed his lips. "Do you know what stories I've been hearing, Prater?"

Prater did not answer. He waited for Sebastian to continue.

"I hear this Werko the Wondrous can give a single man the strength of twenty mules."

"Such a man would surely be a big ass," Prater said.

Sebastian blinked slowly at Prater. "I also hear he can make a woman's breasts grow larger just by whispering in her ear."

"Makes me wonder what would happen if he gave

a speech to a herd of cows," Prater said. "Udder pandemonium may ensue."

Sebastian stared at Prater. "You're very droll today, Prater."

Prater bowed slightly. "I do my best to amuse, as well as educate and advise."

Sebastian grunted. "Now do your best to prepare me for travel. We go to Lucor to see what this Werko the Wondrous fuck can really do."

Variana the Virtuoso was not at all virtuous. She was a magnificent wizard, yes, but not a principled one. Anyone who called her a witch, or tried to be cute by calling her a wizardess, didn't survive her wrath for very long; if they did manage to survive, they usually no longer had a tongue to address her as such. Any streak of humanity she might have had left in her had long ago been wiped away by the various vicious battles she had waged against both fellow wizards and humans alike. Nobody fucked with her. Not anymore. She ruled the islands of Stormkeep and Cragmire with a mighty, perfectly manicured, fist. Actually, she couldn't really make an accurate fist because her nails were too long and they would dig trenches into her palm if she squeezed her fingers into a real fist.

She was a tall woman, regal in posture, with high cheekbones and full red lips. Her long hair was black, sleek as a raven's wing because she bathed her locks in raven blood every week to keep her tresses lustrous. Her body was tight and lithe, fully on display at all times beneath a layer of thin gauzy fabric, her flat chest and small nipples barely making any impression on the fabric. Her nether regions were bare, unable to grow hair due to a spell that had shorn her of all her hair between her legs. This permanent aftermath of one of her battles enraged her every time she saw herself in a mirror, so there were no longer any mirrors anywhere in Cragmire Castle wherein she now resided.

She had no advisers, no inner council. She did what she wanted when she wanted without discussing it with anyone. She was a fucking wizard. She didn't need to discuss anything with anyone. If she wanted something, she took it. If she didn't want something, she got rid of it. Life was very simple in that regard.

Variana had spies everywhere. Men, women, children. Even some animals were under her thrall. Well, others would call them animals, but she preferred to think of them as her scouts and information gatherers because they were once human; every few months she would take a few pitiful human wretches and turn them into the forms of animals that would best serve her needs.

With her spies and scouts spread far and wide, it wasn't long before tales of Werko the Wondrous reached her ears and made them burn hot with contempt. She would show him what it meant to truly be a wizard to be feared.

Malandrake the Magnificent showed up in Lucor first. An old merchant recognized him immediately upon his arrival in the village, so Malandrake cast a sealed-lips spell on the man, melting his lips together to keep them from revealing his presence, at least verbally. He wanted to remain inconspicuous for as long as possible so he could observe this Werko the Wondrous acting as he normally would; he didn't want the wizard to strut his powers and put on a show for his benefit. At least not right away.

Zinnia and Grifik accompanied him. They posed as a married couple, and Malandrake acted as their manservant. It was all great fun when they were in the public eye. He especially enjoyed when Grifik kissed Zinnia on the lips because he knew how much Zinnia actually detested the piggish man.

They settled in to their rooms at Tilkin's Tavern and Inn, the only inn in the village, and went down to the dining hall to have a meal. The sun was setting, so nightfall was nearly upon them. Serving wenches bustled about the large common room that served as the dining hall, lighting candles to illuminate the area in flickering waves of golden light. Shadows of the patrons going about their motions of eating and drinking played along the walls and Malandrake resisted the temptation to cast a shadow spell to bring one of the dark shapes to life. Now wasn't the time to indulge his whims. And then he paused. Or was it? Could he flush Werko out into the open by casting a shadow spell? Maybe a little chaos was exactly what was needed? What was he waiting for? He was here to see what this Werko was capable of. So let's see how he reacts to this.

Gino saw the shadow move first. He was at the inn, enjoying a bowl of fresh lamb stew and a mug of warm ale, when he noticed the strange pattern playing out on the wooden panels that comprised the dining area's walls.

At first, Gino made nothing of it. The shadow was just in the shape of Cinderee, the buxom serving wench who always ignored him and never waited on his table. He could tell it was her shadow because she easily had the largest pair of breasts out of all the serving wenches. The shadow flowed along the wall, mirroring Cinderee's movements as she worked amongst the tables. Cinderee's shadow reached down behind the shadowy shape of her buxom figure and slapped away the shadowy fingers of a shadowy hand groping at her ass, the shadow still mirroring the movements of Cinderee herself, still moving as a normal shadow moved.

Gino took a sip of warm ale from his mug. It was just another typical night at the inn; patrons were always trying to cop a quick feel of Cinderee. But when Cinderee's shadow stopped moving even though she herself kept walking, Gino knew the night was about to become anything but typical. Gino had been in the process of lowering his mug back down from his mouth to the table when he noticed Cinderee's shadow was no longer mirroring her actual flesh and blood movement. He stared at the still shadow on the wall, his mug frozen in mid-air.

Then the shadow moved, reaching for the shadow of a sword handle being cast by a man wearing an actual sword nearby. Cinderee's shadow clutched at the shadow blade and drew the shadow sword, gripping it before her as she raised it up.

Gino finished lowering his mug back down to the table and quickly glanced about the large room. Was this Werko's doing? Or was someone else here? Was there another wizard in the village? Had his mad plan actually worked? He knew some of the rumors he had started had spread and had taken on lives of their own because some of the rumors that had come back to him were even more grandiose than those he had started. But he was surprised they might have actually worked as he had planned.

Suddenly, the Cinderee shadow lunged forward, stabbing the groper's shadow in the chest.

The real groper clutched at his chest, his flesh-and-blood-face scrunching in pain, his muscles seizing up tight.

Gino took a nervous drink from his ale, watching the macabre scene play out on the shadows on the wall and within the physical realm simultaneously.

The groper continued to writhe and groan, gasping for breath, looking as if a heart attack was ravaging him because only his shadow had been stabbed, not his actual flesh. And then the groper keeled over, dropping forward. His head thunked hard against the wooden surface of the table before him, knocking over several goblets full of warm ale. The other men sitting at the table quickly rose to their feet, trying to avoid the sloshing, splashing amber liquid, exclaiming loudly in shock and surprise.

Gino pointed to the shadows on the wall. "Look! It's sorcery!"

Several patrons glanced in Gino's direction at the sound of his cry, then followed his pointing finger to look at the dark shapes visible on the wall. Cinderee's shadow still clutched her shadow blade, but then the shadow transformed, moving quickly along the wall, reforming as if trying to become Cinderee's genuine shadow again, the shadow blade now gone from its shadowy hands.

"Did you see that?" Gino asked, raising his voice. "Did you see that?"

Several patrons looked at each other, muttering disbelievingly amongst themselves. They had seen it.

Cinderee stared at her shadow, a look of abject terror filling her face. She dropped the tray of trenchers she was holding and the food splashed on the floor, the hardened bread and its chunks of meat and vegetable contents spilling in all directions. She raced out of the inn, clutching her hand over her mouth in fear.

Gino felt a pang of sympathy for Cinderee, but that feeling didn't last long. He quickly turned his attention back to the interior of the inn. He glanced about the room, trying to be discrete but also trying to take in every patron as quickly as possible. Was he here? Was he in the room right now? There were a few men with thick white beards seated at tables near the front door, but Gino didn't think they were any form of wizard; their eyes were red-rimmed with too much drink and their expressions seemed lackadaisical and indifferent to what was going on around them. No matter. All that mattered was that he continued to stoke the wizard fires. "Did you see that?" he said to anyone who would listen. He pointed to the now empty wall. "It was a shadow killer. That was powerful black magic."

A very drunk man at a nearby table waved his mug dismissively through the air, spilling some ale with his exaggerated gesture. "It was just Werko the Weanie casting a spell." The drunk man pointed to the now-dead groper sprawled across the top of the table. "He never liked ol' Trallavan no how."

Gino shook his head. "That wasn't a Werko spell." Gino paused. "Werko's magic isn't that strong."

<hr />

Variana the Virtuoso clacked her long fingernails on the top of the large ornate table that filled nearly half of the area in the dining room. She had assumed ownership of a large manor home on the edge of Lucor. The previous owners were very accommodating in transferring ownership. In fact, they were so accommodating they were staying on as her servants.

Well, not all of them. The patriarch of the family was hanging from the high ceiling a few dozen feet above, his wrists and ankles secured by thick manacles, his body chained to the ceiling with magical golden hooks. He was naked, spread-eagled, staring down into the dining room. His first bowel movements had been quite disgusting, but now his wife had a better handle on them and she climbed up a ladder to take care of his needs when the time came. The man hadn't been so accommodating at first, but now he was pretty much agreeing to whatever Variana asked of him and his family.

"What do you want!"

Variana stopped clacking her fingernails and slowly turned to look at the hysterical woman shouting at her. "First, I want you to stop crying. I can't stand women who cry." She waved her fingers in the air and muttered a spell.

The woman's tears shimmered, then seemed to elongate and solidify, growing sharp edges. Thin red lines appeared on her skin as the now-razor-edged tears sliced through the flesh on her face as they slid down her cheeks. The woman howled and clutched at her bleeding face, frantically wiping at the tears, desperate to dislodge the stinging, slashing shards from her face.

Variana nodded at the woman. "Yes, you can scream. Just don't cry."

Several of the hardened tears hit the marble tiled floor and shattered with a soft tinkling sound. The woman's fingers were quickly covered with thin cuts as the sharp tears bit into her skin as she struggled to get them away from her face with frenzied swipes of her hand.

"Now, tell me more of this Werko the Wonder Boy asshole," Variana said to the woman who was no longer crying.

Prater returned to Sebastian's side, frowning with displeasure. "This is the only inn in this…" His frowned deepened with disgust. "…quaint little village."

Sebastian waved his fingers dismissively. He glanced up at the inn, his gaze traveling up its several stories. He and Prater were standing in the dirt street just outside the inn's front door, near the swinging wooden sign that read: Tilkin's Tavern and Inn. "It will do. I don't imagine we'll be in this pig-infested shit-stain of a village for long."

The inn was oddly quiet when they entered, nearly empty. An old man slowly rolled a mug between his hands in a corner booth near a fireplace that crackled feebly from a fire that seemed about to go out at any moment. A serving wench with very large breasts was mending a ripped shirt at a table near the bar to their left; there were no other patrons for her to wait on.

Sebastian stopped just a few steps into the inn. He sniffed at the air. He then waved his finger in the air, as if swirling it through a cake batter to get a finger-full of ingredients, and put his finger to his lips. His eyes widened ever so slightly as he turned to Prater. "There's been magic done in here."

Prater looked at Sebastian curiously.

"Pretty strong fucking magic, too, from the taste of it." Sebastian licked at his lips.

Prater motioned to the serving wench. "Should we speak to her?"

"Yes, but first I think we should speak to that old fuck there."

They made their way through the inn, maneuvering around the tables that filled the main dining area and stopped before the booth where the old man was sitting. They stood at the side of the table, looking down at the old man. "May we join you and buy you a drink?" Prater asked.

The man glanced up at them but both Sebastian and Prater knew they would get no useful information from this man. He no longer had a mouth from which he could speak. His lips were melted together. The man looked back down forlornly at his empty mug and continued to roll it between his fingers.

"Is that the magic you tasted?" Prater asked of Sebastian.

Sebastian shook his head. "No, it's stronger than that."

"It was my shadow," the serving wench said from

behind them.

Sebastian and Prater turned to look at the woman. She was guiding a sewing needle through the torn seam near the shoulder of the garment she was working on. She didn't look up from her work. The two men moved over to her and stood next to the table where she sat.

"It was my shadow," she said again. "My shadow killed that man."

Sebastian frowned. He glanced over at the old man in the booth, then back to the serving wench.

"Not that man," she said. She motioned with a toss of her head to an area on the floor nearby. "The man whose blood that belongs to."

Sebastian followed her lead and stared down at a dark stain that marred the wooden floor a few feet away from them. He looked back to the woman.

"My shadow came alive and killed that man that done groped me," the serving woman said.

Sebastian was quiet for a moment.

"Your shadow came alive and killed a man?" Prater asked.

Sebastian exhaled an exasperated sigh. "That's what she fucking said, Prater."

"Where is your shadow now?" Prater asked.

The woman raised her hand and pointed to the wall nearby.

Prater glanced in that direction to see a shadowy shape on the wall. The shadowy shape raised a hand and gave a cheerful wave with a few quick shakes of its hand. Prater looked down to see that the woman was still busy sewing her torn garment; neither of her hands were waving at all. Prater looked nervously at Sebastian.

"Once your shadow is detached from your body, it can never be re-joined to you." Sebastian frowned at Prater. "Do you never fucking listen to anything I tell you? Why am I always the one doing the teaching when you are supposed to be my advisor?"

Prater hung his head.

Sebastian was quiet for a moment. He glanced at the old man. "This Werko is crafty. He knew we were coming." He looked at the serving wench. "Woman, we need a room." He looked to Prater. "We must prepare for battle."

Gino was excited. Scared as shit, but still excited. There was at least one new wizard in the village - the shadow killer was definite proof of that, but he suspected there were more. Two strangers had come to the inn, both with an air of smug superiority that was a hallmark of wizard arrogance; it didn't definitively prove that they were wizards, but there was clearly something about them that gave everyone who had encountered them pause.

And he had heard talk of a tall elegant woman taking up residence in the Narkozi manor home. He knew the reclusive Narkozi family hadn't had a guest to their estate in years, so it was mighty suspicious for some mysterious woman to show up just as all the strange happenings were occurring. Perhaps she was a wizard. Or did you call them a witch if they had titties? Or maybe wizardess? Or sorceress? Yeah, a real sorceress. He felt a twinge in his groin. What would it be like to fuck a sorceress? How crazy would that be? Would she turn into some wild beast, literally, when he pounded her into orgasm? Maybe she could adjust the size of herself to make his cock feel big to her? How tight could she make herself? She was a sorceress. She could probably do whatever the hell she wanted with her own body, right?

Right, like some sorceress is gonna wanna fuck your little dingus? She'd be better off putting her pinky in her pussy and diddling it around. She'll get more pleasure from that, for sure.

Shut up, you damn fool. Quit insulting me. It ain't my fault Werko fucked me up like this.

You shut up. Your sad little twitching dick doesn't even make your pants move.

Gino clenched his teeth, but refused to engage in any more internal battles. "I need a drink," he muttered and headed for the inn.

Werko the Wondrous was worried. He was a short, stocky man, bulbous in the stomach, thick in the chest and thick in the thighs. He had a thick brown beard and bushy eyebrows. His eyes were a deep brown, sunk deep in his sockets, giving them a hint of a hollowed-out skeletal look despite the beefiness of his cheeks. Stories of a shadow killer in the village had reached his ears. He had heard of such a power years ago, but he had no idea how to accomplish such a deed. Who had done such a thing? And why?

He had also heard other stories lately, stories about him. Some of the stories had hints of truth to them, but other tales were so outlandish that he had a hard time imagining someone actually believing them; they were stories that had been so grossly exaggerated in their telling that they were almost absurdly humorous. Regardless of their veracity, they certainly had painted him as a wizard of immense power. Where had those stories originated and why? From whom?

Bu his thoughts kept drifting back to the latest story he had just heard. The more he thought about the possibilities such a power could bring him, the more his nervous fear turned to an excited thrill. A shadow killer! How exciting was that! He had to learn that spell. If the villagers were making fun of him by spreading grossly exaggerated stories of his skills, they would certainly be respectful of his abilities after he learned *that* skill. He would show them how powerful he truly was.

He donned his brown cloak and raised up the hood to shield his face in a coating of murky gloom. He headed towards Tilkin's Tavern and Inn.

Variana caught a few drops of blood in her goblet, maneuvering the drinking cup underneath the man hanging from the high ceiling dozens of feet above her. One of the manacles around his wrist was biting a bit too harshly into his flesh and drawing blood. She waited patiently while two more drops of blood splashed softly into the goblet with a faint plopping sound.

Behind her, the woman of the house lay dead on the floor. Her eyes were shredded, with strips of eyelid and eyeball and other bits of flesh dangling down out of her eye sockets. She just couldn't stop herself from crying again. Even to save her own life. The diamond-edged tears had savaged her eyes.

Variana leaned her head over the goblet. She raised one of her sharp fingernails to her own eye and gently poked at her tear duct, causing a single tear to form. The tear dropped into the goblet, the milky whiteness of her tear swirling in with the blood. She inserted her finger into the liquid, mixing the tear and the blood with a few twirls of her finger, turning the liquid into a softer shade of lighter red, nearly a pink but not quite.

Before her, half a dozen different animals waited patiently. Two sparrows sat patiently atop the table, one on either side of a fat calico cat sitting on its haunches. Three rabbits waited behind the sparrows and the cat. A robin fluttered down to the table, taking up a position behind the rabbits.

Variana lifted her finger out of the goblet, scooping a small amount of the liquid into the curved underside of her fingernail, using the fingernail as a tiny spoon of sorts. One of the sparrows hopped closer to her and she tipped her finger, dripping the mixture into each of the sparrow's eyes. The sparrow blinked at her and Variana blinked back. And then it was done. That's all it took to synchronize her vision with the sparrow's. Now she would be able to see what the bird saw. She waved her fingers and the sparrow fluttered upwards, then headed towards an open window, the bird disappearing out into the day.

She performed the same ritual with the other animals and they all disappeared into the bright light of the day.

She really had no idea what lay ahead for her, but there was something in the air that gave her a delicious shiver. There was an anticipatory foreboding that made her tingle. She had sent her animal spies out weeks earlier when the first stories of Werko's prowess had reached her, but they had delivered no conclusive evidence one way or the other as to the extent of Werko's magic skills. She suspected Werko was casting blocking spells on her spies, preventing them from reporting what was truly happening in his village. But now that she was in the actual village itself, she would be able to keep very strong ties on her spies and she would be able to detect if their skills were being tampered with.

She expected a report from the sparrows within the hour.

It didn't take the sparrows more than a quarter hour to relay useful information to Variana.

Malandrake the Magnificent had taken a room at the inn in the village. She thought of him as Malandork the Mundane in her head. What the hell was he doing here? The sparrow sat perched on a nearby windowsill, watching the wizard; Variana watched the wizard through the sparrow's eyes. He was soaking in a hot tub of water, his muscles glistening with moisture, tiny wisps of vapor draping him in a soft cloud of steam.

And then within moments, the other sparrow reported in. Sebastian the Spectacular (Sebaceous the Stupid in her head, or sometimes Sebastian the Slimy) was also at the inn, situated in a room on the opposite side of the building, on a floor above the floor Malandrake was on. Wait a moment, she thought. Sebaceous the Slimy was even better. She grinned coldly at her own cleverness.

Variana dipped her finger once again into the goblet. She lifted a blood-stained finger and wiped a line of blood-tears beneath her left eye. War paint, some had called it when they saw it on her face. She raised the goblet to her mouth and drained its contents, reddening her lips with the liquid as it passed them.

⚜

Gino sat in a far corner booth in the inn, off to the right of the hearth. The booth was situated deep in the corner, the edge of the table even with the brick wall that lined the hearth so the light emanating from the fire burning in the hearth didn't reach the booth. It gave him a great vantage point on most of the dining room area, while keeping him mostly hidden. He couldn't see the booth on the opposite side of the hearth, or a few of the tables on that side of the room, but he could still see about ninety percent of the room from where he sat.

He thought about his unfortunate encounter with Werko, playing it over again in his mind as he had done a thousand times already. Sure, he stole the bag of gold. That's what he was supposed to do, right? He was a thief. You see a bag of gold, you take it. It was just sitting there in a pouch on a table, right there in the open. I mean, who leaves a pouch full of gold just sitting out unless they don't really need it, right? Who does that?

A wizard you shouldn't have fucked with, that's who.

"You stink of cheap magic."

Gino froze, afraid to look away from the mug of ale he had been nursing.

62

Then he heard a shuffling sound and saw two shapes out of the corner of his eye slide into the booth seat opposite him.

"Is he deaf?" Gino heard a second male voice asked.

"No, just afraid. I can smell that on him, too," the owner of the first voice said.

Think fast, you idiot.

"You'd be afraid, too, if Werko the Wondrous was after you. He has the strongest magic in the world," Gino said. He kept his head down, still feeling very uneasy, still nervously afraid to see who was now sitting across from him.

"And what spell did he cast upon you that makes you fear him?" the first voice asked.

"He took something from me that no one has the right to take," Gino said. "No man, no wizard, no one."

The two men sat quietly, waiting for him to elaborate.

"He took two inches off my cock," Gino said, keeping his head down, avoiding looking anywhere in their direction.

Absolute silence.

"So that leaves you with one?"

Just a moment of silence hung in the air before riotous laughter exploded out of the men's mouths, the bellows and guffaws coming from deep within their chests.

Gino gritted his teeth, but kept silent. *Let them laugh. Turn it back on them.* He finally glanced up ever so slightly, catching the ends of the oily strands that hung down over the first man's chest, now seeing that the man was dressed in an ornate crimson robe. "He's promised to do that to every wizard who dares challenge him."

The laughter stopped abruptly, as if invisible hands just clamped themselves down over the men's mouths. Sebastian the Spectacular was no longer amused.

Werko the Wondrous stepped into the inn. He glanced about the room. As was customary when he entered the inn, all conversation stopped. No one looked in his direction, but everyone knew he was there. The patrons looked down at their hands, or stared at their mugs, or absently eyed the food on their plates.

Sebastian looked up at Werko, sensing his presence. He nearly laughed aloud. Werko was wearing an invisible shield that Sebastian knew he could crack in a matter of seconds with one dynam spell. Did the man really think that shield would protect him? Sebastian frowned. Or was he being devilishly clever, trying to provoke him?

Werko made his way deeper into the inn, waddling like a huge fat duck. A small booth was empty to the right of the doorway as one faced the interior of the inn, and Werko made his way towards that booth. It appeared to be his booth, reserved for him and him alone. There were two short benches within the booth, positioned on opposites side of the small table centered in the middle of the booth, each bench with just enough space for only one person.

Sebastian contemplated his next move. The man had done him no wrong, yet his very presence felt like a veiled threat and that did not sit well with him. The tales of Werko's wizardly prowess grated on him.

Gino cautiously approached Werko, feeling an anxious twitch in his crotch area, feeling himself turtling and shrinking even smaller. He had left the booth where he had been sitting when he saw Werko entering the inn, leaving the two men without uttering a word. He bowed as he neared the booth, doing his best to appear humble as rage and shame and all manner of fury threatened to overwhelm the calm demeanor he struggled to maintain.

"What is it, Gino?" Werko asked, impatience clipping his words. "Or should I say Gina?" Werko laughed.

"Forgive the intrusion, Master Wondrous, but I think there is something you should know," Gino said.

"I already know you are an idiot," Werko said, with true sincerity in his voice.

Gino nodded. "Yes, of course." He paused, but just for a brief moment. "There is also something else you should know."

Werko waited.

"There are other wizards in town," Gino paused. "Looking for you." Gino looked up at Werko and caught just a quick flash of alarm in the wizard's face. It was a fleeting expression, visible for just the briefest of moments, but he was certain he had seen a hint of fear on the wizard's face. And that gave him an immense feeling of satisfaction.

"Looking for me?" Werko asked. "Why would

other wizards be looking for me?"

"I..." Gino let his voice trail off, but then continued. "I'm hesitant to say, Master Wondrous." He bowed his head, averting his gaze from the wizard.

"Just tell me, or I'll snip off your last inch," Werko said, snapping off his words.

"They want this village for themselves," Gino said.

"This hovel?" Werko frowned.

"And the woods that surround it," Gino added, keeping his head bowed, but tilting his head just a bit to glance up at Werko.

"There's nothing of value here." And then Werko paused. He looked at Gino, but his words came out more for himself than for Gino. "Or is there?" Were they here for the Tree of Tarturus? Maybe some of the stories he had heard were actually true. Werko had casually searched the woods himself a few times, just on a lark, but he had never found the tree. But just because he didn't find it, didn't mean the legends weren't true. The roots of the Tree of Tarturus were rumored to reach into the depths of Hell and infuse the tree's sap with a dark power that a trained wizard could use to augment the power of his spells. Werko focused his gaze directly on Gino. "Are they here for the Tree?"

Gino softly shrugged his shoulders and gave a faint shake of his head. "I don't know for certain." He paused. "But that is what I have heard."

"So it *is* real," Werko said, exclaiming the words with a growing wonder and excitement. He glanced upwards, looking at nothing, just thinking of the powers such a tree could bring him. He quickly brought his gaze back down to stare sharply at Gino.

"Where is it? Where is the Tree?"

"I don't know." Gino met his gaze. "But don't you think you had better stop them before they find it first?"

Two black cats slinked into Tilkin's Tavern and Inn, their small furry heads casually looking left, then right as they entered the establishment, their eyes gleaming in the gloomy areas that shadowed the wood plank floor, their ears perked up and alert to absorb any sounds that might be of interest to their master. No one in the inn paid them any attention; cats meandering about doing whatever cats did was a common sight in the village.

One of the black cats started to slink up the wooden stairs to the left of the inn's entrance, padding up towards the second floor where numerous rooms designated for travelers and other town guests were located, but the clatter of booted footsteps approaching made the animal pause. She sat back on her haunches at the bottom of the stairs and waited, keeping her head up and her gaze focused on the top of the stairway where the second floor landing began.

The sound of leather boots slapping against wood grew louder and then a man appeared at the top of the stairs. A man the cat's controlling master recognized immediately as Malandrake the Magnificent. The cat received a mental command to flee so she turned abruptly away from the stairs and bounded towards the inn's open front door; the second cat quickly joined her and they both raced out into the night.

Variana entered the inn just as her two cat scouts fled the building, stepping in with purpose, a clear determination etched into her stern features. Her arms were down at her sides and she clutched a sparrow in each hand; the birds' tiny heads were the only part of their little bodies that were visible as they peaked out from her closed fingers.

Malandrake saw Variana when he was halfway down the stairs, but by then it was too late. His eyes went wide and he immediately cast about in his mind for a protective spell, but he had no time to utter it.

Variana shot her arms forward, opening her fingers, releasing the sparrows, sending them rocketing towards Malandrake with the blazing speed of cross bolts being released from a tightly coiled crossbow.

Malandrake crossed his arms in front of himself, throwing up a shield of his own flesh and bone in front of his face. He managed to block one of the sparrows with his left forearm; the bird's sharp beak sank deep into his arm, drawing red hot blood. He didn't have time to cry out in pain as the second sparrow soared just beneath the area where his arms were crossed, the little bird slamming violently into the tender exposed area on his throat, penetrating deep into his neck. More blood spurted out, raining down on the stairs, sounding like rain splattering against a rooftop as it struck the wooden planks.

Variana didn't even watch Malandrake fall and tumble down the stairs. She continued walking into the inn, heading for an open table near the hearth.

Zinnia and Grifik stood motionless at the top of the second floor landing, then quietly and quickly turned around and hurried back to their room.

Gino looked away from Werko as he heard a loud crashing sound. He saw a body tumbling end over end down the stairs, arms and legs flailing. At first he thought it was just another drunk taking a fall (which had happened quite often in the inn over the years), but the amount of blood flying about seemed a bit extreme for a man just falling down the stairs. A large splash of blood splattered against the wall, blotting out the painted portraits of several previous owners of the inn that hung there.

The tumbling body reached the bottom of the stairs, twitched a few times, then lay still. Blood continued to ooze out of a ragged gash that had been ripped into the man's throat. What looked like part of a small bird, and a smattering of feathers, appeared to be still lodged in the man's neck.

Gino looked back to Werko, feeling both terrified and incredibly excited all at the same time. "They're here," he said. "They're coming for you."

Sebastian didn't even need to swirl his finger in the air to taste the magic that was so evidently in the air. He muttered a protective spell, putting up a shield around his body that would at least prevent him from dying immediately from a surprise attack.

He glanced over to Werko. The man was so calm! Sebastian didn't think he himself could remain so calm after unleashing such an attack. He would be to hopped-up with power to sit still.

And then he saw Variana crossing the room and

taking a seat at a table near the hearth. She was a thin waif, but very beautiful. She had a red marking on her cheek, the symbol running down from her left eye to the level of her mouth. A witch! A witch with her war paint on! What was she doing here? Was she the one behind the attack?

Sebastian didn't sense the cats coming in for the kill. His spell would protect him against magic, but not against the physical strikes of animals. One of the cats slinked under the table, extended its claws, and sank them deep into Sebastian's leg. Sebastian howled in pain, throwing his head back, exposing his throat. The second cat leaped, slashing at his tender flesh, slicing through his skin. Blood erupted in a powerful geyser as Sebastian's heart pumped blood into his severed arteries, the red liquid shooting upwards, the crimson spray spreading out as it exploded away from him, showering nearby occupants of the inn in a sheen of dark liquid.

Sebastian clutched futilely at his slashed throat, unable to stop the blood from jetting out of his body. His eyes filled with confusion. This can't be happening. He was a powerful wizard. And then fear ripped away the confusion, filling his eyes with terror. He keeled forward, dropping to the table top with a loud clunk, his head cracking against the wooden surface.

Prater bolted for the door, racing out of the inn without a single glance behind him.

Variana waited patiently at her table as chaos erupted around her.

Patrons scrambled away from Sebastian's corpse, desperate to get as far away from it as possible; most of the patrons continued running right out the door of the inn to disappear into the night. A few old hands remained. They looked at Sebastian's motionless, bleeding body for a few more moments, their curiosity only slightly piqued, then returned to their drinks or meals or to their quiet conversations.

"What does a girl need to do to get a drink around here?" Variana asked.

No one waited on her.

Variana looked over at Cinderee, who was still standing frozen, transfixed by Sebastian's dead body; even Cinderee's separated shadow appeared to be too afraid to move. Variana snapped her fingers at Cinderee, finally able to draw the serving wench's attention. "Tell Werko to join me."

Werko sat across from Variana, his hands down in his lap, his fingers twitching nervously under the table as she studied him.

Gino sidled closer, moving very slowly around some nearby tables, doing his best not to be obvious about his movements.

"So, I hear you think you're all that," Variana said. "You're the big shit with the big powers."

Werko immediately shook his head. "I never said that."

Variana clacked her nails on the table. "Well, somebody is saying it." She paused, stopping her fingers in mid-clack. "A lot."

Werko shook his head again. "Wasn't me. I'm not

a braggart."

"Do you have any powers?" Variana asked. "Or is it all just rumor and hearsay?"

Werko hesitated. "I have some powers, yes." He nodded his head. "I've been practicing."

"He's been practicing on me," Gino blurted out. He couldn't help himself. He had to say something. "He took two inches off my cock! That's just not right!"

Variana slowly turned to look at Gino. She blinked slowly. "So that leaves you with one?"

Gino thrust his finger at Werko. "He did it. He said he wants to take over the whole country! He said he's going to destroy every wizard one by one until he's the only one left!"

Variana studied Gino for a moment, then turned to look at Werko. "Is this true?" she asked of the wizard sitting opposite her.

Werko shook his head adamantly. "Absolutely not. It's not true. I never said that."

"He's a liar!" Gino said. "He told me that very thing a dozen times. He boasted that once he found the Tree of Tarturus nothing would be able to stop him."

Variana frowned at Gino. "The Tree of Tarturus does not exist."

Gino nodded his head. "Yes, it does." He pointed a finger at Werko. "He knows. He knows where it is."

Variana turned her gaze on Werko, her face questioning, but her lips remaining silent.

Werko again shook his head. He glared at Gino. "He's a damn fool and a liar. And a thief." He turned back to Variana. "That's why I snipped his cock! He's a damn thief and a liar!"

Variana was quiet for long moment. "Let me see it," she said.

Gino pointed at Werko. "He knows where it is. I don't know where it is."

Variana sighed with annoyance. "Not the Tree. Your cock. Show me your cock."

Gino hesitated, but only for a moment. He untied the rope belt holding up his pants and pulled them down to reveal his crotch area.

Variana put her hand over her mouth. "Oh, my." She looked back over at Werko. "Are you sure you didn't take the whole thing?"

Gino grunted and pulled his pants back up, quickly re-tying his rope belt.

Variana scowled at Gino. "I didn't tell you to pull your pants back up."

Gino just looked at her.

Variana waved her fingers at his crotch. "Pull your pants back down."

Gino looked to Werko, as if looking for help, but the fat wizard just glared at him. Gino untied his rope belt and slid his pants down to again reveal his stunted cock.

Werko chose then to strike, producing a blade and slashing at Variana's throat. Variana leaned out of the way of the slashing blade and struck back, lunging quickly towards Werko, sinking her nails into Werko's throat, using her clawed fingers like the prongs on a fork.

Werko gurgled and choked as his own blood oozed down his throat. His warm blood spilled over Variana's fingers. She pushed her fingers in a little deeper into Werko's throat, her smile growing slightly larger as she did so. Werko gagged, his eyes widening to big saucers. He swiped the dagger through the air, desperate to strike Variana. The blade cut through nothing but residual pipe smoke that had drifted towards them from a nearby table.

Gino glanced down as the dagger sliced past him, the silver metal just missing the tip of his exposed cock. Had the blade been one inch higher he would have lost even more of his manhood. He quickly pulled his pants back up, stepping back away from the table as he urgently tied his rope belt back into place.

Werko dropped his blade and clutched at Variana's hand with both of his, desperate to dislodge her clawed fingers from his throat. And then his head just drooped; his hands went limp and dropped back down to the top of the table with a soft thud.

Gino stood motionless for a moment. Then, he checked his cock, peering down into his pants. He reached into his pants, gripping his member. He frowned, immediately realizing that his lost inches hadn't grown back. His cock remained stunted. Maybe Werko wasn't really dead? He glanced over to look at Werko and quickly came to the realization that he was indeed dead. The wizard's eyes were open, glassy, vacant; his chest no longer moved with breath. Gino glanced back down into his pants, studying his crotch area. The wizard was dead, but his cock had not returned to its normal length.

Variana eyed Gino checking on his cock. She tilted her head slightly, keeping her gaze locked on him. She studied him for a long moment. Then a realization swept over her. "You wanted Werko to get killed," she said to Gino. "You've been crowing about him for months, trying to draw attention to him." She looked at him with a growing respect. "You were trying to get him killed."

Gino remained quiet, silently fuming at his unchanged plight.

"You were trying to reverse the curse he put on you by killing him." She looked at Gino, then gave a soft, tittering laugh. "It doesn't work that way. Only a living wizard can remove a curse."

Gino's scowl darkened.

Variana looked at Gino and softly shook her head. "You want a big cock? You should have just asked me." She gave him a warm smile. "I'll make you a big cock."

Gino's face lit up.

The rooster crowed just as dawn peaked over the horizon, its voice loud and deep.

A young farmer stopped raking the soil to glance up at the carriage slowly moving past him on the dirt road next to his fields. "That's a mighty fine rooster you have, lady," the young farmer said to the carriage's passenger.

Variana nodded and smiled. She glanced at the rooster perched on the side of her carriage, its legs bound by a cord of leather, the bird attached firmly to the frame of the carriage, its golden brown eyes staring up at the sky. "The biggest cock in town!"

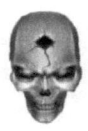

TERRORSTORY #63
OPEN UP A CAN OF WHOOP ASS

Ellis Taggart was thirsty. His tongue felt both dry and sticky at the same time. His eyes felt just as dry, and every time he blinked his eyelids seem to get stuck closed and he had to make an extra mental effort to get the lids to move back up again.

He stumbled past a restaurant, glancing up at the sign that overhung its entranceway as he moved clumsily past. Most of the letters looked blurry to him, but he could make out a big 'D' and a big 'L' in the name. A distant thought burst into his conscious mind - *didn't I used to go to fancy restaurants like this?* - but then the thought zoomed out of his consciousness just as abruptly as it had surfaced.

His brain registered a rumbling sound in the distance, but he didn't know if that was coming from an impending storm or if it was the rumble of a truck passing by in the city street just off to his right. His stomach growled in response to the rumbling noise, reminding him that he was also hungry.

Ellis paused for a moment, glancing about him. *Where am I?* He didn't recognize any of the landmarks. There were a few trees dotting the sidewalk on his right, a row of parked cars beyond them. He looked up ahead and noticed a dark pocket of shadow on his left. The darkness looked cool and inviting to him. He needed to sleep. He was so tired. So very tired.

But he was also damn thirsty. So damn thirsty.

He staggered forward, stumbling towards the dark entrance, turning left into the darkness when he reached it. He found himself in an alley that ran along the right side of the restaurant he had just passed. He suddenly realized what had drawn him into the alley. It was the enticing aroma of spaghetti sauce and garlic bread. Follow your nose!

There were several large green dumpsters set against the red brick wall near a small side door. He stumbled over to them and scrounged in one of the green dumpsters, somehow finding the energy to clamber halfway into the refuse bin and poke his hand around inside. He found several discarded pieces of garlic bread, and even a few half-eaten meatballs. It was a feast! It all tasted delicious to his indiscriminate palate.

After his meal, Ellis ripped off a piece of cardboard from a nearby pile of discarded boxes and made himself a nice mattress to lay on. He was still feeling very thirsty, but fatigue and exhaustion overwhelmed him.

❦

Salamander Smith looked down at the homeless guy sleeping underneath a tattered shred of damp cardboard that he appeared to be using as some kind of blanket. A large folded piece of oil-stained cardboard was serving as the guy's mattress. The guy's face was thick with a tangled growth of black hair, his greasy hair flecked with aging slivers of silver. Salamander guessed maybe he was in his fifties, or even his sixties. The guy's cheeks had a ruddy complexion, the exposed parts of his face heavily wrinkled; what skin Salamander could see looked like somebody had peeled a whole bunch of raisins and spread them all over the guy's face.

Haudie Johnson stepped up next to Salamander and stared down at the dude, but he didn't say nothing. Haudie was in his early twenties, a few years older than Salamander. He had a few more inches of height and a few more pounds on Salamander as well.

They were in the alley outside DeLacort's restaurant, a local Italian joint. A few aging lights positioned higher up on the side of the restaurant bathed the alley in a pale yellowing light. The rain had stopped several hours earlier so the alley pavement, and just about everything in it, including the two green dumpsters and an old piece of discarded equipment, looked like they were all coated with a layer of varnish that had just been laid down. But the alley didn't stink like no furniture cream. To Salamander, it smelled of old spaghetti sauce and stale garlic bread that reminded Salamander of the fat Italian guy who used to come round and see his Momma. Sometimes, the fat fuck would come see him, too. Later at night when his Momma was asleep. Salamander pushed that out of his head. Don't want none o' that shit messin' up my night. Sometimes, his bung hole felt sore just from the rememberin'. He shook his head. No, sir. None o' that shit gonna fuck up this night. No way. The night was his. And he was gonna take that bitch by the throat and shake her till she saw stars swimmin' around her fucking head.

"Nobody gonna miss him," Haudie said, finally speaking up.

"So why him?" Salamander asked as he stared down at the man. He heard a soft snoring coming from the guy.

Haudie stared down at the sleeping man and pointed at him. "Look at him twitchin' and mumblin'. Prolably having some nightmare or somethin'. You's gonna be doing him a favor. Puttin' him outta his misery, so to speak." Haudie smiled. "Nobody gonna care. Don't matter who. It's for the doin', man. For the deed."

Salamander looked back over at Haudie.

Haudie nodded his head as he spoke. "For the notch on your belt, man. You gotta start somewheres."

Salamander nodded. "How should I do it?"

Haudie shook his head. "Ain't for my lips to speak." He tapped Salamander on the head. The back of Haudie's hands were a dark brown, but his palms looked like he coated them with hazelnut creamer. "For your sponge to figure out. I know you's seen the deed being done many a time." Haudie wagged his finger. "But don't be no copycat. Nobody likes a lazy copycat." He smiled a big fat smile.

Salamander scowled at Haudie. "What you goofy faced for?"

Haudie raised his head proudly. "Just memberin' my first."

"Yeah? What was it?"

Haudie shook his head. "You gonna steal it."

"You just tol' me not to be a copycat," Salamander said with a frown. "I ain't gonna steals it."

"I drowned the fuck. In a barrel of rainwater. Tipped his body right in, then shoved his head right under and held him there till no more squirmin'. Easy peasy. It was beautiful. Clean. No muss. No fuss." Haudie paused. "Well, the dude fussed. But not for long. And he mussed a little in his pants, but the water done cleaned that up." Haudie's lips split open wider, and he even showed a little bit of his tobacco-and-tea stained teeth.

"Ha." Salamander bobbed his head up and down in approval. He thought about Haudie's telling. Killed the dude with rainwater. Drowning. Killed with water. Killed with something he used every day. He needed to do something else just as smart. And then he thought of something. Something he in fact did use every day. Hell, he probably used it twenty or thirty times a day.

Salamander smiled a big fat smile. He flicked his lighter to make a tiny flame, lit up his cigarette, and kept on smiling.

Ellis Taggart sometimes forgot who he was, let alone where he was. He had vague flashes of a woman, children, a house. Loud crunching noises sometimes exploded into his head. Metal crunching. Glass shattering. He always expected to hear screams with those noises, but he never heard any screams. Just the metal crunching and the glass shattering. Sometimes the noises got so bad he felt like the sounds of the glass were turning into actual shards slicing through his head. He used to pound on his head and yell and shout when that happened, but that never helped any, so now he just tried to silently endure it as best he could.

Sometimes, though, the sounds still got the better of him and he would regress back into a screaming paroxysm of anger and confusion and then more anger. The agonizing physical torment would move through his body as the skin on his face rippled and warped as if the pain was a wave moving down from the top of his forehead, over his cheekbones, past his chin and down through the rest of his body until it expended itself out of his toes. One time the pain wouldn't leave his toe, so he finally had to cut it off. That action give him a slight limp, and sometimes the pain came back as if a ghost was hammering on a toe that was no longer there, but there was nothing he could do about that because he had already cut that toe off. He just endured it as best he could.

He muttered and moaned in his fitful attempt at sleep, dreaming of foul-smelling acid rain falling on him.

"You gonna roast marshmallows on him?" Haudie asked.

Salamander frowned. "No, I ain't gonna toast marshmallows on him." His frown deepened. "You think I'm some kinda sick fuck?" He shook his head. "I ain't gonna do that."

"Man, you'd think that smell o' gasoline would wake his ass up," Haudie said.

Salamander glanced at the red plastic gasoline container he was holding. It was about one quarter full still. He could tell how much was left because the remaining liquid was visible as a dark mass inside the semi-transparent container. The rest of the gasoline was soaking into Ellis Taggart's clothes. "Yeah, you'd think. I can smell it hard from here." He set the gasoline container down on the alley pavement.

"I like that smell," Haudie said. He looked away from the sleeping homeless man to glance at Salamander. "You like that smell?"

Salamander shrugged. "Don't like it. Don't hate it. It's just what it is."

"I like it. It reminds me of Stilt's garage. I put some good hours in that place."

"You was a mechanic, right?" Salamander asked.

Haudie nodded. "For a little bit. About six months."

Salamander lit up a cigarette, puffing out a stream of smoke after sucking in a big inhale. "Six months." Salamander nodded his head. "That's pretty good. What kind o' cars you work on?"

Haudie shook his head. "Didn't work on no cars.

Just cleaned up the place."

"Sounds mo' like a janitor than a mechanic to me."

Haudie nodded. "Yeah, yeah. Least I had a job for a while." He looked at the gasoline-saturated form of Ellis Taggart as he lay asleep on his cardboard mattress. "You gonna flame him, or what?"

"Yeah, yeah." Salamander exhaled another cloud of smoke. "I'm enjoying the moment, bro. Taking it all in.

"Hey, make one of them trails." Haudie pointed to the container of gasoline on the ground next to Salamander. "Make a trail from here to him." He traced an imaginary line leading from Salamander's sneakers to the homeless guy snoring on the ground. "Then toss your cigarette down. The fire will shoot down that line and light him up. I seen that in the movies a few times."

Salamander nodded. "Yeah, yeah." He shoved his cigarette in his mouth and kept his lips pressed together to keep it in place. "Like a fuse on a bomb." As he spoke, he nearly lost his mouthy grip on the cigarette and it started to slide out from behind his lips. He quickly pressed his lips tight, keeping a grip on his lit cigarette. He grabbed the gas container and poured out a trail from where he had been standing up to the sleeping man, darkening the pavement in a slightly straight line. There had been just enough gasoline left to make the line. He stared down at the empty gas container in his hand; the curly wisp of cigarette smoke drifting up from the cigarette in his mouth stung his eyes for a second. He moved over to a nearby dumpster and tossed the empty gasoline can inside.

Haudie stared at him curiously.

Salamander grabbed his cigarette with two fingers and blew out a mouthful of smoke. "I ain't no litterbug."

Haudie shrugged.

Salamander shifted his body, turning to face the homeless man straight on. He pulled on his cigarette and the end of the cigarette flared up with red heat. He tossed the cigarette down on the alley pavement and a spark flew off the end as it struck the hard ground. But the gasoline-fuse did not light. Salamander frowned. "What the fuck?"

"Try it again," Haudie said.

Salamander headed towards the fallen cigarette that rested on the ground near a stack of discarded pallets leaning up against the restaurant wall, but Haudie grabbed his arm, stopping him. "No, man. Fire up a fresh one."

The homeless man snorted and grunted as he turned over.

Salamander and Haudie froze, staying motionless as the homeless man curled himself into a fetal position. They waited for a few moments longer, staring at the man, but he seemed to be content with his new sleeping position.

"Hurry up, man," Haudie hissed in a low voice.

Salamander fumbled at his cigarette pack and pulled out a smoke. He quickly lit the cigarette and took a deep drag. Before he even finished exhaling, he crouched down and put the red hot tip of the cigarette to the edge of the gasoline trail he had made moments earlier.

The gasoline caught fire this time and a line of flame raced towards the sleeping man.

Ellis Taggart dreamed of Hell. It was the hell of his Catholic upbringing. Full of hopelessness and despair. Full of fire and fear. Full of screaming souls. It felt so real. He could feel the heat on his hands, on his chest, in his face.

Something compelled him to open his eyes, to escape this nightmare he found himself in. And only then did he realize that he was the one on fire. And he was the one screaming.

Salamander danced around excitedly, keeping himself in one spot but jumping quickly from foot to foot. "You look a little hot," he said to the burning man, who was now standing up, twisting and twirling his body, desperately patting at the flames that were starting to fully engulf him. "You better buy yo'self something to cool off." Salamander tossed a handful of loose change at the man. Some of the coins sailed past the burning man, other coins bounced off his chest or arms or face.

Haudie hooted with laughter, his face bathed in the glow given off by the man in flames a few yards away. "Look how much you brightened up his day!"

"I can smell his stanky hair burnin' from here," Salamander said, wrinkling his nose.

"What the hell are you two doing back here?" a voice shouted.

Salamander snapped his head towards the bellowing voice, seeing a big beefy man staring at them from an open back door that led into the restaurant's kitchen. "Oh, shit." Salamander turned to look at Haudie, but Haudie was already twenty steps ahead of him, sprinting towards the mouth of the alley, not even glancing back. Salamander burst into motion, charging after Haudie.

***

Stop. Drop. Roll. Ellis had no idea where those words came from. They came from somewhere deep within his past, his brain somehow drudging them up from the chaotic swirl of memories that churned far below his conscious thoughts. He stopped screaming. He dropped to the ground. He rolled over and over, moving back and forth. He rolled into a puddle, then rolled out of it, then rolled back into it. The combination of smothering the flames against the pavement and the muddy water dousing the blaze that bit at his ragged clothes helped put the fire out.

He lay in the alley for a long moment, breathing hard; every part of his body still felt as if it were aflame. He rolled along the ground again, moving back and forth, desperately trying to stop the searing pain, thinking he must still be on fire, but soon the movement caused him more pain than it alleviated so he stopped rolling.

He heard footsteps approaching and opened his eyes to see a big beefy man dressed in a white apron staring down at him.

"Goddamn bums," the big beefy man said and turned away to head back into the restaurant.

Ellis closed his eyes, trying not to listen to the whimpering sounds his own lips were making.

Ellis opened his eyes. He was curled up in a ball on the pavement. He could feel the bricks of a wall digging into his back. He was still in the alley. Had he dragged himself into the corner, or had someone else moved him there? He didn't know, and he didn't care. Somehow he was still alive.

The back of his right hand pulsed and throbbed. He raised his arm up shakily and saw the redness, the swelling, and several white-capped, bulbous blisters on the back of his right hand. His shirt was burned, most of the sleeve on his right arm now burned away. There were additional patches of reddened skin along his right arm. Some deeper part of his brain shrieked with the pain that was radiating from what seemed the entire length of his arm, but he was so numb by a life now constantly filled with pain that he barely registered it.

Someone tried to burn you alive. Some motherfuckers tried to burn you alive.

He struggled to a sitting position, grunting and wincing as he moved. His burned back scraped against the brick wall, causing spearing spikes of pain to penetrate deep into his head, reaching pain centers that had long been buried by a decade of mental decline. A wailing cry issued forth from his dry lips.

He was so thirsty. He licked at his cracked lips. He needed to get something to drink. That's all he could think of right now. Just get something to drink. Something. Anything.

A shiny object on the ground drew his attention. It was a coin. A nickel. And then he saw another coin lying next to it. A quarter. And then he saw another two coins nearby. Two pennies. He started to drag himself towards the coins, but the intense burning sensation in his left leg forced him to stop as he felt his skin peeling away as he dragged it along the course ground of the alley pavement. He took a deep breath and gritted his teeth, determined to get those coins into his hands no matter what.

Ellis looked like the victim of a train wreck, stumbling and staggering out of the alley, his clothing in tatters, dark edges of the old torn clothing marking the areas where the edges of the flames had reached before he put them out. His right sleeve was practically nonexistent. The left side of his pants was barely more than tattered strips, looking like he was covering his leg in a vertical blind where each slat of the blind had been burnt at the edges. His shoes were mostly intact; only one edge of his left shoe was burned, the rear portion of the sole slightly blackened from the flames.

A red burn patch marred his forehead. Several parts of his scalp were now devoid of hair; the rest of his head was still covered in his scraggly mass of oily, tangled hair. His beard was partially singed on the right side of his face, some of the hairs curled up into burnt crisps.

"You can't be in here," the liquor store clerk said. He was an Indian man, his black hair cut short and neat, his face cleanly shaven. He waved his hand frantically at Ellis, motioning for him to get out of the store.

"I got money," Ellis said, his words coming out in a hoarse, scratchy voice. He raised up his hand, showing the clerk his change.

"No, no," the clerk insisted. "You are filthy. You are a dirty man. You can't be in here. You scare away my customers." He remained behind the counter, and kept forcefully pointing at the store's exit.

"I got money," Ellis repeated. "I need something to drink." He forced himself to stand taller. "I'm not leaving till I get something to drink."

The clerk frowned at him as Ellis drew closer. "How much do you have?" the clerk asked.

Ellis stopped and opened up his palm to stare at the change in his hand. He saw two quarters, a nickel, four pennies and two dimes. He tried to add them all up in his head, but he was having a hard time holding onto the total as he added them together. He knew he had at least fifty cents because of the two quarters. "What do you have for fifty cents?" he asked.

The clerk scoffed. "Fifty cents? I have nothing for fifty cents. You are a dirty man. You need to leave."

Ellis shook his head. "I need something to drink. What do you have for fifty cents?" He paused. "Water. Give me some water."

The clerk scoffed again. "You think water only cost fifty cents?"

Ellis scowled. The pain from the burns on his body was starting to seep into his brain now and he felt a growing irritation welling up inside of him. "What do you have for fifty cents?"

"Nothing."

"I'm not leaving until you sell me something to

drink for fifty cents," Ellis said. He didn't know where the determination came from; maybe the pain was fueling his courage, or his sense of outrage. Regardless, he was determined not to leave this store until he got something to drink. His tongue felt like a block of dried wood in his mouth.

The disgruntled clerk waved at a dilapidated shopping cart sitting near a back wall to the far right of the register. It was filled with closeout items, discontinued snacks, items in torn packaging. "Get something from in there. I'll sell you one thing in there for fifty cents." He waved his fingers impatiently at the cart again. "Go. Pick something out. Hurry up."

Ellis shuffled towards the beat-up shopping cart and peered inside at its contents. There were a few lighters in ripped packaging, some single packs of crackers, several dozen packs of drink mixes, some candy bars. Numerous loose cans of soda filled the bottom of the cart. He reached in and grabbed a dust-laden can of pop. He raised up the can and tried to read the label, but all he could make out was an HO and two Ss. There looked to be other letters on the can but they were covered in a layer of grime so they were illegible. Didn't matter. It was a drink. He'd settle for drinking anything right about now.

He paid the clerk, dumping all of his change on the counter.

Ellis shuffled back into the alley, moving back into the far corner behind the big green dumpster, moving back into the area that he now thought of as his home. Some charred debris was still littering the ground, but most of the damage caused by the fire had blown away by now.

Some patches of his burned skin started to make their presence known as an ache radiated out of them. Some of the reddened areas also radiated a wave of heat. He eased himself down onto a piece of unburnt cardboard and looked at the can he gripped in his hand. He wiped at the dirty can, clearing away the dust and grime that coated its metal surface. He could make out more of the letters now. HOO ASS. He scrubbed at the can again, revealing another letter, a W. He scrubbed at the metal a little more to reveal a P. He read the can's label again. WHOOP ASS. Something in the deep recesses of his mind thought that should be funny, but the thought stay buried and never reached the forefront of his mind so he didn't even crack a smile.

He fumbled at the pull tab, his dirty index finger trying to get a hold on the thin circle of metal. A thick layer of grime was embedded beneath his fingernails, making it appear as if he had lined the tips of his fingers with black paint. He struggled with the pull tab, unable to get a grip on it, the metal circle clicking back down against the lid as he failed again and again to get a hold on it.

Finally, he was able to hook his finger beneath the pull tab and gave it a sharp tug. The pull tab pressed down into the pre-cut oval and a soft whooshing hiss emanated from the can as it was opened. A citrus aroma tickled his nose immediately as the pent up carbonation erupted out of the can.

Ellis stared at the can in amazement at what happened next.

"You gotta know," Haudie said. "The proof is in the pudding, as they say."

"He ain't gonna be pudding," Salamander said. "He gonna be more like roasted marshmallows."

Haudie grinned and nodded. "Crispy on the outside and all gooey on the inside."

Salamander nodded. "Yeah."

They approached the alley cautiously, wary and alert, both of them darting their gazes about.

"Maybe they already took his body away," Salamander said, keeping his voice down.

Haudie shook his head. "No, man. You hear an ambulance? A fire truck? Even a police siren?"

Salamander was quiet. They had fled the alley when they saw the big fat white man staring at them from the restaurant door, but they still had remained within a few blocks of the restaurant. Haudie was right. They would've heard any sirens if somebody had called it in.

Haudie continued to shake his head. "No, man. Nobody even called it in. He's most likely lying there dead. All burnt up and shit."

"Yeah, like a hot cross bum." Salamander's smile split his face. "Get it? Like a hot cross bun, but bum instead of bun."

"Yeah, I gots it."

They moved deeper into the alley, moving slowly, cautiously.

"What if that big dude comes out of the restaurant again?" Salamander asked, still keeping his voice low. He looked nervously at the restaurant's back door.

"Look, all we gots to do is confirm he's dead," Haudie said. "That's it. Then you can claim the deed."

Salamander nodded. Then his face lit up excitedly. "Hey, man. We can be like Batman and Robin. Except they can call us Fire and Water. You do 'em with water and I do 'em with fire."

Haudie looked at Salamander. "Hey, man, that's pretty good." He nodded his head enthusiastically. "That's pretty good. Except it should be Water and Fire. Like that. Water and Fire."

"Water and Fire?" Salamander frowned. "Nobody say Water and Fire. They always say Fire and Water."

Haudie frowned. "Who say they do?"

"Man, everybody do," Salamander said. "That's just how they say it."

Haudie hushed his talk with an impatient wave of his hand. "Man, whatever, let's just go find your hot cross bum and be done with it."

A fizzy spray of bubbles rose up out of the can as Ellis stared in growing amazement. But these weren't any kind of carbonated bubbles Ellis had ever seen before. They didn't continue to float up into the air. They didn't dissipate. They retained their shape and seemed to hover around the entrance to the can. Ellis stared at the bubbles. They danced and swirled around the lip of the can, shimmering slightly with a silver sheen, their curved shapes catching reflections of light coming off the metal can.

Then some of the bubbles finally drifted higher, and he felt their effervescence reach his nose. The bubbles tickled his nose, but there was more to them than just a fleeting sensation. They seemed to take hold inside his nose, almost aggressively gripping at his flesh as they lined his nostrils.

And then Ellis took a sip from the can of WHOOP ASS. It was just a little sip, but it was enough to change his life forever.

⚜

"Fuck, the dude ain't dead," Haudie said. He stared in amazement at the bum who was standing near the back of the alley just behind a large green dumpster, drinking something from a can.

Salamander stared in disbelief at the homeless man along with Haudie. "That can't be. I lit him up good."

"You gotta finish him off," Haudie said. "He knows our faces."

"That fool don't even know his own face," Salamander said.

Haudie shook his head. "No, man, he can I.D. us. You gotta finish him off. If the cops ever talk to him, we's in trouble."

⚜

Some of the carbonated bubbles floated up out of the can and into the air about Ellis. They should have popped, or at least continued to rise up into the air, drifting to disappear up into the sky, but instead they remained hovering in the air about the rim of the can. He looked closer at one of the tiny bubbles. There seemed to something inside the bubble, a dark shape, some kind of form. What the hell was that? Was that some kind of... thing? Some kind of creature contained within the bubble?

97

He reached a tentative figure towards the bubble. The tip of his finger pushed against the bubble, the force of his finger indenting the side of the bubble. The bubble felt slightly cool against the edge of his finger as he pushed his finger deeper into the bubble. And then the bubble popped! The creature that had been inside the bubble expanded with a loud whooshing sound, growing quickly, quadrupling in size, then again, then again, then again. A vague memory of tiny sponge dinosaurs getting thrown into a bathtub fleeted across his mind, the little sponge shapes quickly expanding to three or four times their original size upon contact with the water. It was kind of like that, but this thing, this creature that came out of the bubble expanded at a much greater pace and grew to a far, far greater height than those sponge dinosaurs.

Within seconds, a creature about five feet tall stood before Ellis. It looked very similar to the creature depicted on the can's logo. Sort of a Tasmanian devil crossed with a Neanderthal man crossed with a reptile, then with a hint of a demon thrown in for good measure. It had a humanoid shape with dark leathery skin on its few exposed pieces of flesh. A thick hide of dark fur covered most of its body. The eyes were what made Ellis think of a demon. They were dark, deeply set, ominous. He couldn't look at them for more than a few seconds before feeling very unsettled. The creature had five fingers on each hand, fingers that ended in very long, very sharp claws. Its fur-covered legs were thin, but muscular, ending in what looked like a twisted combination of paws and cloven hooves. This was not a cuddly creature. This thing was designed to terrify and instill fear in anyone who saw it.

The creature stared at Ellis and he somehow realized that the creature was waiting for him, waiting for him to issue a command.

Ellis heard footsteps on the pavement and he glanced over to his right to see two men approaching him, two nervous men with deadly intent on their faces. These were the men who had burned him. He didn't know how he knew, but he was completely certain that the two men coming towards him were the ones who had set him on fire.

Ellis turned back to look at the creature. It was a simple command. A command that came easily to his lips. "Kill them," he told the creature.

The creature obeyed. It quickly crouched and launched itself at Haudie, the power behind its muscular legs easily propelling it across the few dozen feet that separated Ellis from the two approaching men. Haudie didn't have much time to react. He threw both his arms up protectively over his head as the creature descended towards him. The creature slammed into Haudie, swiping one of its clawed hands towards Haudie's face. Haudie's arm blocked the blow and the claws raked through his clothing, drawing ragged rips across his flesh. Haudie shrieked in pain, dropping to his knees, clutching at his now profusely bleeding arm.

The creature swiped its other clawed hand down over Haudie's face, engraving four deep lines into Haudie's flesh. Blood poured out of the vertical slashes, the red liquid quickly forming pools around Haudie's knees. Haudie shrieked again and clutched at his bleeding face. The creature struck again, slashing through half of Haudie's neck, digging a deep gash in his throat.

And then the creature vanished. It seemed to just dissolve, as if turning into an amorphous cloud of fizz. A dark cloud hovered in the air for just the briefest of moments where the creature had been standing, then a slight gust of wind blew the cloud apart and it dissipated into nothingness.

Ellis stared at the area where the creature had just been, then shifted his gaze to the dead man lying in his own pool of blood, then slowly looked up to see Salamander staring at him. Their eyes locked, held for a moment. And then Salamander turned and bolted away, racing out of the alley at a speed that could only be described as exceptional for a human being.

"Where Haudie?"

"He's gone, man. Gone." Salamander raced about the room, shutting windows, locking them. His eyes were wide, frantic, his movements wild and uncontrolled. He glanced out the big front window of the house, peering out past the curtains. He quickly looked back to the two other men sitting on a couch nearby. They were watching a football game, eating chips, smoking some weed. A few cans of beer and pop rested on the glass table in front of the couch.

"What do you mean, he's gone? Like to the store or something." Little Juicy followed Salamander as he darted about the room. He was a small man, prone to chewing gum at all hours of the day. Juicy Fruit was his favorite flavor, so it didn't take long for his genius friends to come up with his nickname.

Salamander shook his head. "No. Not like he's

gone to the store or something. He's gone, man. Fucking gone. Like fuckin' dead and gone, man." He moved to another window and locked it.

"Yeah, sure, Salamander, sure." Little Juicy took his gum out of his mouth, stuck it to the side of the bong on the table in front of him, lit up a bowl, exhaled a cloud of smoke, then grabbed his gum and popped it back into his mouth.

"What the hell is wrong with you, man? You actin' all crazy and shit." Dumps frowned at Salamander. His full nickname was Sir DumpsALot, but that was far too much effort to keep repeating, so they all just shortened it to Dumps. He was big man, a fat man with a double chin and very thick arms. Dumps had very erratic bowels. He was prone to using the bathroom, often using it three times a day, sometimes even four, but never less than twice a day. Irritable bowel syndrome, his doctor said.

"You'd be actin' crazy, too, if you seen what I just seen," Salamander said, the words gushing out of him in a quick flood of distress.

Dumps' frown deepened. "Yeah? What'd you see?"

Salamander looked out the front window, again peering out past the curtains.

"Seriously, where's Haudie?" Little Juicy asked. "He said he was gonna bring me back some gum. I'm almost out." Little Juicy waved a 15-stick pack of Juicy Fruit in front of him, showing everyone that only a few sticks remained in the pack.

Salamander whirled on Little Juicy. "He's fucking dead, man! The monster got him! It ripped him all the fuck apart, man! And it's probably comin' for me next!"

Little Juicy leaned back away from Salamander, grinning. "Whoa, man. Chillax, bro. You cranked up or what?"

Salamander turned back away from Little Juicy, again peering out past the curtains. His body tightened and he didn't move a single muscle for a long time. He just stared out the window, frozen in place. Then he slowly turned from the window and calmly looked at Dumps.

Dumps wasn't looking at Salamander. He started to rise up off the couch, clearly about to head for the bathroom, grunting and snorting as he got up, just like he always did.

"Dumps," Salamander called out, his voice now calm, almost eerily flat and unemotional.

Dumps turned to look at him as he finished rising up off the couch. "I gots to go, Sal. What you need?"

"Where's your piece? Your snub. I'm gonna need that."

Dumps pointed to a white plastic storage box near the TV. "Where it always is," Dumps said. "In the white box next to the PlayStation."

Salamander nodded. He headed over to the TV and knelt down near the white storage box. He pulled it open and quickly pulled out the gun.

Dumps cocked his head at Salamander. "What you need it for all of a sudden?"

"Oh, you'll see," Salamander said. "You all is gonna start believin' what I been sayin' in about ten or fifteen seconds." He quickly checked the chamber, making sure it was loaded. There were four bullets in the snub nosed .38 revolver.

Dumps waved his hand impatiently at Salamander. "I ain't got time for this shit."

"Yeah," Little Juicy said. "You only gots time for your own shit." He grinned a stupid grin.

Dumps headed off towards the bathroom, moving into the tight hallway that separated the living room area from the bedrooms and the small bathroom.

"Light that candle when you done, you fat fuck," Little Juicy called after Dumps as he entered the bathroom.

A gentle knock sounded at the door, barely audible above the sound of the football game on the TV, but Salamander heard it.

"They's here," Salamander said. He took a few slow steps back away from the door, pointing the gun at the door. His hand shook slightly, so he gripped the gun with both hands, but the gun still quivered slightly in his grasp.

Little Juicy finally frowned a deep, serious frown at Salamander. "Seriously, bro, you are ruinin' my fuckin' buzz. You gotta lay off that pipe. It makin' you a whack nut fuck nut."

The door splintered open with a tremendous booming crack. Chunks of wood exploded into the room, showering the room with shards of pine.

Little Juicy didn't stand a chance under the onslaught that followed. Three creatures burst into the room, two of them immediately going for Little Juicy as he threw his arms protectively over his head. One of the creatures bit his left arm off at the shoulder, while another creature ripped his right arm right out of his socket with one vicious yank. What remained of Little Juicy's shoulders seemed to shake up and down, as if his body still thought his arms were attached and was still trying to defensively wave them about his head. Blood streamed and spouted in all directions, oozing and gushing out of the huge holes in his shoulders. Little Juicy fell forward, crashing into the glass table, spilling the snacks and drinks and bongs and weed everywhere as his head cracked the glass and the table shattered under his weight.

Salamander pointed the gun at one creature, then quickly swiveled the weapon to point it at the next, then shakily moved the gun to the next creature, then moved it hurriedly back to the first creature he had pointed it at, then back to the second. He didn't fire at first. His mind didn't even think about pulling the trigger; he stood transfixed, watching Little Juicy get ripped apart with widening eyes.

Then Salamander finally pulled the trigger, gripping the gun with both hands, firing several shots at one of the creatures, but the bullets had no effect on the beast. The projectiles appeared to just go right through the creature, having no impact on its demonic form. It was like shooting a bullet through a pile of bubbles. One of the bullets struck Little Juicy in the thigh and another grazed his groin, but Little Juicy felt nothing; he was already dead, his body savagely shredded by the attacking hellish creatures.

Ellis stepped into the room, stepping over a big chunk of wood that sat on the floor just inside the entrance to the house. He still clutched the can of Whoop Ass in one hand, the other hand empty. He glanced down at the huge pools of blood that soaked into the carpet near Little Juicy's ravaged corpse. He looked up to see Salamander holding a heavily shaking gun in his trembling hands. "Don't kill that one yet," Ellis said, speaking to the creatures. He took a soothing drink from the can, feeling the liquid rush down into his body towards his stomach, and then rush into his brain, filling him with a surging sense of power.

"What the fuck!" a voiced cried out from a nearby hallway.

Ellis turned to see Dumps standing in the hallway, one hand clutching at the top of his unbuttoned pants to keep them from falling down, the other hand clutching a long-handled candle lighter.

Ellis popped another bubble that floated in the air near him and gave an immediate command to the hellish creature that expanded rapidly, the creature surging to its full height. "Kill that one," Ellis ordered.

A whooper (that nickname for the creatures had just popped into Ellis's head and it stuck) lurched towards Dumps. Dumps instinctively thrust the candle lighter towards the creature, flicking the flame on with a sharp jerk of his finger on the trigger.

The candle flame touched an edge of the whooper and a popping sound rang out, accompanied by an unearthly howling cry. The whooper's left arm burst apart, like a balloon popping when a pin gets stuck into it. Tiny sprays of mist fanned out in all directions, the droplets radiating out in a circle from where the flame had touched the whooper's arm.

Dumps moved the candle lighter, waving the tiny flame about frantically. The flame hit another part of the whooper and another shrieking screech sounded out as the whooper's right shoulder explosively popped, vaporizing into a misty spray.

Salamander saw the effect the flame had on the creature. Fire! Fire can kill it. He quickly glanced around the room and saw a lighter on the ground, resting near a porn magazine. He looked back over to Ellis and saw that he was momentarily distracted as he watched Dumps getting attacked. Salamander hurled his gun at Ellis, then immediately lunged down towards the lighter, snatching the lighter and the magazine with one smooth motion.

Ellis saw the gun sailing towards him out of the corner of his eye. He ducked and the gun sailed over his head to collide against the wall, the heavy metal weapon putting a deep gouge into the wall.

Salamander quickly flicked the lighter, getting a nice flame on the first try. He held the rolled up magazine in his opposite hand, putting the edge of the papers into the flame. The magazine ignited, creating a small torch.

One of the whoopers leaped at Salamander and he thrust the flaming magazine straight into the midsection of the unearthly beast. A tremendous popping sound filled the room as the entire creature seemed to burst apart, splintering into a thick cloudy spray. The scattering liquid drenched the burning magazine, dousing the flame.

Salamander tried to light the magazine again, but it was just too wet to re-ignite. He tossed the soaked magazine down in disgust and looked up.

Dumps was on the floor in the hallway, several whoopers huddled over his body, ripping at his flesh with weirdly white claws that seemed to be comprised of some thick white foam turned into vicious talons. Dumps no longer made a sound; his eyes were open and empty.

Salamander looked back to Ellis. He raised the lighter and flicked on the flame.

Ellis raised the gun he had picked up off the floor and shot Salamander square in the chest.

Salamander grunted when the bullet hit him. The lighter dropped from his fingers.

The whoopers pounced.

❊❦❖❦❊

Ellis sat quietly on the couch, not really seeing the dead bodies and body parts that were sprawled about the room. There was something in the drink that was reaching down into his brain, reaching memories that had been long since buried deep in his mind. The whoopers were gone, all of them popping and vanishing back into whatever hellish dimension they had come from.

Flashes of a woman filled his mind. The word 'wife' floated past the image of her. Angry words filled his head; the words themselves were unintelligible, but the tone behind them was unmistakably filled with rage. Betrayal. Deceit. Lies. Those weren't the exact words being spoken in his head, but something in his mind put those words at the forefront of his thoughts.

Poison.

He didn't know where that word had come from, but it popped up into his mind. Had he been poisoned? Is that what caused the crashing sounds in his head? Had poison made him groggy, causing him to veer out of his lane?

An address popped into his head. Was that where he used to live. Did she still live there?

He raised the can to take another sip, not really consciously thinking about it, but the can was empty. He tilted his head, holding the can to his lips, waiting for at least a drop to ooze down into his mouth from the upturned can, but nothing came out.

He stared at the now empty can he gripped tightly in one hand, the gun still clutched loosely in his other hand. He glanced about the room, eying the pockets of the dead men laying sprawled about him.

Ellis set four battered cans of WHOOP ASS down on the counter. He had just pulled them out of the dilapidated cart filled with closeout items. He produced a twenty dollar bill that had a hint of a blood stain in the upper right corner of the currency. He was wearing a fresh set of clothes he had found at the house; Dumps's blood-stained belt was holding up the pants.

The store clerk frowned at him, but took the offered money.

Ellis impatiently waited for the clerk to finish the transaction and give him his change. He grabbed one of the loose cans and relished the cool feeling of the metal against his burned skin. He was feeling thirsty. Very thirsty.

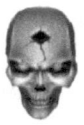

TERRORSTORY #64
STARING CONTEST

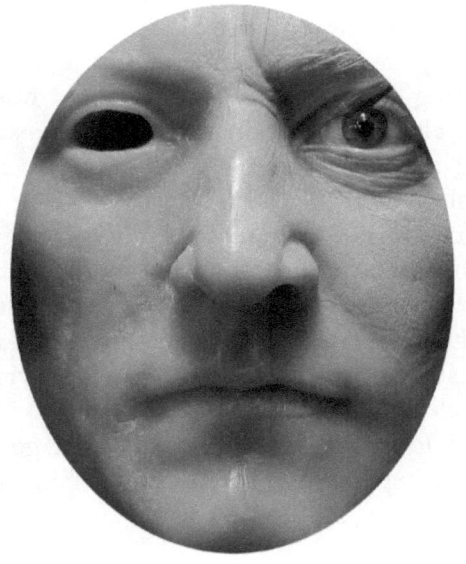

"**K**eep your eyes closed, Patti," Jimmy said. "We're almost there." Jimmy was clean-shaven, his dark hair cut short. He was wearing a dark blue suit, a yellow cream tie, and a sports watch on his wrist.

Patti kept her eyes closed, clutching at Jimmy's arm as he slowly guided her through a doorway. "Where are you taking me?" Patti was dressed in a tight white dress, her blonde hair done up in tight curls. A hint of blue mascara lined her closed eyelids. A topaz bracelet encircled her wrist, the bracelet comprised of a few dozen circular beads.

"Ahh, Mister Jimmy! Welcome, welcome." The booming voice came at them from a nearby hallway.

"Can I open my eyes yet?" Patti asked.

"Sure, babe," Jimmy said.

Patti opened her eyes to see a reedy man approaching them with quick steps. He was cleanly shaven, well-manicured, dressed in a white suit with a crisp red tie and matching cufflinks to give him an extra flash of color.

"Hello, Mister Rifault," Jimmy said to the approaching man and they quickly shook hands.

Rifault beamed a smile at Patti. "And this is your beautiful companion you spoke so much about."

Patti smiled and extended a hand, playing along with the elegant gentleman.

Rifault took her hand and gave it a gentle kiss. Then Rifault spread his arm out before him, gesturing them on. "Come, *my* beauties await."

"Don't tell me," Jimmy said. "They're all going to come to life and attack us."

Rifault smiled. "Oh, no. Nothing so obvious as that." It wasn't necessarily the words the guy spoke that creeped Jimmy out a little; it was more the cryptic smile that twitched at the corners of his lips and the disturbingly gleeful twinkle in Rifault's eyes that gave him an uncomfortable vibe.

Patti grabbed at Jimmy's arm. "This is so cool,"

she said, pressing her breasts tightly against his tricep. "They really do look so real." She gazed up at him, her face flush with excitement, the blue mascara bringing out the deeper blue of her eyes.

Jimmy glanced around the displays. They were in Rifault's Wax Museum, enjoying a special private after-hours show that cost him a pretty penny to arrange. But Patti was worth it. She hated crowds as much as he did, so he arranged for a private tour of the museum after their regularly scheduled hours so they could enjoy the place with a little peace and quiet.

Patti was having a hard time because her sister had died in a car accident a few months earlier and she and her sister had been pretty close. Distractions and amusements seemed to keep her in better spirits, so they had been attending concerts, plays (sitting in private balconies, of course), going to sporting events at the venues where he had his own private box, going to the movies, anything he could think of to keep Patti from dwelling on the despair he knew her sister's death was threatening to well up inside her at any moment.

Rifault's Wax Museum was just something that had come up in conversation a few times; they had always meant to visit it, but had just never gotten around to it. Jimmy wasn't sure that walking around a room full of wax dummies that looked like they were freshly embalmed corpses was a good way to take Patti's mind off the tragedy of her sister's death, but she was the one who had kept talking about wanting to come here.

Jimmy looked at a wax replica of Abraham Lincoln that was positioned in a display just off to their left, the tall man posed as if orating the Gettysburg Address, his long fingers curled around the edge of his coat, and he had to admit all the figures in the wax museum sure did look life-like. Some of the older figures that served as anonymous audience members in some of the displays did have that waxy sheen of a freshly embalmed corpse, but others looked amazing life-life with a texture to their outer coating of skin that looked very much like human flesh. Jimmy knew the visible surface on the wax figures wasn't really skin, but some of them sure looked like they had living human flesh.

Beyond the wax statue of Abraham Lincoln, Jimmy could see the wax replica of George Washington, the first president of the United States, standing heroically at the bow of a small boat, his foot on the edge of the ship, his hand on his thigh, a curved sword strapped to his waist. He was wearing some sort of black hat, covering most of his graying hair, but a few tufts of his hair were visible, covering his ear. The wax figure's face was stern, serious.

Closer to Jimmy on his right, he saw two men and a Native Indian woman. He instinctively knew they were wax statues of Lewis and Clark, the famous team of explorers who navigated the wild west and helped mapped the western lands of the United States. The men were dressed in outdoorsman clothes, each carrying a rifle, while one of the men also clutched a journal. The woman guiding them was Sacagawea, an Indian woman who helped them navigate the lands that at the time were known as the Louisiana Territory before those lands became individual states. She had a papoose on her back and Jimmy vaguely remembered that she had brought her child with her on the expedition. He looked closer at the wax statue of the Indian woman, his attention caught by her dark eyes. They looked sad to Jimmy, forlorn.

"Don't stare at them too long," Rifault said.

Jimmy pulled his gaze away from the wax statue of the Indian woman and looked over to Rifault. "Why not?"

Rifault smiled that damned annoying cryptic smile. "Because you'll swear they blinked at you."

Jimmy frowned at Rifault.

Rifault nodded his head. "Heard it a thousand times. People swearing on their children's souls that one of my wax beauties blinked back at them."

Jimmy looked back up at the wax figure of Sacagawea, then back over to Abraham Lincoln, but purposely avoided looking too long at his face.

Patti shivered deliciously at Jimmy's side, shaking her body up against his arm. "Ooh, that's so creepy. Let's try it," she said.

Jimmy glanced down at Patti, but didn't say anything.

"I would advise against it, but you are your own boss, as they say." Rifault again made a sweeping gesture to indicate the breadth of the room. "I will leave you to enjoy the displays." He raised up a hand and wagged a finger. "Don't touch. The oils on your skin will leave a nasty mark on my beauties." For a moment his cheery face darkened to a somber glare. "I *will* charge you for the repairs." Then his annoying smile returned and the twinkle resurfaced in his eyes. With that, he whirled on his heels and disappeared into some back room somewhere.

Patti tugged at Jimmy's arm, but he didn't respond. "Oh, come on."

Jimmy swept his arm towards the figure of Abraham Lincoln. "Be my guest."

Patti playfully pushed at his arm. "Oh, pooh. I'm not going to stare at that gangly old geezer." She glanced about the room, taking in all the displays, eyeing the figures of dozens of historical people represented in wax. Her gaze flitted past Lewis and Clark, past Napoleon, Alexander the Great, past Julius Caesar, Adolph Hitler, and then stopped on an amazingly beautiful re-creation of the Egyptian queen Cleopatra.

Patti grabbed Jimmy by the wrist and tugged him over to stand before Cleopatra. The wax figure stood between two ornate, sand-colored columns that had Egyptian hieroglyphs etched into them; the wax statue of the famous beauty was dressed in a sheer robe that barely concealed the dark tips of her full breasts. An asp, the deadly black snake that was supposedly the cause of Cleopatra's death, was wrapped around one of her arms, the snake's head angled towards her exposed neck and poised for a strike, its small fangs bared and ready to puncture some holes in her neck and deliver its poison into Cleopatra's delicate throat.

"You don't need to do this," Jimmy said as he watched Patti stare at the wax statue of the Egyptian queen.

Patti looked at him with a bemused grin. "Ha, you're freaked out."

Jimmy said nothing. He was a non-practicing Catholic so he wasn't devoutly religious by a long shot, but there was still that young Catholic boy trapped inside him that got nervous when surrounded by life-like re-creations of the dead. There was just something ominous and unearthly creepy about this whole place that put him on edge. He had felt it immediately upon walking into the wax museum and seeing the displays, but he didn't want to disappoint Patti because she certainly seemed to be thoroughly enjoying it, so he had done his best to ignore his unease and push it aside. But now the unease had returned with a vengeance. There were so many dead eyes in the room, all of them staring blankly. So many dead eyes. It was just damn unnerving.

Patti let go of Jimmy's wrist and moved up to Cleopatra, stopping a few feet from her. A red velvet rope attached to two stanchions kept her from getting any closer. Patti was slightly shorter than the wax statue of Cleopatra so she had to glance upwards to stare into Cleopatra's smoldering dark eyes. Patti stood motionless for a long moment, looking more and more like a wax figure herself the more Jimmy watched her stare at the long-dead Egyptian queen.

"She blinking yet?" Patti asked.

Jimmy felt obligated to give her a formal answer. "No, Patti, she is not blinking yet."

Patti continued the staring contest she had no chance of winning. "How about now?" she asked.

"Nope," Jimmy said. "I don't think they carved in moving eyelids on her wax statue."

Patti pushed her face a little bit closer to Cleopatra, keeping her gaze riveted on the wax woman's eyes. "How about now?"

"Patti—" And then Cleopatra blinked. Jimmy saw it plain as day. Her eyelids went down and then they went back up. "What the fuck?" Jimmy staggered a few steps backwards, nearly tripping over his own feet.

"What?" Patti asked. "She blink?" She quickly looked over at Jimmy, then back to Cleopatra. "Did she blink? I didn't see it. Shit, I didn't see it."

No way. That wasn't possible, Jimmy thought. It was just a trick of the light. He had just imagined it.

"Jimmy, did you see her blink?"

Jimmy slowly looked over to Patti. She stared at him with her big blue eyes. Eyes that didn't blink. At all. He looked intently at her face, waiting for her to blink, but her eyes remained open and wide. Maybe he was just blinking at the same time she was. Maybe he just wasn't seeing her eyelids go up and down.

He stared at Patti, trying to make himself not blink so he could see her blink. He felt his eyelids trying to force themselves down and he fought back, pushing his eyes open even wider. Her face started to blur and he felt his eyes actually starting to dry out. He couldn't fight it any longer. He had to blink. A soothing relief flushed over his eyes as his eyelids moved down then back up. He blinked a few more times in rapid succession, then closed his eyes.

He felt a hand shake his shoulder and he opened his eyes to see Patti scowling up at him.

"You okay?" she asked. She sounded more concerned than annoyed.

"Yeah," he muttered.

"What the heck happened to you?" Patti asked. "You looked like you saw a ghost. Your eyes got all bugged out and shit."

"Nothing. I'm good."

Patti stared at him. And still didn't blink.

Jimmy had to look away from her.

"You saw her blink, didn't you?" she asked. "You saw Cleopatra blink."

"Of course not," he answered immediately. "She's fucking made of wax. She can't blink."

"Don't lie to me, James McGilliot," Patti said in a scolding tone that was both playful and serious. "You saw something."

Jimmy glanced over at the wax statue of Adolph Hitler, doing anything he could to avoid looking anywhere near Patti's face. *And her unblinking eyes! She wasn't blinking! What the hell was that about? She wasn't fucking blinking!* The former German ruler of the Nazi regime was dressed in his military uniform, his famous tiny black mustache adorned on his face above his upper lip. The man was responsible for more human deaths and suffering than anyone who had ever lived. And Jimmy found himself wanting to look at his face more than he wanted to look at the face of his sweet girl Patti.

"Jimmy, look at me," Patti said.

Jimmy shook his head. It was an abrupt, involuntarily gesture, but it came out as a sharp head shake that couldn't be confused with anything but an absolute refusal of her request.

"What the heck is wrong with you?" Patti asked.

He felt her fingers on his shoulder as she reached for him, but he shrugged off her hand with a quick lowering jerk of his arm. He kept his gaze focused on Hitler, staring into his dark beady eyes; he didn't mean to look at them this long but his gaze just stopped on the wax Hitler's eyes and he couldn't break their gaze. He desperately wanted to look away, mentally begging himself to look away, but something, some force kept his gaze riveted on Hitler's fucking wax eyes.

"Okay, seriously, what the heck is wrong with

you?" Patti asked.

The wax statue of Adolph Hitler blinked and Jimmy exclaimed, "Oh, fuck!" with a level of fright he had never felt before in his life. He staggered back away from the wax figure of Adolph Hitler, this time tripping over Patti's legs, tumbling to the floor. He looked at the figure of Hitler with wide eyes, knowing that he wouldn't at all be surprised if Adolph took a few step towards him and reached for him with groping fingers.

"Shit, Jimmy, what the fuck?"

He could see Patti's legs moving around him as she maneuvered towards the front of his body. Jimmy looked up, looking anywhere but at Patti, to see the wax statue of Julius Caesar staring down at him. Was Caesar's head pointed down like that when they came in? He couldn't remember. Yes. Yes, it was. His head was tilted that way. Wasn't it? Jimmy kept staring at Caesar's wax face, dreading what he knew was about to happen, but knowing that he had to wait it out. He couldn't look away. He had to know.

"Jimmy, why are you acting like a total ass?"

Julius Caesar blinked and Jimmy felt as if that gesture released him, as if that up and down movement of eyelids that shouldn't have even been possible let loose a shackle that had been binding his head and forcing him to keep staring at the wax statue of the Roman ruler. He looked away from the wax statue of Julius Caesar, turning his gaze to his girlfriend.

Patti loomed over him, staring down at him with her big blue eyes. Eyes that didn't blink.

He quickly averted his gaze from hers. He knew he should leave this place. He should get to his feet and run as fast as he could out the door and never look back. But he couldn't. Not yet. Not until she blinked. Not until Patti blinked her fucking eyes. He reached up towards her, avoiding looking at her eyes. "Help me up."

She grabbed at his hand and tugged, helping him get back to his feet, grunting a little with the effort.

The lights in the room flickered for a few seconds. Jimmy quickly looked at Patti's face as she glanced about the room. Was that a blink? Did she just fucking blink? Damn it, he wasn't sure because of the flickering lights. He stared at her face for a moment longer, waiting, watching. But there was no blink. How were her eyes not watering like mad right about now? How the fuck could she keep them open so long without blinking?

He saw the scowl appear in Patti's face, drawing deep lines into her skin.

"What? Why are you staring at me like that?" she asked, her voice tight. "Now you're starting to freak *me* out."

"You're not blinking," he blurted out. There, he said it. And then he decided he needed to say it again. "You're not blinking."

"What?" She frowned at him, looking at him as if he was a complete idiot. "Of course I'm blinking."

Jimmy shook his head. "No you're not." His next words came out in a jumbled rush. "You were staring at Cleopatra and then she blinked and then you stopped blinking. And then Hitler blinked but you're not blinking. Then Julius Caesar blinked. But you're still not blinking. You're not blinking." The pitch in his voice continued to rise as he spoke, quickly elevating to a nearly hysterical screech. "You're not blinking!"

"Yes, I am," Patti said, her voice rising along with his. "Look, I am!"

Jimmy stared at her face, focusing on her left eye.

"There," Patti said. "I just did it."

Jimmy shook his head slowly. The tone of his voice was quieter now, calmer. "No. You didn't."

Patti stomped her foot, nearly breaking off the heel of her shoe. "Yes I did, goddamnit!"

Jimmy continued to shake his head. "No. You didn't." The last words came out in a muttering mumble. "You're not blinking."

A nearby light flickered for a second. It was only for a second, but that was time enough for everything to change. Patti's face suddenly looked shinier to him, glossier... as if her flesh now had a freshly waxed sheen to it. Without even really thinking about what he was doing, impulsively feeling an undeniable urge to do so, Jimmy reached up and put his index finger against Patti's cheek. The thing he noticed immediately was that her face felt cool to his touch. Not warm like human flesh should feel. It was cool, almost cold. He pushed his finger firmer against her cheek, but he felt no give; he only felt a solid resistance to the pressure he was applying. He curved his index finger and dug his nail into Patti's face. She didn't cry out, or even resist, as he dragged his finger down her cheek, the rough movement digging a line into her face.

Jimmy withdrew his finger and brought his hand back towards himself. He turned his hand over, curling his index finger to get a good look at its tip. What appeared to be a thin chunk of wax was embedded beneath his fingernail.

The lights flickered again and suddenly Patti was screaming in pain, clutching at her face with her hand, blood oozing out between her fingers. "What the fuck did you do that for?" she cried out. "Are you fucking crazy!"

Jimmy just stood dumbly mute for a moment, trying to get his bearings. What the hell? He quickly glanced down at his finger to see a trail of blood sliding down his finger, and what looked like a piece of flesh dangling off to the side of his fingernail. He quickly shook his hand, desperately trying to dislodge the piece of skin that was hooked onto his fingernail.

"Are you fucking out of your mind?" Patti screamed at him.

Jimmy, still feeling somewhat in a daze, slowly looked up at Patti. Blood was still oozing out from between her fingers, little crimson droplets dripping to the tile floor.

Patti put both hands over the gouge in her face, pressing firmly against her cheek. "You're fucking crazy!"

Jimmy stared mutely. Then, he finally uttered, "Your face..." His words trailed off and he was quiet for another moment before continuing. "It was made out of wax."

"Does it look like my face is made out of wax?" Patti's words came out in a shriek, her face contorted in a mask of pain, her voice full of a shrill rage. "I'm bleeding all over my fucking dress, you crazy motherfucker!"

Jimmy stood mutely for a moment, just staring at her. He reached his hands up clumsily towards her face. "I'm sorry. Let me help you."

Patti swatted his hand away with a quick slap,

smearing some of the blood on her fingers across his hand. "Don't touch me!"

"You're bleeding all over the place," Jimmy said.

"I know! Because you scratched my face, you crazy fuck!"

"I'm... I'm sorry," Jimmy said. He stared at Patti, at her face, at the blood on her fingers. Then, he chanced a quick glance up to her eyes. Surely, they would be blinking now. He stared at her blue eyes, those wide eyes, eyes that were full of anger. But they were not blinking.

She motioned to her tiny yellow purse that was resting near her hip. "I think I have a band-aid in my purse. Get it!" She turned slightly, thrusting her hip towards Jimmy to give him easier access to the purse.

Jimmy reached for the purse, going for the little zipper, but stopped as his fingers touched the purse. The purse should have felt soft, like the fabric it was made out of, but it didn't. It felt much more solid, cool to the touch. He quickly jerked his hands away from the purse. It felt like wax. It was made of wax. Patti's purse was suddenly made out of wax.

"Give me the band-aid! Jesus, hurry up!"

Jimmy took a step back away from Patti, staring with alarm at the little yellow purse, keeping his gaze focused on the fucking yellow purse made out of fucking wax.

"What the fuck, Jimmy? Give me the band-aid!" Patti said, her tone increasingly more irritated and demanding.

Jimmy slowly took another step back from her, slowly raising his hand to point at the purse at her waist. "It... I can't... It won't open," he said, stuttering, unable to put together more than a few words at a time.

"God damn it, you are so fucking useless right now!" Patti kept one hand over the bleeding gouge in her cheek and fumbled at her purse with the other, smearing blood all over the outside of the purse. She snatched at the zipper, yanking the purse open. She rummaged inside the purse, but came up empty-handed. "Shit, I thought I had a band-aid in here."

Jimmy stared at the now-open purse, somewhat amazed and startled that Patti had been able to open it. He glanced up to her face. And immediately regretted it. He stared at her eyes, unable to look away, praying for her to blink. Just once. That's all he wanted to see. One blink. That's it. Just one fucking lowering and raising of her eyelids. But she didn't blink. Her eyes stayed open, never blinking.

"Don't you have a handkerchief or something?" Patti asked, but he didn't really register the question the first time she asked it. "Jimmy," she said with more insistence, raising her voice, "don't you have a handkerchief or something?"

Jimmy didn't answer. He was too absorbed in what was happening just over Patti's left shoulder. A Mongol warlord dressed in fur, wearing a rounded fur hat, blinked at him. Genghis Kahn. Jimmy remembered him from a history class. Why the fuck were the eyes on his wax statue blinking? He hadn't even been staring at him. Not that any of this insanity was supposed to follow a set of rules.

"Jimmy! Fucking answer me!" he heard Patti shout. The vehemence in her tone caused him to shift his gaze back to her.

"Genghis Kahn is blinking," he said. He pointed over Patti's shoulder at the wax statue of the

Mongolian leader. "He's blinking at me."

"You have lost your fucking mind," Patti said. "Did you do drugs before we came here? God damn it, Jimmy, are you on something?"

Jimmy shook his head. "No. I'm clean."

Patti frowned at him. "You sure?" She took her hand away from her cheek to glance at it. Her fingers still glistened with fresh blood. She put her fingers back over the gash, pressing hard against her flesh. "Cause if you did this when you're straight, I'm gonna have serious doubts about this relationship."

Suddenly, Jimmy lunged forward towards Patti. He put his fingers on her face, just below her eyebrows, touching the tips of her eyelids. He pulled his fingers down, forcing her eyelids to close over her eyes. He moved back away from her just as abruptly as he had surged towards her. *There, now her eyes are closed,* he thought with a feeling of triumphant relief. He was going to go mad if she didn't close her eyes.

But that feeling of relief did not last long.

"I can't see!" Patti shrieked. She put her bloody fingers up to her eyes, rubbing them against her eyelids, smearing blood all over them. "You blinded me! You crazy motherfucker!"

"Just open your eyes," Jimmy said to her.

"They are open!" Patti shrieked.

"No, they're not. They're closed," Jimmy said. "I closed them."

"You blinded me!" Patti shrieked again.

"Just open your eyes, Patti," Jimmy said. His voice started to take on an odd, almost pleading tone. "Just open your eyes."

"They're fucking open! I can't see!"

"They're not open," Jimmy said, trying to keep his

voice calm.

"They're fucking open, Jimmy."

Jimmy shook his head. "They're not open, Patti. You have them closed. Just open them."

"You telling me I don't know when my eyes are fucking open or closed? They're open, goddamnit!"

"They're not open!" Jimmy shrieked back at her, matching her intensity. "Open your fucking eyes, Patti! They're not open! Open them!"

"You blinded me, you crazy fuck! I can't see!"

Jimmy reached forward, putting his fingers on the bottom portion of her eyelids. He flicked his fingers upward, raising her eyelids up over her eyes.

"Oh my God," Patti said, breathing a massive sigh of relief. "I can see. I can see again."

Jimmy just stared at Patti.

Behind Patti, the wax statue of Marilyn Monroe blinked at Jimmy.

"Let's get out of here," Jimmy said. "This fucking place is cursed or something."

Patti reached out a hand and Jimmy took it. He could feel the wetness on her cool fingers, but he didn't look. He knew there was blood on her hand, but at this point, he didn't care. He just wanted to get out of this fucking freaky wax museum.

⚜

Jimmy breathed in a full dose of the night air, savoring the feeling of being out of that fucking museum. The city bustled with life around them. Cars filled the streets, their headlights throwing beams of light out before them. Dozens of people walked the sidewalks, clustered in numerous groups. The neon lights of restaurants and bars gleamed in a rainbow swirl of glowing colors.

A man and two women walked past Jimmy. He gave them a polite nod. They didn't nod back. They just seemed to be staring at him curiously. Without blinking. No, they blinked. They blinked. Didn't they? No, they didn't. They just stared right at him and not one of them blinked. Get a grip, Jimmy. It's dark. They blinked. You just didn't see them.

Patti's hand felt cool in his. He curled his fingers tighter around hers, feeling reassured by her presence.

A group of teenagers walked past. One of them thumped his friend in the chest, indicating Jimmy and Patti with a quick jerk of his head in their direction. The teenager's friend looked over at Jimmy and Patti and broke out into a hushed laughter. Jimmy stared keenly at the teenagers, waiting for them to blink. Just one of them. That's all he needed. Just for one of them to blink.

But they didn't blink. Not a one. They just stared at them with their creepy always-open, never-blinking eyes.

Jimmy turned to look at Patti. She stared back at him, her skin giving off a lustrous sheen in the swirl of colored lights that filled the night. He quickly looked away from her eyes, not even wanting to know if she was blinking or not — because of course she was blinking. To think otherwise was just crazy. "Come on, let's go home," he said to her.

Jimmy started to walk, but then stopped as he felt an odd tug on his arm, a resistance. He turned to look at Patti. Her face looked odd, stiff in a way. Her flesh looked... waxy.

"You understand the charges against you, Jimmy?"

Jimmy didn't answer. He sat with his eyes closed, his eyelids clamped firmly shut.

The voice continued on. "Breaking and entering Rifault's Wax Museum and stealing a wax statue,"

"She wasn't a statue," Jimmy said, his voice resolute. "She was my girlfriend." He quickly corrected himself. "She *is* my girlfriend." His voice became more agitated. "And he let us in. I paid extra for it! We didn't break in."

Jimmy heard rustling, bodies shifting in chairs, people muttering, papers being shuffled.

"We really need you to look at us, Jimmy," another voice said, a woman's voice. "It's really hard to carry on a conversation if you won't look at us."

Jimmy shook his head.

"Why won't you open your eyes, Jimmy?"

"I already told you," Jimmy said.

"Tell me again," the woman's voice said. "I wasn't here when you were first brought in."

"Because none of you blink," Jimmy said. "None of you fuckers blink, that's why."

More rustling noises, more muttering.

"That seems pretty absurd, doesn't it?" the woman asked, not doing a very good job of hiding the derision in her voice.

"You don't blink!" Jimmy shouted, thrusting his body forward, but keeping his eyes shut. "None of you fucking blink!"

Yet more rustling noises, more shifting of bodies, more mutterings.

"He knows," a strong male voice said. "It's no sense lying to him anymore."

Jimmy thought for a moment it might be Rifault's voice, but he was too afraid to open his eyes. Too afraid of seeing them all staring at him with their wide, unblinking eyes.

"We can't let him go," the woman said.

"Of course not," the male voice said. "I did warn them."

It *was* Rifault's voice. It had to be. But Jimmy was still too afraid to open his eyes to confirm his suspicions.

"We can use him for a crowd scene," the man who Jimmy was pretty certain was Rifault said. "Put him in the crowd at Lincoln's Gettysburg address. You can fill that one empty spot near the front with him."

"But he won't open his eyes," another voice protested.

"He will. He won't be able to help himself. Once he does, he'll be ours. Just leave his lovely Patti in here with him. Put her right here, right next to him."

More mutterings, but this time the noises were of an approving tone.

Jimmy felt a presence move near him, could hear breathing, could feel a rush of warm breath on his face.

"Don't fight it, my beauty," Rifault whispered to him. "Don't fight it."

Jimmy squeezed his eyes shut tighter.

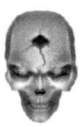

TERRORSTORY #65
PENNY FOR YOUR THOUGHTS

A penny for your thoughts. That's how much they paid when this all started. One penny for one thought. Times sure have changed since then. They moved it up to a buck or two after a few months, somewhere around there, I'm not sure, after they realized the machine's potential.

But it went up to ten bucks if your thoughts had enough juice behind them. Ten dollars for one thought. Of course, it had to be the right kind of thought. It had to be the thought worth paying for.

Oh, they still hooked you up to the same machine. They still stuck you with the same electrodes, still inserted those tiny micro fiber relays into your head. That didn't change much at all. And why should it? It still worked. In fact, with advances in nanotechnology now, it works even better. Those same electrodes can extract the thought in milliseconds instead of seconds. Hell, it used to take minutes.

You still just sit in the chair, pop in the electrodes, think the thought, collect your ten bucks, and go on your merry way in a matter of a few minutes total. Hell, you don't even have to sit anymore. You can just stand there for a few minutes and get it all done without even bothering to sit. Ten bucks ain't bad for a few minutes of work. Heck, it isn't even work. It's just... well, I don't even know what to call it. It's more like a donation, but not really a donation because you get paid for it. Work for hire, I guess. No contracts, no commitments. Just walk into one of PTS offices, do the deed, collect your dough, and be on your way. As easy as pie. Nobody gets hurt.

That's what I thought until I found out what they were really up to. But I'm getting ahead of myself here.

Some scientists claim that human brains are more interconnected than everyone realizes. They believe the brain picks up tiny micro-signals that communicate what a person is thinking or feeling. These signals go far beyond the role written or verbal language plays. They say that explains how so many people have gut feelings or intuition about a person, or a place, or an idea, or a situation. They say this form of connection explains how some superstitious beliefs can become established as societal norms. How else can you explain why some architects purposefully omit the thirteenth floor from their blueprints, or why ancient Roman leaders once made decisions about important events based on the flight patterns of birds, or why some people will go to great lengths to avoid walking under a ladder, or letting a black cat cross their path? These thoughts and behaviors are not rational, but they are accepted as normal because they reside firmly entrenched in that ethereal world of human thought.

I know some of you have heard of the collective unconscious. For those of you who haven't, the collective unconscious was a term coined by Carl Jung. Jung was a Swiss psychologist who lived in the early 1900s. He originated the concept of introvert and extrovert personalities and the concept of the four psychological functions of sensation, intuition, thinking, and feeling. Collective unconscious refers to structures of the unconscious mind which are shared among beings of the same species. I took that right off Wikipedia. These structures are real. They exist. They may only exist as ephemeral wisps of thought in the minds of all mankind, but they still exist. And because of the very fact that these unconscious structures of the mind exist means they can be manipulated and exploited.

That is what those fine folks at PTS are doing. They are paying you to help them manipulate the collective unconscious of the human race by buying your thoughts. They are seeding their ideology deep inside all of us. This goes beyond the manipulation of history, goes beyond re-writing textbooks, goes beyond using AI to wipe out any knowledge of events whose outcomes go counter to their beliefs. This is far more insidious because it lurks beneath your conscious awareness.

If enough people think something is true, then it becomes true in their minds. The actual facts don't count. It is the belief that drives changes in behavior, not what actually happened, not the actual events. And if enough people think something is true, then that changes the structure of the collective unconscious. Let that sink in. It changes the very nature of the collective unconscious. It changes the fundamental core of what humanity believes.

And do you know why they are doing this? I wish I could say the reason they were doing it was to change the world for the better, but you know it isn't. Human nature just doesn't allow for such a thing. They are using it to sell products. Kind of anticlimactic, isn't it? They just want to sell all of us more of their shit.

Cow's milk is bad for you. That's one of the seeds they planted. Hell, they paid me ten bucks just to think that thought. They showed me some propaganda video, convinced me momentarily that cow's milk was indeed bad for you, then collected my thought on it to feed it back into the collective unconscious. Once they collect enough thoughts on a particular topic and feed them into the collective unconscious, a tipping point is reached. Once the tipping point is surpassed, it now becomes an officially recognized part of the collective unconscious. Now, everyone *knows* that cow's milk is bad for you. They don't really have facts to back up their feelings; they just *know* it's bad. Heck, everybody knows it. It's just a given now. It wasn't like that a few years ago. Millions of people were enjoying cow's milk with no adverse effects, but PTS wanted in on that action. PTS - that's the Planting The Seed corporation if you weren't aware of their acronym.

So now sales of cow milk have dried up, replaced by their synthetic milk. Synmilk. You would think a product with a name like that would be a turn off to many people, but the exact opposite happened. People got off on drinking something synful. It was funny. It was dangerous. It was exciting. It provoked different reactions in people, but the most important part was that it provoked a reaction at all. No reaction was the kiss of death for a new product. No publicity is worse than bad publicity. It's an old adage, but still true.

So how do I know all these things? I used to work at PTS, but not anymore. I suppose you could call me a whistle blower.

Some people have a deeper reach into the collective unconscious, sometimes referred to as the Collective, just as some people are born with increased intellectual capacity, or increased capacity for physical strength, or increased longevity, or higher levels of disease resistance. Me? For whatever reason, I was born with deeper roots that reached farther into the collective unconscious than most people. It makes my thoughts more valuable than most because my thoughts have a greater influence, because they spread wider and faster than the thoughts of most people.

Think of the Collective as a gigantic pool of thought that all humanity swims in, that all humanity shares. Every thought a person thinks makes a ripple in the pool, but most of these ripples are so weak that they barely travel any distance before fading away; they are like one minuscule particle from a very fine mist hitting the water, leaving no telltale impact and vanishing within microseconds. But if you get enough of these particles, enough of these thoughts, to hit the collective unconscious pool then they will have an effect. Hence, that's why PTS puts on so many thought drives to get as many people involved as possible. The effect may not last long, but they don't need it to. Sometimes, they only need the effect to last a few weeks to capitalize on it. Remember the fidget spinner craze? They caused that. The original manufacturer of those made a killing before the copycats destroyed the market.

My thoughts are like chunks of hail hitting the Collective. There is an obvious impact when my thoughts hit the collective unconscious pool of thought, and the ripples travel far and wide. I can think a negative thing about a certain celebrity and within hours social media posts will start appearing across the web, maligning the celebrity for the very thing I just thought. It's quite a fascinating effect, really.

My thoughts turned out to be worth far more than a meager penny, far more than ten dollars. Every one of my thoughts was worth thousands of dollars to them. Of course, I wasn't even aware of this power my thoughts had. At first.

And that's why they recruited me. Well, I guess I shouldn't say they. It was just one guy. It was why Gerald Gracy recruited me.

Talk about plush offices. The PTS business offices were the epitome of corporate comfort. Sleek furniture, vibrant colors, free coffee, free food, dozens of relaxation rooms, game rooms, quiet reading rooms with soundproofed walls. Hell, they even had dedicated massage rooms with professional massage therapists on hand to cater to that little crick in your neck. Everything was super shiny, super clean. No one was wearing a suit; everyone was dressed in corporate casual attire.

But I didn't have too much time to take it all in because Gerald assaulted me with a fake smile and a quick limp handshake within minutes of me walking in the door. He was of medium height, about five foot eight, with short brown hair and the slouching posture of someone who spent far too much time sitting in an office chair. "So glad you could make it. Come on, this way."

Gerald immediately steered me into a corridor to the left of the small reception desk, ushering me forward with a hand on my back, guiding me to a small extraction room. It wasn't a typical thought extraction room. It didn't have the leather couch, or the bright lighting, or the tranquil music playing from hidden speakers. It was a stark room, painted a blueish gray, with one chair that looked more like the patient's chair in a dentist office than a lounger. A very high-tech-looking piece of equipment was positioned next to the chair. This, I later found out, was the next iteration of the thought extractor. It was the TE 5000 model.

Gerald pointed to the chair. "Sit, sit."

"What exactly is it that you want me to do?" I asked him. The promise of a thousand dollar payout, payment upon delivery of the thought, was enough to motivate me to come in, but the invitation I had received to come to the PTS Chicago office was rather cryptic so I wasn't quite sure what Gerald had in store for me.

Gerald again pointed to the chair. "Sit." He glanced past me at the open doorway to the room, looking over my shoulder. He was clearly nervous about something. He brushed past me and closed the door, then returned to his previous position next to the TE 5000 extraction machine. He again motioned to the chair. "Please, sit. We need to get started."

I remained where I was. I thought about crossing my arms in a defiant gesture and forcing a deep frown on my face, but I didn't do that. I just looked at him.

"I am paying you well," he said, as if that was all that was important to me, as if that's all that mattered.

I sat in the chair. Heck, he was paying me well after all.

The TE 5000 only had one slender electrode. It was by far the most advanced thought extraction machine I had ever seen. It was still tall, but it was much less bulkier, much slimmer than the older models. It was about four feet tall with a small touchscreen that displayed the various control commands in different colors. The single electrode was attached to the machine via a single clip.

Gerald unclipped the electrode and held it firmly in his grasp as he waited for me to settle into the chair.

"So," I said, "what do you need? You guys launching a new product?"

Gerald shook his head. "No." He hesitated for a long moment. "I need you to help me take down..." his voice trailed off. "A scumbag. The guy's a scumbag. He's a woman-beating pedophile."

I put my arms on the armrests of the chair, shifting to get a little more comfortable in the seat. "Who is it? Who do you want me to thought-bomb?"

"His name is Nigel Davenclaw."

That was a unique name, but I had never heard of him. "Don't know him," I said. "He an actor or a politician or something?"

Gerald shook his head. "No."

I waited for a further explanation, but he didn't elaborate on the guy. "You got a picture of him?"

"Of course," Gerald replied. He pointed to the large monitor affixed on the opposite wall. "Show me Nigel Davenclaw," he commanded.

The dark screen buzzed for a split second, then shimmered as a picture blossomed into view. And there was Nigel Davenclaw looking dour. He had a full head of dark hair, but it was greying at the temples. He had a bulbous nose and full lips. He had the appearance of an old English guy you might find in a pub in Wales. At least that's what he reminded me of. "What's he do?" I asked.

"I told you. He beats women and molests children," Gerald said.

I shook my head. "No, what's he do? What's his job?"

"Does that matter?" Gerald asked.

I gave a slight shrug. "It helps clarify the thought."

Gerald was quiet for a moment. He fiddled with a few dials on the side of the TE 5000 extraction machine, tapped a few buttons on the control panel touchscreen. "He works here."

Whoa. I took that in for a moment. "He works here?"

Gerald nodded.

"That's gonna be a tough one to pull off," I said.

Gerald nodded again. "That's why I called you in. You've got the power to push deep into the Collective." He paused. "And this one has to go in deep if it's going to work."

I thought about what he had just told me. He said I had the power to push deep into the Collective. I knew my thoughts were strong, but no one had ever said much about that to me before this. Of course, he was right as it turns out, but I just found it very interesting at the time that he just came out and said it.

A sheen of sweat glistened on Gerald's brow, which was odd because the room was nowhere near being warm. It was quite comfortably cool. He was being awfully cagey, secretive even in his movements, as if he had something to hide, as if he was afraid of being found out at any moment. A sudden realization came to me and I figured I had nothing to lose in saying it aloud. "He's your boss, isn't he?"

Gerald said nothing.

"You want his job," I added.

Gerald said nothing.

I was quiet for a moment, thinking about what Gerald was asking me to do. "Man, that's harsh."

Gerald held the electrode tightly in his hand, hovering the tip near the side of my forehead where the electrode would be attached for the extraction process. His patience had clearly reached his limit and he scowled darkly at me. "Are you going to do it or not?"

"Sure," I said. "But I want more than your measly thousand dollars."

Gerald was quiet, waiting for me to continue.

"I want a job. Here." I could see his shoulders relax. I wasn't sure what he had been expecting me to ask for, but a job at PTS certainly didn't seem to be it.

He waved the electrode slightly back and forth in the air. "Let's see how this turns out, then we can talk."

⋘⋅⋅⊱❁⊰⋅⋅⋙

It turned out just fine. As I knew it would. Nigel Davenclaw couldn't go anywhere in the city without someone recognizing him and calling him out for being an abuser and a child molester. He denied everything as vicious, slanderous rumors on the first few talk shows that gave him an allotted five minutes to defend himself, but soon even the talk show hosts grew weary of his groveling and pleading for them to believe that he was innocent. You see, everyone just *knew* he was guilty. Facts be damned; they all knew Nigel was guilty. They felt it, thousands of people felt it, tens of thousands of people, hundreds of thousands of people felt it. I had pushed that thought pretty deep into the Collective, so even the mention of Nigel Davenclaw evoked feelings of disgust and abhorrence. After a few rounds of talk show appearances turned into more of the same old same old boring pleading chatter, the talk show producers just ignored Nigel's requests to clear his name of these alleged falsehoods and stopped granting him interviews. Nigel was terminated from his job at PTS within a few days.

It was amazing to me that Nigel didn't even try to pin the blame on someone in PTS. He must have surely known it had been an inside job. I can only imagine some kind of juicy severance package kept him quiet. He probably lives off the grid in some cabin in the woods now. Regardless, Nigel was gone and I got the job I had requested, working under Gerald, who was now the new department head at the PTS Chicago offices.

Things went well for a time. We put the fear of contracting Lyme disease into the Collective, and that drove sales of Lyme disease preventative sprays up six hundred percent in one month. The repellent sprays didn't really work all that well on repelling ticks, but that didn't matter. All that mattered was that people were so terrified of contracting Lyme disease from ticks that they'd buy anything that helped give them more peace of mind.

Fear was the biggest motivator that drove sales. Not trust. Not a sense of fairness. Not good will. Good old fashioned fear. That was the driver. You put the fear of something deep enough into the Collective and there will be millions of people who will buy anything to help them alleviate that fear. Gluten is a great example. PTS planted that one before I even started working there. That one took off like wildfire. Millions of people are now terrified of gluten. Stores that once used to have maybe half a dozen gluten-free products now had entire aisles devoted to gluten-free foods. Most people can't really explain what's wrong with having some gluten in their diet. They just know, they just have this feeling, that it's bad for you. That's all it takes. Just that sense of knowing *for sure* that something is bad for you. Facts be damned. They just know it's wrong, it's bad. Facts can never override emotions, not if those emotions are planted deep enough into the Collective.

The war between the United States and Canada was what really made me think twice about what I was doing.

I have no particular love for Canadians, nor any animosity. I'm pretty much indifferent. They're hardly in the news. Oh, there was a spike in interest in Canada when they decided to legalize marijuana and when they had a mass shooting a few years back, but that's about it. Other than that, you never really hear about Canada much. They're not really a global player.

That all changed the day Gerald came into my office with a seriously stern look on his face. I could tell this was going to be a big one. Really big.

"This one comes from the top, so don't blame

me," he said.

Gerald starting out immediately on the defensive was never a good sign. I looked away from my computer monitors, giving him my full attention.

"She wants to build a wall," he said.

"A wall?"

Gerald waved his hand impatiently. "Not a physical wall. A mental wall."

"Where?"

"Across our northern border."

"The President wants to create a mental wall between us and Canada?" I rubbed at the stubble on my chin. "Why?"

Gerald frowned at me. "Don't you keep up with the news?"

"I depend on you to tell me what's important." I smiled at him.

Gerald grunted. "Now that their country is about seven degrees warmer than their historical average, they're able to grow more crops, feed more of their own livestock. They're posing a threat to the entire life blood of the Midwest. We can't let that happen."

I was quiet for a moment. At that time, I was all for protecting our country from the unwanted influence of outsiders. "So what's the play?" I asked.

"Salmonella and E coli. Maybe a little bit of that flesh-eating disease, but we'll make that only if you eat Canadian beef or pork, maybe chicken, too."

"So anything edible coming down from Canada is tainted with some foul disease or bacteria or what have you?"

Gerald nodded. "We'll start small, but quickly escalate. Maybe an outbreak on some Canadian cattle farms first. A few dozen deaths directly related to the tainted meat."

I nodded. "The new machine ready?"

Gerald's face actually lit up with a smile. That was a rare occurrence, so it was very noticeable. "Yes, it is. You're gonna be the first to test it."

I nodded. I had been the first to test the last two iterations of the thought extraction machine, so this did not come as any surprise. "When do we start?"

"No better time than the present."

<hr />

I stepped into the extraction room, but was immediately confused by the lack of a big extraction machine. There was only a small computer station set up near a brown leather chair. What looked like a VR helmet of some sort rested on the table near the computer base. I turned a surprised face to Gerald. "That's it?" I asked. "That's the new extraction machine?"

Gerald nodded, beaming like a proud father. "I told you those guys in tech were amazing." He motioned to the chair. "Go on, have a seat, get comfortable."

The leather chair crinkled softly as I sat in it and maneuvered myself into a comfortable position. As I looked closer I could see the chair had a joystick embedded on each side of the chair's arms.

Gerald grabbed the VR helmet and handed it to me. "Just put it on and it will automatically activate."

I grabbed the black helmet and put it on. The VR device covered my entire head, cocooning my head like an astronaut's helmet. True to Gerald's word, the unit activated immediately. I was instantly immersed in a field of dead cows, their bloated corpses littering a field full of dead and decaying foliage. The smell hit me in a rush of stench and decay and rotting meat. It was the first time smell had been incorporated into the process, so it caught me off guard for a second, but I recovered quickly. Flies buzzed everywhere, sometimes swarming so thick they turned some portions of the surroundings completely black. I turned my head, taking in more of the virtual scene. A few cows were still alive, lying on their sides, and they flapped their black-tipped tails weakly at the flies swarming all over them to little avail.

Two big, burly men dressed in white butcher's outfits came into view, their apparel smeared red with blood. They grabbed the legs of a bloated, dying cow with bare hands and dragged it into the meat processing plant that was positioned right next to the field.

I fumbled about with my hand, seeking out the joystick. I quickly clutched the cool metal shaft of the joystick and wrapped my fingers around it. I pushed the joystick forward and followed the two men dragging the cow into the plant.

Inside the plant was like some Hieronymus Bosch painting of Hell. There were intestines lining the floor, half cut cow bodies hanging from hooks, chunks of cow bodies piled up in what looked like haphazard columns of bleeding meat. Flies buzzed everywhere inside here as well. A very large rat raced out of a hole in a nearby wall, grabbed a chunk of loose intestines in its teeth, then raced back into its hole, the intestines leaving a swerving trail of blood and internal gunk along the concrete floor as the rat raced back to safety. I glanced up at the high ceiling of the plant, somehow not surprised to see blood splatters even on the ceiling.

I continued to follow the two men dressed in their blood-drenched butcher's outfits as they dragged the cow deeper into the meat processing plant. The cow raised its head and bleated out a weak cry for help. None of the other workers in the plant stopped what they were doing, nor even paid any attention whatsoever to the cow being dragged across the blood-smeared floor of the plant.

The cow was ultimately put out of its misery with a heavy hammer blow to its skull, then cut up into select portions of meat, and then packaged into Styrofoam-like containers wrapped in cellophane. The packages were earmarked for USA customers.

That's disgusting, I thought. What this company was doing to create the meat they were selling to the USA consumer was downright foul. It didn't really matter if what I was watching was real or just some sick fabrication created by the imagery team on the second floor of PTS. I thought long and hard on the repulsive things I was seeing and smelling, pushing deep into the Collective, spreading the feeling of disgust and anger, and then layering in an additional element of raw revulsion. All of the meat from Canada being sent to the US was processed just like this. Avoid it. Avoid it like the plague. Avoid it like your life depended on it. I spread those thoughts far and wide into the Collective. It didn't matter if my thoughts were true or not. Once they took hold in the Collective, their power would only grow, magnified by fear, magnified by the power of social media. I just needed to, you guessed it, plant the seed. PTS. These people knew exactly what they were doing.

I finished thinking my thoughts and then removed the VR helmet. Coming back to reality after that dose of strong virtual reality took a moment to get used to. The experience inside the VR helmet had felt very real, especially with the element of smell now added into the mix.

Gerald glanced down at the smartwatch on his wrist, tapping at the screen. "Thirty-seven-hundred posts already." He glanced over at me. "That's a new record. Congratulations."

I gave the virtual reality helmet I still held in my hand a little shake. "This made it even easier."

Gerald smiled. "Congratulations to us both, then," he said.

And so it went. We kept planting more seeds against Canada's exports, spreading the fear of bacterial-contaminated food, and the Canadian authorities soon accused the US of spreading fake news on purpose. A full blown trade war escalated, with hefty tariffs issued on both sides. Soon, it came to physical blows as fights broke out within numerous border towns, then those skirmishes exploded into small scale military strikes.

After fifty thousand soldiers and civilians died in the Battle for North America, I really began to question if I was doing the right thing.

But the biggest change occurred when PTS wanted to go global. It was just too much. It was all just too much for me to handle. Well, plus those cheap bastards weren't willing to pay me what I thought I was worth. More on that in a moment. The PTS bigwigs weren't content with just the manipulation of one group of people, or just the citizens of one nation. No, they had to go global. The board of directors at PTS insisted upon it. It was the only way to keep the corporate growth train accelerating. I don't think they had any idea of their ultimate destination; they just wanted to keep going faster and faster.

Think about the entertainment business. There's something about these experiences that millions of people, sometimes hundreds of millions of people, share that creates this invisible, intangible sub structure in our thoughts. All these superheroes don't exist anywhere but in our imaginations. Sure, they exist in physical forms in comics, in pictures drawn by talented artists, in films created by talented filmmakers, but they don't really exist as we all understand our true human experience of life. Yet, hundreds of millions of people collectively share the stories of these imaginary beings, collectively debate their merits, their strengths, their weaknesses. These fictitious heroes thrive in the collective unconscious.

PTS understands that and they know how to tap into it. I know I may be repeating myself here, but it's important you understand. Somehow, they know where the collective unconscious of humanity exists. Somehow they discovered this invisible spectrum, this ethereal cloud around which all human thought orbits, this wavelength that is linked to all human beings. Think of the mind of a crowd during a riot; the madness is contagious. Somehow all of these people who would never consider committing any kind of crime, would never even contemplate looting a store, or throwing flaming bottles at police officers, get caught up in this maelstrom of manic behavior. It spreads like a contagion, as if the wind just blows the thought from one person to the next, whispering to them, goading them into an action that would seem reprehensible if looked upon as an individual acting it out.

Think about that for a moment. Think about the power PTS has with this knowledge. Think about how swiftly they can sway public opinion. What is so insidious about PTS is that they don't do it openly. Sure, they have thought drives, trying to recruit new people so they can purchase their thoughts, but even those efforts are somewhat self-contained; they don't publicly advertise - word just spreads and people show up at the PTS pop-up sites and sit in extraction chairs, or wear the new extraction VR helmets. PTS attacks from the subterranean depths of the mind, just steering actions in the direction they want them to go, spreading their own beliefs, spreading their own insidious agenda without ever rising up to the surface to reveal themselves.

When this next thought hits, everyone's gonna sit up and take notice. Not just a few thousand people. Not just a few million. Not just the inhabitants of one country. Not just the inhabitants of one continent. I'm talking about the whole world. Every person living on Earth is going to notice because everyone on Earth is going to think their neighbor is infected, or their office co-worker is infected, or the lady at the cash register is infected, or their house is potentially contaminated, or their grocery store is contaminated. Think Ebola times a hundred. One sneeze from an infected individual can infect an entire building within minutes; that's how fast rumors will say it spreads. It can linger in the air for up to twelve hours after its been expelled by a single sneeze. It can live on any surface for up to forty eight hours after contact; store-bought disinfectant cleansing wipes won't kill it. Even hospital-strength cleansing agents won't kill it.

And PTS is going to be the only one with the cure. It'll be cheap, only about twenty bucks for a shot. But when everyone on the planet feels compelled to get the vaccine, that's a lot of dough. Even if only half the planet get the shot, that's still well over seventy-five billion dollars in profit.

So why am I blowing the lid off this whole fucking thing? I'll tell you why. They were only going to give me a measly fifty million dollar bonus. Well, fuck them. I think I deserve a cool two billion at least. That's why I'm blowing the whistle on these fuckers. They're taking advantage of me. They don't appreciate my talents. No one else can reach as deep into the Collective as I can. Yeah, I'll still plant the seed of their pathetic little disease because I'm under contract and I don't feel like going to court for a breach, but that doesn't mean I have to take it lying down.

I've got something much bigger planned after those PTS fuckers pump everybody full of their useless vaccine. So why am I giving myself away, too? Call it pride, ego, whatever you want. I just want everyone to know it was me. You can't stop me anyway, so who cares? Remember, it doesn't even matter if you know the facts because the emotional waves sweeping through the collective unconscious of humanity are going to sway your reactions; the power of the Collective dwarfs any individual.

Brace yourself. Pay close attention to the news. Keep checking your social media accounts. Keep watching your neighbors. Keep your eyes on your family. I'm going to push this baby deep into the Collective, and it's going to be coming in hot. It's bigger than contaminated food. It's bigger than a measly virus. This baby's gonna spread like wildfire. This one's going to hit the Collective with the power and force of an asteroid slamming into the planet. It's going to be my masterpiece. And it's worth a fuckload more than a penny, that's for sure.

If you want to be saved, it's gonna cost you.

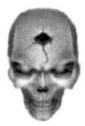

TERRORSTORY #66
THE CANDY JAR

It wasn't the candy jar itself that was terrifying.

It was what came out of it.

"Cool! Look what Mom got us," I said to my two sisters. My excitement erupted out of me before we even knew its purpose. It was just a cookie jar. Well, really a candy jar in our case because we never put any cookies in it. It was in the shape of a medieval castle, with the removable top adorned with painted ceramic turrets. It had a light brown color for the main part of the container, the bottom portion painted to look like the stones of a castle wall. The lid had four triangle shaped turrets above its base, the uppermost turret festooned with a tiny ceramic flag, each turret painted a sky blue.

It was only after we filled the jar with actual candy that the weirdness started. It was as if the candy jar needed to be filled in order to activate it, because if the candy jar was empty then nothing came out of it. I know that may sound a little obvious and confusing at the same time, but you'll see.

I was the first one to pull out something... fucked up. That's the best way to describe it. It was just fucked up. We really didn't know what it was at first, but it became obvious pretty quickly that it wasn't a piece of candy. Okay, that wasn't true for all of us. My older sister Ivet and I knew what it was right away, but we tried to reassure Laura by telling her that it was just a big candy grape covered with cherry sauce. Laura was only three years old, so she didn't know any better and would pretty much believe anything we told her. She really looked up to me and Ivet and worshipped us, believing every word that came out of our mouths.

You might have already guessed what it was that I pulled out of the candy jar. It was an eyeball. A human eyeball. How on earth it had gotten in there was anybody's guess. We certainly didn't put it in there. Heck, I'd admit it if I did for the sake of claiming ownership of the prank. But I didn't do it. Pulling it out had felt a little strange, too, because it felt like it was stuck on something at first and I had to give it a sharp little tug to get it to come free from whatever had been pinning it down inside the jar.

My sister Ivet and I just stared at the eyeball sitting there in my palm. Ivet was older than me. She had really long black hair that flowed halfway down her back. Her hair was always straight, super smooth and shiny like a raven's wing. She had a bit of acne, but she was pretty skilled at covering it up with her makeup. I was the middle child, sandwiched by two girls.

Laura made a move to grab at the eyeball and I quickly reached over to her and stopped her, pulling her arm down away from my hand. I may have jerked her wrist too hard because she gave out a little whelp. "Don't touch it," I said, curling my fingers over the eyeball, but not too tightly so that I would squish it in my grip.

"I want to see it," Laura said. She had dark hair, too, but it wasn't straight like Ivet's. Laura's hair was curly, and it seemed to be getting curlier and curlier the older she got. She was as cute as a button, as the saying goes, always easy with a smile. She had little dimples in her cheeks that ratcheted up her cuteness a notch.

Ivet made a sour face. "Laura, it's just gross."

Laura frowned at Ivet.

The eyeball felt warm and wet in my palm. I opened up my fingers to get a better look at it, turning my body to shield the eyeball from Laura's gaze. A thin layer of blood covered portions of the eyeball, and a few trailing strands of veins or ligaments or something dangled down from the eyeball. I was absolutely fascinated by it. I just stared at it. And it stared back. It was a blue eye, streaked with tiny red veins within the white portions. I had no idea where it had come from. No idea how it could have gotten into our candy jar.

"Go wash your hands," Ivet told Laura.

"But I didn't touch it," Laura protested, putting both her little hands on her hips, imitating one of Ivet's poses to the T.

Ivet pointed a firm finger towards the bathroom. "Go. You can pick something out of the candy jar later."

Laura frowned, but she still jumped off the chair she had been standing on and scooted off into the bathroom. The sound of running water could be heard seconds later.

"It's a fucking eyeball," I hissed at Ivet, keeping my voice low but putting a tight edge on my words. "How the fuck did an eyeball get in the candy jar? It was empty before we filled it." And we had only put in mini candy bars. We had dumped in bags of mini Hershey bars, mini Mister Goodbars, mini Butterfingers, and mini Snickers. That was it. That's all that should have been in there.

"Maybe it was already in one of the candy bags," Ivet said.

I shook my head. "No way. We would have seen it when we were dumping the candy in there." I stared down at the eyeball in my hand for a moment, then looked up at Ivet. "What am I supposed to do with this?"

"Jesus, throw it in the garbage," Ivet said. She scrunched up her face, the left side of her upper lip curling up. "It's freakin' disgusting."

"Should we call the police or something?" I asked.

"And tell them what? Tell them we found an eyeball that somehow just appeared in our candy jar?"

I looked down at the eyeball again. "It sure looks real."

"And you know what an actual eyeball that's been plucked out of someone's eye really looks like?" Ivet pursed her lips in miss-know-it-all-style.

I shrugged. "I guess not."

"Seriously, throw it away and go wash your hands."

I moved to the garbage bin near the back screen door and tossed the eyeball in. The eyeball vanished into the dark bottom of the black garbage bag with a soft plunking sound, disappearing into some folds of the plastic bag. I passed Laura coming out of the bathroom on my way into the bathroom. "Wait for me before you pick something else out," I said to her.

She just raced on past me.

I quickly washed my hands and moved back into the kitchen to rejoin my sisters. They both were just staring at the candy jar. They had these weird, almost vacant looks on their faces, like they were staring at the candy jar but also staring into space at the same time. The top of the candy jar was still resting on the kitchen counter near the base of the castle-shaped jar. Neither one of them was making any move towards it. They just stared at the open jar.

"Did you pick something else?" I asked Laura.

She shook her head.

"The other candy's probably all blood—I mean, all wet," Ivet said, quickly altering her proclamation. She kept her gaze riveted on the castle candy jar as she spoke. "We should probably just throw it all out."

I frowned at that. "Mom would be pissed."

Ivet didn't say anything, but I knew that she didn't want to encounter Mom's wrath either.

"Well," I said. "Let's find out." I reached out and put my hand into the jar. I felt the packaging that surrounded each mini candy bar, rummaging my fingers through dozens of mini bars, hearing the wrappers crinkle as I shuffled through them. I pushed my hand in deeper, continuing to move my fingers around, trying to feel any wet spots. But I didn't feel any. Nothing felt wet at all, which was damn weird because that eyeball had been thoroughly coated in blood. There's no way some of it could not have been smeared on at least a few of the candy wrappers. I pulled my hand out and looked at it. It was clean. No sign of any blood on my fingers. Not even a tiny speck.

Laura didn't waste any time to follow my lead. She climbed up on the chair that was positioned next to the kitchen counter and thrust her little hand into the castle candy jar before we could stop her. And pulled out a mini Snickers. She whooped with delight since those were her favorite.

Ivet and I exchanged glances, then both gave a little shrug to each other at the same time.

We each had a few pieces of scrumptious chocolate, then put the lid back on.

"Look at Mister Reynolds," I whispered to Ivet. I motioned with a subtle toss of my head to let her know not to be too blatant with her gaze.

Ivet slowly turned her head to see what I had been looking at. "He looks like a pirate," she muttered as she turned back to me.

Mister Reynolds, one of our gym teachers, was

wearing a patch over his left eye. He seemed very agitated, constantly pointing to the patch over his eye. He was a little wide in the waist for a gym teacher, and his brown curly hair was a bit more disheveled than normal. He was talking animatedly to one of the priests from our church.

We were in the grocery store, tagging along with Mom. She had given us a list of things to find so Ivet and I had gone off together to gather up the items. We had already found the spaghetti sauce and the penne noodles that were on the list, so Ivet was clutching those. We were in the chips aisle, looking for generic corn chips (which taste even better than some brand names, by the way) when I saw Mister Reynolds. His head had been turned away from me, but I still caught a glimpse of the thin black band that ran across the back of his head. Only when he turned his head did I realize he was wearing a patch over his eye. He did look like a pirate, what with the thick beard he always sported. Actually, he looked like a very angry pirate because his face was flush and the movements of his arms were wild and exaggerated as he discussed something heatedly with Father O'Callan.

Father O'Callan was doing his best to calm Mister Reynolds but the priest didn't seem to be having the desired effect on the very agitated man. Father O'Callan was young for a priest, slender in build, tall, with short red hair and a few freckles dotting his cheeks. He kept holding his hand out palm up at Mister Reynolds, clearly encouraging the gym teacher to stop his crazy animated waving of his arms.

Ivet and I moved closer, trying to avoid looking at them, pretending to scour the shelves for something.

They were standing towards the end of the aisle, near all the peanut products. We inched our way past the potato chips, moving towards the corn chips section, which was next to the peanuts section.

"What did the police say?" Father O'Callan asked. The young priest kept his voice calm, even.

"They have no idea," Mister Reynolds said, his voice huffing indignantly. "There was no sign of forced entry, nothing on my security system. They've got nothing. They haven't got a fucking clue!"

"Just calm down, Jim," Father O'Callan said, his voice soothing, relaxed.

But Mister Reynolds was having none of the priest's pacifying attempts to tone him down. "How the fuck can you explain it?" He again pointed to the patch over his eye. "I woke up four days ago and my fucking eyeball was missing! Have your God explain that to me!"

"Are they giving you anything for the pain?" Father O'Callan asked, still keeping his voice calm, his tone even in that way priests were really good at.

Mister Reynolds grunted harshly. "I don't want anything for the pain. I want my fucking eyeball back!"

"Please, come and see me at the church. We can talk further about it there."

Ivet and I found the corn chips we were looking for, and I grabbed them as quietly as I could from the shelf, trying not to let the bag make any crinkly noises as I gingerly removed it from the shelf. We moved back away from them, going the opposite way up the aisle away from Father O'Callan and Mister Reynolds.

"I told you we should have called the police," I said to Ivet. We were back at home, sitting on Ivet's bed in her bedroom.

Ivet frowned. "What? You really think that was Mister Reynold's eyeball in our candy jar?"

"You heard him. He said he woke up four days ago and his eyeball was just gone. That's the same day we found the eyeball in the candy jar. There is no way that was just a coincidence." I paused before delivering the bombshell. "He's got blue eyes." Then I added, "Well, now just one."

"That's not even funny, Tobias."

I lost the start of my smirk before it could form.

Ivet sat up straighter in her bed, lifting her back away from the headboard she had been leaning against. "So how the fuck would his eyeball get into our candy jar?" Ivet asked.

Ivet doesn't curse much, so her harsh language caught me off guard for a moment. I didn't answer right away. Besides, I didn't really have an answer anyway. I had no idea. Okay, well, that's not really true. I did have the semblance of an idea. I just didn't want to share it with Ivet. Not yet. It was still... too painful to share at that point in time, too awkward. I was too ashamed to tell her what had happened to me. I didn't want her to look at me differently. Like I was some sort of victim. Or, even worse, that I was somehow to blame for what had happened. "I don't know," was all I said to her in response to her question.

Everything that happened between Mister

Reynolds and me would come out later.

"Oh my God," Ivet muttered. Her hand was deep inside the castle candy jar, her wrist beneath the castle's rim. Her whole body seemed to freeze. We both knew we couldn't stay away from the candy jar. Its perverse allure was just too much for us to deny. We did at least wait until Laura wasn't home with us, though; our baby sister was off playing at a friend's house.

"What is it?" I asked. "Is it..." I knew I didn't need to finish the question. I knew the hand she had buried deep into the castle candy jar wasn't clutching at a piece of candy. Somehow, I just knew it. And, to be fair, I was morbidly curious, seriously morbidly curious about what she would pull out. "Let's see," I said. I could feel a rush of excitement spread through me as I prompted her to reveal what she was clutching.

Ivet hesitated. She shifted her gaze to me, and I could see the nervous fear in her eyes, and then she shifted her gaze back to the candy jar. "I think it's... a hand. I think it's somebody's hand."

"Holy shit," I said. "Let's see. Take it out. Take it out."

"It feels like it's stuck," she said.

I nodded. "So did... mine," I said. "Just tug on it a little. That's what I had to do."

She gave a little tug with her hand, then followed that with a bit stronger of a yank. Then she slowly withdrew her hand from inside the candy jar, raising it up for me to see what she clutched in her fingers. It was indeed a hand. Ivet gripped three of the hand's fingers, pinching them together as she clutched at the severed hand. Loose hanging tendrils of veins and arteries and ripped flesh dangled down from one end of the severed hand; part of a sharp piece of bone jutted out from the end of the hand. The hand appeared to have been yanked off very roughly at the wrist.

"Holy shit!" I said again, this time with a bit more disbelieving emphasis.

Ivet stared at the severed hand. I knew my eyes were as wide as hers as we both marveled at what had just come out of the candy jar. Then she quickly moved the severed hand away from her body as she gazed at it. It was a right hand. That much we could tell by the position of the bloody thumb. "Jesus," Ivet muttered. "I know whose hand this is."

"What? How do you know that?"

"Look," she said. She turned the severed hand slightly to give me a glimpse of the hand's index finger; she was clutching the hand by the last three fingers so the index finger was clearly visible. A word was tattooed along the length of the index finger; the letters were spattered with blood but the word was still easily legible. It read: SUPERSTAR, all in small caps. I didn't know what kind of font it was, but it had a bit of a stenciled look to it.

I read the word aloud. "Superstar." I looked curiously at Ivet.

"It's Joanna's hand," she said. "Joanna Jovisich."

"The softball pitcher? The one who pitched the winning game at the state finals?"

"Yeah, that one," Ivet said.

I was quiet for a moment, just staring at the

severed hand, reading the tattooed word over and over again in my head. I knew Ivet had tried out for the softball team last year, but she had been cut because her batting skills were pretty poor, so her not making the team was still a very sore topic for her that I did my best to avoid at all costs.

"She's a nasty bully," Ivet said with a deep scowl, still staring at the severed hand.

I only knew Joanna by the stories Ivet told me about her. I had never actually met her, let alone seen her much. I did remember the time Ivet told me that Joanna had shoved her into a locker and she had cut her forehead on the edge of the metal locker door. She still had a ghost of a scar from that incident. There were many other stories like that about Joanna's bullying and physically abusive behavior, none of them ending very well for Ivet.

"Umm," I finally said after a moment, "you're dripping blood all over the floor."

Ivet glanced down at the tiled kitchen floor. Sure enough, a few splatters of blood were visible on the tiles. She cupped her other hand beneath the severed hand, blocking any more blood from dripping to the floor, and quickly moved over to the garbage can near the side of the counter. She plopped the severed hand into the garbage and grabbed a few paper towels off the roll to wipe off her blood-stained fingers. She looked over to me as she wiped at the blood. "We've got to get rid of that. Take the garbage out. Throw it in the garbage bin in the garage."

"Shouldn't we bury it or something?" I asked.

Ivet shook her head. "Just get that garbage out of here before it starts to stink. Tie up the bag tight."

I did as she asked. I tied the garbage bag tight and

brought it into the garage to dump it into the big garbage can that we pulled out to the curb every week.

I cleaned off my hands in the bathroom, then came back into the kitchen to see Ivet taking a bite out of a mini Hershey bar. I looked curiously at her. The floor was already clean, so she had already wiped up the blood splatters and probably cleaned her hands in the kitchen sink.

"I had to see if there was anything else in there," she said. "There wasn't. Nothing was bloody. Nothing was even wet. Just candy."

I nodded at her. The same thing happened with her as it did with me. After the candy jar lid was removed, whoever reached into the jar first was the one who pulled out the... well, I'll just call it the fucked-up object. Then anyone who reached into the candy jar after that would just pull out a normal piece of candy. When the candy jar lid was put back on, it seemed to re-set itself, priming the jar for another fucked-up object to be pulled out of it.

"So are you going to tell me about the eyeball you pulled out of the candy jar?" Ivet asked between bites.

I just frowned at her. The question set my heart racing a bit faster and I felt a weird lightheaded sensation floating inside my head. I could actually feel a thin layer of sweat forming on my forehead.

"I know why I pulled out what's-her-name's hand from the jar," Ivet said. "She's just a nasty bitch to everyone."

"So you really think it's her hand? Her actual hand?" I asked.

"What do you think?" she asked.

I didn't say anything. I could see the topic of her

arch nemesis was getting Ivet a little riled up, so I just waited for her to continue.

She finished her mini Hershey bar and reached back into the candy jar, pulling out a mini Mister Goodbar. I loved those; the nuts really went well with the chocolate. She unwrapped the wrapper and just stared at the small chunk of chocolate. "That's the hand she slapped me with," Ivet finally said. "She humiliated me pretty much in front of our entire English class. That's the one I pulled out of the candy jar." She popped the entire mini Mister Goodbar into her mouth and stared at the castle candy jar. "Who's humiliated now, bitch?" she said in the middle of chewing the chocolate.

She reached into the candy jar again and this time pulled out a mini Butterfinger. Can't say I was a huge fan of those. The chewy inside part always seemed to stick to my teeth. "So?" she said, obviously prompting me to answer her question about the eyeball I had plucked out of the candy jar.

I didn't really want to answer, but I knew Ivet would never let up until I did. "He… watched us. In the showers." I felt unclean just talking about it.

"Like a peeping tom?"

I nodded. "We found a spy hole. I'm pretty sure there were a bunch of mirrors set up behind the walls so he could watch us from his office. Or maybe they were little spy cameras. I don't know. I just know he was watching us."

Ivet frowned. "Did you tell Principal Thomas?"

I shook my head.

"Why not?"

"You know those guys are really good friends, right?" I said. "We always see them talking together.

Sometimes, Principal Thomas came out of Mister Reynold's office right when we were coming out of the showers, and he always had this weird look on his face, and he always seemed sweaty."

"Gross," she said.

I nodded. She didn't prompt me to go into any more detail, so I was grateful to her for that.

Ivet finished her mini Butterfinger. She was quiet for a long moment, then she looked at the candy jar again. "If thine eye offends thee, pluck it out," she muttered.

I looked curiously at her. "Where'd you get that from?"

She shrugged. "I think it's from the Bible or something."

⚜

The more I thought about it, the more I came to the realization that what was happening was not just happening randomly. There seemed to be a purpose behind what was going on. The candy jar was offering up psychological treats, sweet tasting pieces of revenge or justice or whatever you want to call it. How it worked, I had no idea. I don't even remember where it had come from. It had just shown up on our kitchen counter and we all had assumed Mom just bought it at the store for us; she was always doing nice things like that for us. But now I wasn't so sure about that.

Ivet and I felt a strange calm come over us after we realized what was happening. It was a nice feeling. A strange, yet comforting feeling. Like maybe the universe really was looking out for us after all.

Somehow, the castle candy jar was connected to all things. Maybe there was some dark matter curtain buried in the bottom of the jar. Maybe there was some miniature wormhole that distorted space and time somehow contained within the castle jar. The candy jar clearly fed off some emotional triggers. Or our emotions were triggering doorways, triggering these wormholes that allowed us to reach across space and time. I didn't really know the answer then. But it was pretty damn cool, if you think about it.

We debated letting Laura have a turn, but then we figured why not. Heck, she was only three years old. What could she possibly pull out of the candy jar? Maybe the body of a mouse? She had seen a mouse in the basement just the other day and it had scared her. Or maybe a spider? She hated spiders. One of them had crawled over her hand a few months ago and she still seemed a little freaked out by it. It had just been a harmless daddy longlegs, but it still had spooked her.

So we gave Laura a turn. I still wonder if we did the right thing. We honestly weren't trying to be cruel. The three of us did practically everything together, so it just didn't seem right not to let Laura have a turn. Maybe we shouldn't have. Because it wasn't a mouse she pulled out of the jar, or even a spider. It was something worse. Something horribly, horribly worse.

"It's my turn to go first? Really?" Laura's hazel eyes were as big as saucers. She could barely stand still, fidgeting from one leg to the other.

172

"Yep," Ivet said.

"Go ahead," I urged, pointing to the castle candy jar. "Take off the lid."

Laura climbed up on the kitchen chair we moved next to the counter so she could reach the candy jar. The lid was a bit heavy and oddly shaped with the castle turrets on it, so Laura had to use both hands to grip it and lift it up and off the main body of the jar. She set the lid down on the counter next to the jar. She stared at the open candy jar for a moment.

I looked over to Ivet and she looked like she was actually holding her breath, waiting for Laura to reach into the jar. I shifted my gaze back to Laura. "Go on," I urged her again.

Laura stuck her small hand into the jar and immediately made a sour face. "I feel something yucky," she said.

"It's okay," I said, encouraging her to keep going. "It won't hurt you."

"It's all wet and slimy," Laura said, still making her sour face.

I looked over to Ivet and she looked back at me. I could see the nervous excitement and maybe a bit of the fear that I know was mirrored on my face.

"It's okay, Laura," Ivet said. "Just pull it out. Let's see what it is."

"Okay," Laura said and started to lift her hand out of the jar. But then her hand seemed to get stuck, as if she was tugging on something but couldn't get it to come out. Exactly like what had happened to me and Ivet. "It's stuck," she said.

"Pull harder," I told her.

My little sister made a tight little grimace and jerked sharply, pulling with all her little might.

On the other side of town, Father O'Callan shrieked. Had we been there we probably would have needed to cover our ears because we heard people say that his scream could be heard from several blocks away. Had we been there, we would have seen him writhe and moan at clutch at his groin. Had we been there, we would have seen a darkening stain spread across his crotch. Had we been there, we would have seen his fingers turning a deep crimson.

I know you don't need me to tell you we immediately disposed of what Laura had pulled out of the castle candy jar.

Ivet and I cried as we did our best to comfort her. For a little kid, Laura was surprisingly strong. She was just disgusted by all the red goop on her hands and the little sausage-like thing she had pulled out of the jar, but after we helped her wash her hands she was all smiles and giggles.

Later that night, Mom walked into the kitchen and beamed us all smiles. "How are you enjoying that candy jar?" she asked.

I just looked at her. There was something in her eyes, something in her tone of voice, that told us in not so many words that she knew, she knew exactly what the candy jar was doing.

Laura bit into a mini Snickers bar and chewed

noisily. "I love it, Mommy."

Mom's smile grew. She came over to us and gave us all a big group hug. We all hugged her back. She was just trying to protect us the only way she knew how. We knew that after Dad died she had a rough time adjusting to life as a single parent. Just because she read palms and interpreted tarot cards and read tea leaves didn't mean she was a bad person. That didn't automatically make her a witch. That didn't automatically mean she could summon dark forces for her own purposes.

I mean, she is a witch and she can summon dark forces for her own purposes, but that still doesn't make her a bad person. She's a good mother, and that's all we care about.

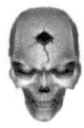

TERRORSTORY #67
PERILS OF POORISM

"They're so filthy." Vanessa Foreland waved a wrinkled pamphlet in front of her expertly mascara-painted face as she peered out of the window of the small mini-van they were riding in. She was dressed in an elegant peach-colored pantsuit. Her blonde hair (very professionally dyed to hide every single black root) was coifed up, leaving just a few strands (on purpose) dangling down along her slender neck. She was forty-seven, the widowed wife of a wealthy tech magnate, looking for some new thrill to alleviate the utter boredom she felt living a life of pure luxury. "Look at how awful their lives are."

There was a glee in Vanessa's tone that the three others in the van found infectious. They all smiled and nodded along with her.

Fernando Rivera silently read the words emblazoned across the front of the pamphlet that Vanessa continued to wave in front of her face. *Slum Tours* was the headline on the pamphlet, written in large black type. *See Ravihada - the biggest slum in Asia!* was the second line on the pamphlet. A smaller line at the bottom revealed the company behind the tours - *Real World Real Tours.* Fernando was a handsome Hispanic man in his forties, a friend of Vanessa's from the old days before he joined the one-percenters with his real estate deals and venture capital successes.

"Look!" Diana Duport shouted. "Look at that little boy. He's trying to steal food from that old man!" She was also a friend of Vanessa's, a dark-complexioned woman in her forties. She and her brother William owned a medical company that devised medications to help people fight off addiction to meth, or crack, or heroin, or the dozens of different painkillers that were ravaging American lives. She had a delicate round face with wide, expressive brown eyes.

Everyone moved to the right side of the van, ogling the event playing out in the streets. A young boy of about eight, dressed in what truly looked like a soiled shirt and pants set made out of rags, was trying to pry what appeared to be an apple out of the wrinkled hands of an old man sitting in a battered steel chair near the crumbling wall of a dilapidated stone building.

"Are you sure they're human?" Vanessa asked. "They act like animals." She continued to wave her pamphlet in front of her face like a fan, her movement getting a little faster, the motion of the fan increasing, her attention glued to the little thief and his victim.

William Duport snorted. He was tall, very stern looking, his face long and thin, his expression usually quite serious. He tried to force himself to relax and enjoy the moment, but his thoughts often drifted back to work and how much he had to do when he got back to the States. He was a few years younger than Diana. He often felt compelled to out-do her simply because she was his older sister and she always played the *but I'm older card* with their parents when they were young. That had irritated and angered him to no end; he thought he was well over it, but something always seemed to trigger those combative emotions no matter how hard he fought to dismiss them.

Out in the dreary streets of Ravihada, if one could even call the crumbling pothole-laden, look-out-for-that-crater-pavement a street, the young boy managed to wrench the apple out of the old man's hand and raced off into a dark alley. The old man raised his hand and yelled after the boy, shaking his unsteady fist, his face a mask of outrage.

Diana giggled. "It's like watching the beginning of Aladdin in real life." She turned to beam a smile at Vanessa. "This is *so* exciting."

The van continued on, moving cautiously through the muddy streets, the driver doing his best to avoid the numerous potholes that pockmarked the crumbling roadway.

Fernando stared out the back window of the van. He looked on with growing curiosity as the young boy re-appeared out of the dark alley. The boy moved back to the old man and handed him the apple back. The old man beamed a smile at the young boy and patted his head affectionately. Another man, dressed in clean clothes, looking very out-of-place in this shabby environment, appeared out of the alley and moved over to the old man and the boy. He appeared to make some kind of transaction, and it looked to Fernando as if the cleanly-dressed man was handing some coins to the boy and to the old man.

Fernando looked back towards the front of the van and caught the driver watching him in the rearview mirror.

"You saw that, eh?" the driver asked, not turning around. He glanced forward at the road in front of him, then back up at Fernando in the mirror. The driver was a small man, Indian or Pakistani maybe, sporting a thin black mustache.

Fernando said nothing.

"Saw what?" Vanessa asked. She looked at Fernando, then at the driver, then back to Fernando.

"That little boy gave the apple back to the old man and then some other guy showed up and paid them some money or something," Fernando finally said.

"What?" Vanessa's face took on a crestfallen look. She looked out the back window to catch a fleeting glimpse of the young boy raising his middle finger towards them just as the van turned a corner and he disappeared from view. Vanessa turned back to face forward. "He just flipped me the bird." Her voice held a tone of disbelief.

"What?" Diana asked.

"That little fucker flipped me off," Vanessa said, the indignation growing stronger as she spoke.

"What?" Diana quickly turned to get a glimpse out of the back window of the van, but they were already on a different street, the boy and the old man gone from view. She turned back to look at Vanessa. "Are you serious?"

Vanessa frowned. She waved the pamphlet a bit more vigorously in front of her face.

Diana laughed. "Well, you did say they act like animals."

William nodded. "We did pay to see the uncouth denizens of the biggest slum in Asia, after all."

"This area is over-toured," the driver said. "The residents have learned to put on fake shows for the tour groups."

William frowned and pursed his lips. "Well, that's a little disappointing."

The driver tilted his head up so they could see his smiling face in the mirror. "Oh, don't worry. This is just the beginning. We're going to go into some real slums very soon. You'll get to see how some of the poorest people on the entire planet actually live. No running water. No proper sanitation. Many have no electricity. They barely have a roof over their heads."

Diana clapped her hands gleefully.

❦

"We have to walk?" Diana asked.

The driver nodded. "There are no roads that go into the heart of the slum. All the buildings are too close together for vehicles. Not even bicycles are of much use. Everyone just walks."

Diana frowned. She glanced down at her heels.

The driver followed her gaze. "I did tell everyone to wear comfortable shoes."

Diana looked up at him. "These are comfortable. They're just not made for walking long distances."

The driver shrugged. "You can just take them off," he said. "Many of the residents around here don't even wear shoes anyway. They can't afford them."

Diana shook her head. "No thanks. I'll manage."

The driver looked at her for a moment, then shrugged again.

Vanessa glanced out the window of the minivan. She waved her pamphlet near her face, fanning herself. "Are they..." She turned away from the window to look at the driver. "Are they... dangerous?"

The driver glanced out the window, then back to Vanessa. "Them?" The driver laughed. "No. None of them have enough energy to be dangerous. Most of them live on the very edge of starvation."

"So they won't try to rob us?" William asked.

The driver shook his head. "Oh, no. Money has no value here. They barter for goods. They make things for each other, trade services."

"How delightfully barbaric," Fernando muttered.

The driver motioned for them to exit the van with a sweep of his hand. "Shall we go?"

"How many people live here?" Diana asked as they continued their walk. They passed several rows of shacks that looked like they were made out of cardboard. Thin tin sheets acted as the roofs. There were dozens of slum dwellers milling about, many of them looking listless and drained; all of their clothes looked like they had been worn for weeks, if not months, straight without being washed.

"Over six hundred thousand," the driver said.

"Six hundred thousand?" Fernando asked, the question nearly coming out in a gasp. "Six hundred thousand people live like this?"

The driver nodded. "This is only one of India's slums. There are dozens more."

As they walked through the slums, they passed numerous slum dwellers who had cracked lips. Vanessa eagerly took pictures of a few of them, zooming in to get close-ups of their parched mouths, zeroing in especially tight on the mouths that looked like they were formed out of the cracked earth of a parched wasteland. They were so abundant that even Diana noticed them, pausing at one point when she was taking a selfie to mention it.

"There's not much fresh water here," the driver explained. "Some of the residents have to walk half a mile a day and then wait for hours in line just to get fresh water for their families, and even then sometimes they come back home empty-handed."

Fernando absently licked at his lips.

William unhooked his water bottle from his belt and took a sip.

They continued on their walk. All of the matchbox-size houses were about the size of one of the smaller bathrooms in Vanessa's Florida retreat, all of them crammed together nearly on top of another. Every house, if you could even call them houses, looked as if it would fall down any second. Some of the walls on the houses looked to be made of clay, others of chipped stone, others of crumbling bricks, and yet others of wood. There was no rhyme or reason to the building structures; they all looked as if they were haphazardly put together with whatever materials were available at that moment.

Scattered pieces of garbage of all shapes and sizes and textures and colors seemed to be everywhere, just as flies and other buzzing insects seemed to be everywhere. The air was thick and humid. Smoke emanated from nearly half the houses, rising up out of holes in the roofs or up out of open doorways. All sorts of smells wafted to their nostrils, most of them not too unpleasant as they smelled of meals being prepared, but every once in a while a noxious stench would assault them, carried by a slight breeze.

Vanessa took more pictures, snapping off photos of crooked houses, of crumbling walls, of slum dwellers sitting on rickety chairs or sleeping on the ground, of colorful piles of garbage. With every new encounter, her excitement grew. She took a perverse pleasure in the decay, the filth, relishing her life of ease compared to the horror of how these people (*savages in her mind*) actually lived their lives.

⋘⋙⊰❂⊱⋘⋙

"What is that building?" William asked, pointing off to their right. It was a dilapidated structure made of wood that was leaning heavily to the left, looking as if it might collapse at any moment. In fact, every single structure they had seen or come across in the slum seemed to be in imminent danger of collapsing at any moment. There was a rare building-less space in front of the structure, but that space was occupied by what looked like hundreds of people standing outside the slanted doorway of the building, most of them young children. From his vantage point, William could see dozens more people just inside the building. One child exited the building, his food cupped in his hands since he didn't appear to have a bowl to put it in.

"It is a feeding center for the children in the slums," the driver said. "There are over ten thousand of these, probably more."

"Ten thousand?" Fernando echoed.

The driver didn't bother to respond to the question. He pointed to one of the children waiting in one of the long lines. "She looks extremely malnourished," he said. "Look how thin her legs are. You can see how her bones stand out, especially there around her shoulders and neck. Hopefully, she turns to look at us."

"Why do you want her to look at us?" Diana asked.

The driver didn't get a chance to answer. The young girl turned and they were all immediately drawn to her eyes. They stood out from the rest of her face, but not because of their beauty or the innocent sweetness of youth; they stood out because of how hollow they looked, how deeply set into her face they looked, how immensely tired they look. Even though she was no more than nine years old, the young girl had the look of a ninety year old with one foot in the grave and the other foot about to join in.

"Oh my God," Diana said, putting her hand over her mouth as she whispered the words.

"Your God is afraid to set foot here," the driver said. He suddenly sounded very bitter, his tone angry. But then he quickly recovered and put a jovial look on his face. "Hurry, you'll miss your picture."

Vanessa reacted to the driver's insistence. She quickly raised her phone and took several photos of the gaunt, emaciated girl.

"Come, Navala is probably waiting for us," the driver said.

"Navala? Who is she?" Fernando asked.

"She's going to make a meal for you," the driver said.

"A meal?" Vanessa frowned.

"We're actually going to... eat something?" Diana asked, then glanced around the area. "Here?"

"Of course," the driver said. Then he noticed Diana looking about the area. "No, no, not right here. This is for the children. We're going to get a home cooked meal. I'm hungry. Aren't you hungry?"

"Not really," Diana said.

"You paid for a meal with your tour, so you might as well eat," the driver said. "We still have a bit of a walk to go before we get to her house, so let us continue on."

They continued on, walking cautiously over a few planks of rotting wood that protected them from a shallow rivulet of filthy water flowing between a row of the closely packed houses.

William fought back the hint of claustrophobia that threatened to unnerve him as they continued to move through the slums. Everything was so tight and confining, the houses packed in like sardines. He looked up at the sky every so often, the open sky and lazily drifting clouds above him helping to calm his nervousness.

⟡

"What are they doing?"

The driver followed William's gaze to a group of children rummaging through a massive pile of garbage that was situated between a few houses. Flies and other insects buzzed about the mound of refuse. The stench of rotting garbage was strong in the air.

"Looking for scraps of food, most likely," the driver replied. "They're pretty good at figuring out what is still edible. But sometimes they're just playing games, though."

"They… they play in the garbage?" Diana asked. She wrinkled her nose. She didn't think the slums could get any worse, but somehow they did.

"Oh, yes. Sometimes the girls make paper dolls out of some of the wrappers." The driver looked at the group and smiled. "Just because they are poor does not mean they are not creative." The driver looked back to the children sitting atop the pile of garbage. "Sometimes, they make clever little traps to catch some bugs."

"Catch bugs?" Vanessa frowned. She swatted a fly away from her face. "Why even bother?"

The driver frowned. "To eat them, of course. They are very nutritious." He nodded at the children. "For some of them, that is the only source of protein they have."

"We're…" Diana hesitated. "We're not going to be… eating bugs, are we?"

The driver shook his head. "Not unless you want to."

189

Diana made a disgusted face.

The screeching cry of a child drew their attention.

Diana looked to her right, her head shifting toward the sound of the cry. She saw a small girl scrambling down a mountainous pile of what looked like rusty discarded cans, soiled boxes, ripped wrappers, wooden crates in various states of damaged condition with most of them missing slats or having broken slats. The girl didn't appear to be in pain. She seemed happy almost. Her dark brown skin was marred with various splotches, like greasy stains a mechanic might have on his fingers. She was naked but for a ripped pair of red shorts. Her feet were clad in well-worn sandals that looked like they might just shred into strips of leather at any moment. She nearly slipped as she careened down the gigantic pile of garbage, but she was remarkably agile and kept her balance, only needing a quick readjustment when she put a hand down on the edge of a crate to steady herself.

"Are they... really playing in garbage?" Diana asked.

The driver nodded. "I think they are playing a game of hide and freak."

Fernando frowned. "Hide and freak? Don't you mean hide and seek?"

The driver looked at Fernando. "No, I mean hide and freak."

Fernando's frown deepened.

The driver motioned with a quick toss of his head at the garbage hill. "Watch."

Suddenly, a small hand jutted out of the garbage near the young girl in the red shorts, its curved fingers snatching and clawing at the air.

Diana clutched at her brother's arm, gripping

William tightly and pulling herself closer to him. William hesitated a moment, but then put his arm around his sister, holding her tightly to him; now didn't seem like a great time to get a leg up on her by making fun of her meekness.

The young girl scrambling down the pile of garbage shrieked again, her voice a mixture of startled fear and delight. She deftly avoided the groping fingers, continuing to move down the scattered mass of refuse. She reached the bottom of the garbage pile and leaped onto a smooth patch of dirt. She turned triumphantly back around to face the garbage hill, her face filling with a proud smile. She said something to the garbage pile in her native language.

"What did she say?" William asked.

"She said she won," the driver replied.

"She won?"

The driver nodded at William's question. "She won. The monster in the garbage didn't tag her."

"What monster?" Diana asked, her voice cracking slightly. "There's a monster in the garbage?"

The driver laughed. "Not a real monster. Just one of her friends. They take turns being the monster." The driver pointed to the garbage pile as a young boy of about twelve pushed his way out of the garbage mound, shoving aside rusted cans, clumps of paper, a tangle of wires and other debris to free himself of the filthy clutter. "See."

"They really play in the... garbage?" Diana asked, repeating her earlier question as if she refused to acknowledge the answer.

The driver nodded. "They take turns being the monster. One of them hides in the pile, then the others have to make it down from the top without getting touched."

"But they are playing in… garbage," Diana said, her words coming out in a protest.

The driver shrugged. "There's not many other places they can go where they'll be left alone to play. Most adults don't linger here after they dump off their trash." The driver was quiet for a moment. "Don't you want to take any pictures of them?"

Vanessa raised her phone to take a few pictures as several other children joined the young girl in the red shorts and the boy who just came out of the garbage. They smiled at the half-naked young girl, clapping her approvingly on the back.

Fernando just stared at the garbage, leaving his hands down at his sides, his phone clutched in his curled fingers.

William felt a tug on his arm and glanced down to see a young boy smiling up at him with dried, cracked lips. The boy's face was smeared with dirt. He clutched what appeared to be half of a large bug of some sort in one hand. The boy chewed for a moment and William realized where the other half of the bug was. The boy pointed to William's water bottle. "No, go away," William said. He frowned at the boy, waving him away with a few quick jerks of his hand. "Shoosh. Go on, now."

Fernando frowned at William, seeing him wave the boy away. "He just wanted a drink of water."

William frowned, scrunching up his face. "Jesus, who knows what kind of diseases he has."

"You could have just dripped some into his mouth," Fernando said.

"Be my guest," William said. "Call him back and give him some of yours."

Fernando just looked away from William, moving his attention back to the garbage mound.

The young girl moved back to the garbage mound and started digging into it, making a path for herself to move deeper and deeper into the pile. The other children turned away from the garbage and put their hands over their eyes. They started to count.

"What is she doing now?" William asked. Diana was still clutching at his arm, keeping herself close to her brother.

"It's her turn," the driver said. "She's the monster."

"Don't they have toys to play with?" Diana asked.

The driver didn't answer. "Come. We must be going."

"Wait," Vanessa said. "I need a better angle." She moved a few feet to her right and raised up her phone, continuing to take more selfies of herself, making sure to frame in the children and the giant pile of garbage that was their playground.

<hr />

"I have to pee," Diana whispered to William.

"Can't you hold it?"

Diana shook her head. "I've been holding it. I really need to go."

William exhaled a disgruntled breath. "Okay." He glanced around the area but could only see row after row of small dilapidated structures extending as far as he could see in the direction they were moving. The slum residents milled about, doing whatever it was they needed to do. Some of them cast wary glances in the group's direction, but most of them just ignored their presence. There was nothing nearby that looked like a public facility as far as William could tell. He looked towards the driver. "Where is the nearest bathroom?"

The driver pointed towards a nearby stream that ran between a row of the small dwellings. The stream was only a few yards wide and didn't appear to run very deep, perhaps two or three feet at most. The water slowly moved downstream, the movement of the current barely visible.

The group just stared, both shocked and somewhat in awe of what was happening a few yards upstream. A middle-aged man was clearly defecating into the water, his buttocks hovering a few inches above the surface.

"Is he... in the middle of the stream?" Diana couldn't believe what she was seeing, but she couldn't bring herself to look away.

"That's disgusting," Vanessa said, then raised her phone to take a picture.

The driver shrugged. "It's the nearest bathroom." The driver was quiet for a moment.

William glanced about, taking in all the houses around them. "What about them? Can we use one of their bathrooms?"

The driver shook his head, giving William a condescending smile. "No one has a toilet in their home. Or if they do, it doesn't work. There is one toilet for about every five hundred people in this slum. Most of them have no doors. No running water." He was quiet again. "They are not safe."

"The toilets are not safe?" William said, questioning the driver's words.

The driver shook his head. "Some of them are

death traps."

"Death traps?" William was incredulous. "The public restrooms are death traps?"

The driver nodded. "One of them collapsed last month and four men fell into the septic tanks. Three of them were so covered in feces they were unrecognizable when they pulled them out. Two of them died."

"That's awful," Diana said. Her face blanched for a moment, and she fought back a gag. She watched the man rise up out of the water, seeing his nakedness from his waist down. He shuffled through the stream to the shore. Once on land, he brushed as much as water as he could from his legs, then started donning his stained pants.

Vanessa raised her phone and took another picture of the man.

"It happens several times a year." The driver pointed to the man who had been defecating into the stream. The man finished pulling his pants back on and stood motionless near the bank of the stream, returning their gazes for just a brief moment before turning away and heading off. "One of the men who died was his brother." The driver was quiet for a moment. "Not a way I would like to die..."

Fernando pointed a few yards down the stream. "What is she doing?"

The driver followed Fernando's pointing figure. A woman was on the edge of the stream, on her knees. She appeared to be squeezing out some piece of cloth, wringing it dry. "Cleaning her family's clothes, most likely," the driver said.

Fernando watched the woman near the stream's edge for a moment, then looked back to the departing man who had just been squatting in the stream a few yards away, then looked back to the woman. "In the same water? They... do it in the same water?"

"It's the only source of water she has," the driver said. "Where else is she supposed to wash her clothes?"

"That's just disgusting," Vanessa said. She raised up her phone and took a picture.

The group was quiet for a moment.

Diana leaned in closer to William. "I still have to go pee."

William looked at Diana, then glanced at the stream, then back to his sister. He gave her a slight shrug, widening his eyes ever so slightly.

Diana stared incredulously at her brother, then straightened up, stiffening her back. She marched over to Vanessa. "You take a picture of me pissing in the stream, I will ring your fucking neck." She glanced down at the phone in Vanessa's hand, then back up to Vanessa's face.

Vanessa wordlessly handed her phone over to William.

Diana stomped towards the stream, walking awkwardly in her heels.

William cast Vanessa a sly glance, then wordlessly slipped Vanessa's phone back to her.

Navala was a plump woman with a pleasant face, which seemed incredible in such a place, but she was clearly not going hungry for lack of something to eat. She bustled about the tiny stove she was cooking over, the meal cooking in a heavy metal skillet. She wiped her black hair away from her eyes as she prepared the meal. Her home was very small, with a kitchen area on the left that had a small table and a few chairs, and a sleeping area on the right. What were clearly very old and worn mattresses rested on the floor, with a few pillows resting atop each mattress. A small television set was positioned on a crate near the foot of the sleeping area.

"No one in this area of the slum has a refrigerator. Nothing is stored or kept. Nothing is pre-cooked. Nothing is frozen. No canned sauces," the driver explained. "Everything is made fresh. Every day."

"What is she making?" William asked. His stomach growled. Whatever the Indian woman was cooking did smell delicious.

"An eggplant recipe, handed down by her mother to her," the driver said. "She grinds the coriander seeds with her pestle only when she is ready to use it in a meal. It gives a meal much more flavor that way than sprinkling it from some plastic container that's been sitting on a shelf for a year ever will."

"Will it... make me sick?" Diana asked.

The driver laughed. "Only if your body is not accustomed to very fresh food."

⊰⋙⊱

"Should we... give her a tip," Fernando asked. "Pay her for the meal? It was actually very delicious."

"You are surprised?" the driver asked. "Because they are forced to live like this, you think they cannot appreciate a fine meal?"

"No, I didn't mean it that way," Fernando said quickly. "It was good. I just want to show my appreciation."

The driver shook his head and raised his hand. "Oh, no. Your enjoyment of her cooking is payment enough. I will tell her you very much enjoyed it."

"How does she pay for the food?" Vanessa asked.

The driver was quiet. "Let's just say she is very friendly towards many of the men who live in this area."

"She fucks for food?" Vanessa asked.

"I wouldn't put it so vulgarly," the driver said.

"I'll give her a dollar for a blow job," William said with a grin.

Diana elbowed William in the side.

William feigned a wince. "What? A dollar is a lot of money to these people." He looked over at the driver. "Isn't it?"

The driver just smiled. "Come, we must keep moving. We don't want to be caught here after the sun goes down."

"Why not?" Fernando asked. "What happens after the sun goes down?"

"Then there is no light and we will not be able to see where we are going," the driver said. "There are no streetlights here like in America."

"Oh," Fernando said.

"Plus the local gangs come out at night and they might take an interest in your women."

"What?" William blustered out the question.

"Yes, but don't worry," the driver said reassuringly. "We can probably pay them to leave us alone if we encounter them."

"Nobody said anything about gangs," William said.

"Nobody asked," the driver replied. "Come, we really must be going. We have maybe two hours of light left."

"But we've been walking for four hours," William countered. "How are we going to get back in two?"

"Oh, we're not going back in the same direction."

"Then where are we going?"

The driver pointed towards a steep hill in the distance. "That way."

"What's over there?" William asked.

"You could say the climax of the tour," the driver said.

"What the hell?" William muttered.

The building looked like a very small version of an old English mansion one would find touring the wealthier outskirts of London. It was situated at the bottom of the steep slope, opposite the steep hill they had just walked up, positioned just a few feet beyond where the ground leveled out at the bottom of the slope. It had two stories and was wide enough to accommodate half a dozen large bedrooms on each level.

"Is that real?" Diana asked.

The driver nodded his head. "They just finished it. The top floor is just a facade, but the ground level is real. They built it inside this old bomb crater. It's a secret project they don't want the government to find out about."

William frowned. "Who's *they*?"

The driver didn't answer. "The best part's on the inside."

William felt eyes on him and craned his neck around to see someone quickly ducking back down out of sight behind a pile of garbage. He turned back to the driver. "Is someone following us?"

"I would say waiting would be a better term," the driver said.

"Waiting?" Fernando asked.

The driver nodded. "Come. Let's go inside."

"It's beautiful," Diane cooed as she walked deeper into the large foyer area. The interior was indeed beautiful with a high ceiling adorned with thick wooden beams and a tiled floor that had the sleek and glossy appearance of marble. Fine works of art adorned the walls. A sterling silver tray with a silver pitcher resting atop it was seated on a mahogany end table near the door, accompanied by several crystal goblets.

"Make yourself comfortable," the driver said.

"What is this place?" Vanessa asked.

"Please, just be yourselves," the driver said. He pointed to a room on their left. "There's a study in there with some English books. You can sit in a big comfy chair and smoke a pipe and have a snifter of brandy."

Fernando and William exchanged amused glances.

A wrinkled clump of paper on the floor, blown in from outside, drew Vanessa's gaze. She reached down and scooped up the paper, grabbing the paper just ahead of the driver who was also reaching for it.

The driver withdrew his reaching hand and stood back up straight. He smiled at Vanessa, but it was a bit of an awkward smile, almost a nervous smile.

As Vanessa unfolded the paper it was apparent

that it was a pamphlet of some sort. It was written in Hindi so she couldn't understand it. She took out her phone, opened up her favorite translation app and centered the pamphlet on her screen. The translated words sent a numbing feeling flooding throughout her body. *"Come, see how the rich live!"* The rest of the pamphlet was smeared with dirt and grime, making any of the other words unintelligible.

Behind them, the front door they entered through softly clicked closed.

Vanessa held out her phone so William, Diane, and Fernando could get a look at the translated pamphlet. None of them said a word as they read the translation; they exchanged confused looks with each other. Vanessa looked up at the driver.

But he was gone.

Vanessa quickly scanned the area, turning left, turning right, searching him out. She did a full circle, her eyes darting about as an oddly urgent desperation filled her gaze. "Where is he? Where's our driver?"

The others joined in her visual hunt, taking a few steps deeper into the house as they scanned their surroundings.

"Hey!" William shouted. "Where are you?"

"What was his name?" Fernando asked.

William looked at Fernando, then shrugged. "I don't remember."

Fernando stared at William for a moment, then lifted his head. "Hey! Driver, where are you?"

Vanessa shook the handle on the door they had entered to gain access to the small mansion replica. The door did not budge. "It's locked." She kicked at the door. "It's fucking locked."

Fernando brushed Vanessa aside, gripping the

handle as he stepped up to the door. He tried to twist the handle, but it didn't move. He shook it angrily, but the door still remained locked tight.

William stood near one of the darkly tinted windows, quickly realizing they weren't windows at all. They were fake. They had no latches on them, no visible means of opening them. They were just solid pieces of some black reflective material.

Suddenly, one of the outer wall panels slid down with a loud whooshing, sucking sound, revealing dozens of slum residents pressed up to a window, all of them eagerly peering inside.

William couldn't hear what they were saying, but he could see them smiling, laughing, pointing in his direction. William stormed up to the window, which reached from the floor up to about seven feet high, and angrily pounded on the glass with clenched fists. The force of his blow only made the window material vibrate for a brief moment.

Several onlookers looked startled and quickly moved back from the window, but many others stayed glued to their spots, laughing, smiling, and pointing at William. One of the onlookers pretended to raise up a camera and take a picture.

"What the fuck?" Fernando said.

"Oh my God," Vanessa muttered. She stared at the onlookers outside. "They put us on display. We're like some animals in their twisted fucking zoo." She shook the pamphlet she clutched in her hand and said, "See how the rich live," then threw the scrap of paper disgustedly to the floor.

The four of them stood silently, staring at the onlookers outside.

The onlookers stared back, some of them

pounding half-heartedly on the glass; others just peered in quietly at them.

The sound of a creaking door opening broke the silence.

"Did you hear that?" Diana asked, turning to look to her left. "That sounded like a door. Maybe there's a way out of here."

The others let a glimmer of hope seep into their expressions.

But that glimmer quickly turned to a wide-eyed expression of fright as a man dressed in tattered, soiled clothes came charging into the room brandishing a butcher knife. It was the man they had watched defecating in the stream. His face was oddly expressionless as he charged at them, which somehow made him seem all the more frightening.

Vanessa screamed. William clutched at Diana, pulling her protectively to him. Fernando just stared slack-jawed at the quickly approaching attacker.

The onlookers pounded excitedly against the window, the sounds of their fists banging against the glass increasing in tempo.

The attacker continued his charge, racing straight up to Fernando and shoving the large steel blade straight into Fernando's stomach. Fernando appeared too stunned to even move, or cry out. The attacker withdrew the blade, now red and wet with Fernando's blood, and slashed it across Fernando's throat, cutting a deep gouge in his neck. Blood spurted out forcefully, showering the attacker in Fernando's blood. Fernando just stared straight ahead, his eyes not blinking. Fernando's hands seemed to move independently of any willful action as they rose up instinctively, shakily, to cover the gaping hole in his throat. Blood oozed between his fingers. Fernando didn't make a sound as he collapsed into a lifeless heap on the floor.

The attacker took a step back, trying to avoid being tangled up in Fernando's falling body, the dripping butcher knife held down at his side.

William surged forward and chopped down hard on the man's wrist, the surprise move knocking the knife out of the attacker's grip. The steel blade clattered against the tile floor. William lunged for the fallen knife, grabbing it before the attacker could pick it back up. He waved the blood-stained blade in front of him, gripping it with both hands.

The attacker shouted at William in a language he didn't understand, pointing at the blood-streaked butcher knife in William's hands.

William gripped the knife firmly, keeping it raised in front of him.

The room became quiet. Even the pounding on the window stopped.

Somewhere in the distance, the sound of a door opening again could be heard.

Then there were more whooshing sounds as more panels in the walls slid away, revealing more windows, revealing more gatherings of onlookers clustered around each window.

"Oh, fuck," Vanessa whispered. She quickly grabbed Diana by the wrist and maneuvered towards William, tugging Diana along with her, positioning themselves behind William. William continued to hold the blade out in front of himself, his hands trembling despite his best efforts to keep them still.

The pattering of feet sounded, the footsteps echoing softly in the large room. It was the sound of more than one person.

Diana watched in disbelief as three raggedly-dressed children moved slowly into the room. Two of them were boys, the other a girl. Each boy carried a rusty implement of some sort in his hand, some loose scrap of metal with sharp edges. The girl appeared to be carrying an old TV antenna. The two boys barely had any clothes on at all, their ripped and ragged pants containing just enough cloth to cover their genitals, their flimsy soiled t-shirts draped over their torsos. The girl was topless, wearing ripped red shorts. Diana knew she was looking at several of the children they had seen playing in the garbage heap.

The attacker shouted at the new arrivals and the children moved over towards him.

William looked beyond the attacker and the children, the flurry of motion at the windows catching his attention. Many of the onlookers appeared to be holding some sort of cup in one hand; they banged on the glass with a clenched fist formed in one hand and with the cup they clutched in the other hand.

The ragged children stood in front of the man. He barked a command to them and they started forward, shuffling slowly at first as if pretending to be zombies, but then suddenly lurched forward with quick bursts of speed. One of the boys slid feet first, sliding through Fernando's trail of blood, his momentum carrying him beneath William's blade. He slid past the terrified group of tourists and quickly got to his feet behind them, slashing out with his jagged implement, slicing through the back of one of Diana's thighs. She shrieked in pain and buckled, dropping to one knee on the floor. She grabbed at her gushing wound, screaming in pain.

The second boy dropped to his knees, moving quickly to all fours, and the girl leaped onto his back, then sprang off her companion's back as if he had suddenly transformed himself into a mini-trampoline. The girl soared through the air, slashing her weapon like a whip, the former antenna now a deadly implement in her hand. The antenna slashed across William's forehead, drawing a line of blood nearly from one side of his head to the other. William waved the blade he now held wildly in the air, but his efforts were in vain. He missed the girl and she lashed out again with her deadly homemade whip as she landed near him, slashing across William's abdomen, slashing through his shirt, the sharp-edged weapon slicing into his flesh, her weapon drawing another line of blood across his body.

Vanessa started to flee but the man who had first attacked them, stepped into her path, blocking her.

Outside, the gathered crowd was whipped into a frenzy, their eyes wide and brimming with excitement. They pounded on the glass with their fists and banged the bottoms of their cups against the glass until the sound was just a cacophony of mind-numbing noise.

"Let us go," Vanessa begged. "Please, just let us go."

The man curled his fingers into claws, his nails crusted with dirt and grime. He snarled at Vanessa, his dry lips encrusted with white-rimmed cracks.

Several residents of the slum looked up at the sound of the commotion in the distance. A pamphlet fluttered across a man's foot and he reached down to pick it up. If Vanessa had looked at this pamphlet through her phone using her translator app, the rough translation into English would have been something like this, *"Come, see how the rich live! And then see how they die! Watch them scream and squirm! Then quench your thirst on their holy sacrifice!"* In smaller letters on the bottom of the pamphlet it read: *"Bring your own cup."*

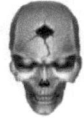

TERRORSTORY #68
NIGHT WATCHMAN

"**Y**ou are listening to Throwback Radio.
Thanks for tuning us in. Tonight on the Night
Watchman we're featuring the true tale of Pavel
Khrushchev, the Russian mobster who boiled his
enemies alive."

Maury Bernstein smiled softly. The Night
Watchman. He remembered listening to that show
when he was eight years old. His entire family sat
quietly around the big radio his father had purchased.

It was a big wooden radio, its polished maple veneer all shiny and glossy. A big speaker was positioned at the bottom portion of the radio cabinet, filling their living room with its scratchy sounds. Sometimes they would invite the neighbors over and all the children would sit on the carpeting in front of the radio, listening raptly to the tales while the parents smoked their cigarettes and drank their bourbon and whisky drinks. The Night Watchman had only lasted a few episodes, but he still remembered the theme song vividly. It had been a mixture of bombastic orchestral thunder, intermixed with an eerie, creepy chorus of whispering voices.

He absently took a bite out of the beef and bean burrito he had just purchased from the drive-through window at Taco Palace. Maury had no one to share a meal with, so he often just bought fast food for himself for dinner.

He didn't remember exactly when he had found the radio station replaying all the old thrillers from his youth, but he was glad he had the sense to program it on one of the selector buttons on his car's radio when he had accidentally come across the show when doing a quick scan of all the available stations. Now, on his way home from the factory where he served as a security guard, all he had to do was jab the appropriate button with his finger and the stirring tales he remembered from his youth would ease the boredom of his drive home. Murder mystery tales, creepy supernatural stories, sordid crime sagas. He loved them all. Performance radio was a lost art that would never be coming back. He was well aware of that. But that didn't matter. He still had Throwback Radio. It was the one thing that let him travel back to the happy memories of his youth. His favorite show, of course, had been the Night Watchman because he had fancied himself as the main character on that show, believing he would have as much bravado as the hero of that show if he ever found himself in similar situations.

Outside his car, a distant gunshot rang out, bringing Maury back to the present. The gangs seemed to be everywhere now. Even after marijuana legalization, there were still plenty of other illicit drugs to sell and plenty of money still to make. Shootings were nearly a daily occurrence in his neighborhood; at least one person was killed every week. He forced his thoughts away from the unpleasantness of modern life, and re-tuned his attention to the story unfolding on the radio.

Pavel Khrushchev was a nasty son of a bitch, but Maury knew he would get his just desserts. The bad guys always did. At least on most of the old radio shows, especially on Night Watchman. The Night Watchman never failed to protect those under his charge. His methods of meting out punishment were unorthodox to say the least, but no one could argue that they weren't effective.

Maury listened intently as the tale played out on his car's radio, absently taking small bites out of his burrito, absently licking a bit of sour cream from his upper lip. As expected, the ruthless Russian mobster got what was coming to him, getting trapped in a coil of wires above a blazing hot vat of molten steel as he fled the Night Watchman's relentless pursuit through a steel factory. The Night Watchman watched the Russian thug blister and bake, the mobster roasting as the hot waves of steam churned up from the blazing inferno of molten steel over which he was trapped. Pavel Khrushchev received the justice befitting the ugliness he had dished out to his enemies.

The story ended, but the announcer continued, as he always did, with a direct sales pitch for a product related to the show. "And remember kids, don't forget to send your quarter to 4554 Glenwood Avenue, New York, New York along with a self-addressed stamped envelope. We'll send you your own Night Watchman ring. You can fight crime alongside your favorite hero!" Maury loved the fact that they left in the old commercials and product endorsements from the old shows. Sometimes, it was an ad for a shaving product, or sometimes an ad for a pain medication, or sometimes an ad for a particular brand of cigarettes. It made the whole listening experience feel so authentic.

Maury drove along, really only paying half-attention to the road before him, listening to the old-time advertisement for a brand of shaving cream that no longer existed. But then the address that the announcer had mentioned at the end of the Night Watchman episode replayed itself in his head. 4554 Glenwood Avenue. Why, that was only a few miles away from where he lived in his apartment now. He wondered if there was anything still at that address, then immediately scoffed at the idea. That was nearly seventy years ago. That's absurd. Surely, there was no one there any more, at least no one that had any affiliation to a radio show long lost to the passage of time.

The address wouldn't leave his head. It was like a song was stuck in his mind, replaying itself over and over and over, and there was nothing he could do to stop it. 4554 Glenwood Avenue. 4554 Glenwood Avenue.

Maury thought about the real-life Night Watchmen from days long past, trying to distract himself from the address that refused to leave his thoughts. In the years before the dawn of the modern era, the Night Watchmen were responsible for the safety of the inhabitants of the walled cities that comprised the height of civilization at the time. The good citizens went to bed early, trusting the Night Watchmen to keep the streets of their fortress-like cities safe. His job was dangerous because most of the people still awake late into the night whom he met on the streets back in those days were the drunks and the thieves and the murderers.

To protect himself, and to show his authority, the Night Watchman of old carried an intimidating weapon called a halberd. A halberd was a two-handed pole weapon, usually five to six feet long, consisting of an axe blade topped with a dagger-like spike mounted on a long shaft. It always had a hook or thorn on the back side of the axe blade for grappling mounted combatants.

The Night Watchman on the radio show didn't use a halberd, but he was an expert at wielding daggers and axes, and he did only patrol the streets at night, so there was some vague hints of similarity with historical facts. The only place the halberd was mentioned in the radio show was in relation to what was on the Night Watchman's ring. The halberd was his sigil, representing a brotherhood with the original

Night Watchmen of the past.

4554 Glenwood Avenue. Like a damned ear worm, the address kept crawling through his ear, looping in a circular track, repeating itself over and over and over. 4554 Glenwood Avenue.

Just go take a look. What the hell else do you have to do? Maury smiled the silly smile of a dotty old man.

Maury sat in his car and stared at the building. At least there was still a building at the address. It could have easily already been torn down, turned into an empty lot full of weeds and ragged clumps of concrete and broken bricks. The address was faded but still visible on the side of the aged bricks. 4554. It was abandoned, though. That much was obvious from the overgrown plants, the abundance of weeds, the chipped paint, the broken windows on the upper floors.

Maury sat in his car for a long moment, just staring out the window at the building. Now what? You're here. There's the building. You just gonna stare at it? He put his car into park and turned off the ignition. He sat for another long moment in his car, continuing to stare at the building. He felt a weird nervousness overcome him, but he didn't understand where that nervousness was coming from. It was just an abandoned building. A brooding corpse of brick and metal and glass that once held a vibrant life. He suddenly felt very sad, almost morose at the loss. And then he felt a sadness for himself, for his own lost life. He had never really done much of anything, had never really amounted to much. He had never married, had no children. He didn't have his own business, had no legacy to pass on even if he had someone to pass it on to. He was just a lonely old man lost in the memories of his childhood.

Snap out of it, you old fart. Get out of the car and at least go take a look. You've only got a few hours of daylight left before it gets dark out.

He took the keys out of the ignition and climbed out of the car.

The front door of the derelict building was slightly ajar, knocked off one of its hinges. Maury shifted the door, making the opening wider so he could fit through it.

Once inside, he paused, taking in the interior of the building. It was a large expanse, maybe half the length of a football field and mostly empty. A few old wooden desks were stacked in the far left corner. A bird fluttered high above and he glanced up into the rusted metal rafters to see several bird nests perched up on the flat metal beams high above. Several dirt-smeared windows let in enough sunlight to give the room a soft golden ambience, but the room was still murky. Several beams of light coming down from some small holes in the roof also dotted the room in columns of brighter sunlight, the beams filled with swirling dust motes.

The floor was caked with dust and he kicked up a tiny cloud with each step as he moved deeper into the building. Several stacks of cardboard boxes were stacked along the back wall to his right. They piqued his curiosity so he moved towards them, shuffling slowly as that was now his normal walking speed. He suffered from severe arthritis in just about every joint in his body and on some days the pain seemed to concentrate itself in his knees, but today he was feeling okay and his knees weren't giving him too much trouble. His silly childish excitement seemed to be masking any pain he usually felt.

Maury reached the cardboard boxes and stopped before them. He stared at the words stamped on the side of the boxes in crude black stencils, not really believing what he was seeing.

His memory flashed back to his youth. He remembered asking his father for that precious quarter because he had wanted to get his official Night Watchman ring, but his father had refused. "You don't need that junk," his father had told him. "I'll get it for you and a week later it'll be forgotten or thrown in the garbage."

Maury sighed. He had never gotten his official Night Watchman ring. Oh, Nicky Kravitz had gotten his, and flashed it at everyone and anyone who would pay attention, but poor old Maury Bernstein never got his. Maury stared at the words on the cardboard boxes, still not believing what he was seeing. How could they still be here after all these years? It just didn't seem possible, yet here he was, standing before box after box labeled Night Watchman Rings.

He shuffled closer to the boxes, stopping just before them. Could there really be Night Watchman rings inside those cardboard boxes? After all these years? His mind still refused to even accept the possibility. He reached out his shaking, wrinkled hands and grabbed one of the cardboard boxes from the top of one of the stacks. He gently set the box down on the ground, then awkwardly moved down to his knees, nearly falling over before he caught his balance with the flat of his palm against the concrete floor; a billowing puff of dust exploded out from beneath his hand as it hit the floor. He righted himself, knowing that he was going to regret the pain kneeling was going to cause him when he moved to get back up, but he didn't care about that now. All he cared about was opening the sealed cardboard box that rested on the ground before him. He tugged and poked and ripped at the tape that was affixed to the box's flaps, managing to get a finger under a portion of the yellowing tape, then triumphantly ripping it off with one mighty yank.

He stared at the cardboard box, afraid of the disappointment he would feel if the box was actually filled with something else, but he refused to let that fear stop him. The box clearly held some kind of contents, so he knew it wasn't empty because of its weight. He grabbed one of the flaps and flipped it up to reveal the contents of the box. His eyes widened in sheer delight and he nearly clapped his old wrinkled hands in glee.

The box was full of rings. Night Watchman rings.

On the radio show, the ring was what gave the Night Watchman his powers. The ring was activated by the night, sort of a reverse solar-powered object. It bequeathed all sorts of powers to the wearer. There hadn't been too many episodes of the radio show created before it was cancelled, but Maury still remembered the Night Watchman's ring had granted the user the power of turning night into day. It wasn't that weird green effect that modern-day night vision goggles created; the radio show narrator described it more as a golden glow, more of a truer turning night into day effect. The ring had also augmented the wearer's strength, giving the wearer the strength of ten men.

And it had done something else, too, he remembered. The ring somehow created the illusion of the wearer being bigger than he truly was, as if his body looked as if it took up twice as much space to an observer when it really didn't. The intent of the illusion was to create fear amongst those denizens of the night who came upon the Night Watchman, to make their terror so intense that it drove them back to their homes and off the streets.

Delicious tremors of excitement raced up Maury's spine as he reached into the box and his aged fingers curled around one of the rings. He was even more delighted to find that the rings were solid, made of some metallic material; they weren't cheap plastic rings at all. He pulled the ring out of the box, raising it up into what minimal light was available to marvel at it.

"You supposed to be in here, old man?"

Maury looked up, turning his head to his right towards the source of the voice, to see four young men stepping into the building. The youths strode straight towards him. Their forms were shadowy and dark and ominous as they loomed closer, moving in and out of patches of light.

"It's a good thing you're already on your knees," one of them said, cracking his knuckles as he spoke, "'cause it's gonna take all your prayers to get out of here without getting your ass beat." He was wearing a baseball cap backwards atop his head, covering a mop of greasy-looking black hair. BaseballCap was about six feet tall, with some old acne scars dotting his face. He had a visible tattoo of a baseball on his right shoulder, with some undecipherable markings etched into his skin below the ball. Maury thought it might be Japanese characters, but he really had no idea.

Maury started to get to his feet, struggling to do so, but the four youths quickened their pace, moving quickly towards him.

"No, no, don't get up," another one of them said, quickly reaching him and pushing Maury back down to his knees. This youth had a gold tooth for one of his front teeth that just looked odd on the youth. Maury knew he was just painting a stereotypical picture in his head, but the gold tooth seemed more appropriate to a dark-skinned man than to this pale-looking white boy.

"What you looking at? What's in them boxes?" BaseballCap asked. He cracked his knuckles again.

"You shouldn't do that," Maury said to BaseballCap, indicating his hands with a slight nodding of his head. "You're gonna give yourself arthritis."

"I don't need your advice, old man," BaseballCap said with a snarl. "I need to know what's in them boxes."

"Nothing," Maury said. "Just some old junk."

"One man's junk is another man's treasure," another one of the youth's said. He was a skinny kid, his clothes hanging loose, his brown hair long and wild and unruly. He smacked the back of his hand against another youth's chest. "Ain't that right, Ritchie?"

"I don't know, man." The youth called Ritchie grabbed at his crotch. "All I know is that my junk is every woman's treasure." Ritchie was the biggest one in the group, broad-chested, quite muscular. He sported the beginnings of a dark mustache and beard.

GoldTooth and Skinny hooted with laughter.

"Seriously, what you looking at?" BaseballCap asked Maury.

"Just some old rings," Maury said.

"Rings?" BaseballCap frowned. "Rings ain't junk. You trying to steal from us, old man?"

Maury shook his head. "No, no."

"Why you tellin' us they junk then, old man?" BaseballCap asked, putting an even deeper snarl into his words.

"Yeah, what's up with that?" GoldTooth asked. He tried to crack his knuckles like BaseballCap, but his fingers didn't make a sound.

Maury closed his fingers around the ring he still held in his hand, shielding it from their view.

BaseballCap snatched at the box, ripping it away from Maury. He looked into the box. "Damn, man, these are sweet!" He reached into the box and pulled out a couple of rings, holding them out in his palm to show his buddies.

The youths crowded around the box, all of them reaching in to get their own samples.

Maury slowly slid the Night Watchman's ring onto his ring finger on his right hand, sliding it down until it fit snugly against the base of his finger. He wasn't sure if anything would happen, but something inside him compelled him to put the ring on. Some silly dream of becoming the Night Watchman like he had wished for when he was a child. Whether it was sheer desperation, or the foolish fancy of the hopeful child still existing somewhere inside his heart, he couldn't deny the pull of the ring.

He wasn't disappointed with the results.

At first, Maury felt a sharp stinging of pain in his hand, centered right around his ring finger, then the pain flared out wider, spreading throughout his entire body. Dark spots threatened to completely fill his vision and a wave of nausea threatened to overwhelm him. Then, for a brief moment, everything did go black and silent. He couldn't see anything, couldn't hear anything. But then the pain and the queasiness quickly vanished as he felt an odd surge of energy flow through his entire body; it felt as if he had been emptied but was now being replenished.

There was no denying the ring had some form of power. It could have just been his childish imagination rearing back to the forefront of his thoughts, but he didn't think that was it. There was definitely something happening to his body. He easily rose back up to his feet, feeling no pain whatsoever in his knees, not even a slight twinge. He felt taller, wider, as if his presence spread higher and wider than just the physical dimensions of his body. He had thought the ring wouldn't yield any effects until it was dark, but perhaps the murkiness of the large expanse gave off the appearance of night and thus activated the ring's powers. Which was still completely and utterly absurd. It was just a piece of junk. It was just some toy ring meant for eight year olds. How could it be having any effect? But he knew it was because his vision became stronger, turning the murky interior of the building into a brightly illuminated room.

"Hey, man," GoldTooth yelled at Maury, "I told you not to get—" His voice cut off as he turned to look straight on at Maury, then the youth finished with a weak, "—up." He took a step back, knocking his hand purposefully against the shoulder of one of his gang.

Skinny looked up at his thug-brother slowly backing away from the group, then turned to glance over his shoulder at Maury. "Oh, fuck," he muttered. He, too, started to drift slowly back away from Maury, keeping his gaze locked on the old man.

Maury could see Skinny's gaze shift, could see him look above Maury's head as if he were seeing something above Maury. And then Skinny's gaze would look to Maury's sides as if Maury was flanked by other people. Was the ring actually working just like it had worked on the radio show? It still seemed so absurd, but Skinny's behavior was certainly making Maury more and more of a believer with each frantic darting of the youth's eyes.

BaseballCap noticed his pals moving back away from him. He looked at Maury and his eyes widened. He stood frozen for a moment, then he also began to take slow measured steps backwards. BaseballCap was the one holding the box of Night Watchman rings, so the youth they had called Ritchie frowned at him because he was still digging through the rings as BaseballCap moved away from him. "What the fuck, man? I'm still looking at that." Ritchie snatched a ring from the box as BaseballCap continued to back away from him.

All three of the other youths pointed behind Ritchie's shoulder, nearly in exact unison.

Ritchie turned to see Maury standing tall near him. A glistening flash caught Ritchie's eye and he looked down at Maury's hand to see one of the rings from the box adorned on the old man's finger. Ritchie immediately followed suit, sliding the ring he held down on his ring finger, pushing it all the way down so it fit snugly on his finger. The youth felt an instant surge of energy coursing through him, as if he had just snorted a thick line of coke. His entire body buzzed. But then something else happened. The ring started to feel tighter and tighter on his finger, as if it were shrinking. The pain was immediate and intense when the edges of the ring cut into his finger, drawing a circle of blood. Ritchie howled and clutched at his finger, desperately trying to get the ring off, but it was too slippery with blood to get a good grip on it, too tight to budge. The ring continued to shrink, cutting through more flesh before reaching the bone of his finger. A loud crunching sound filled the empty space, followed by Ritchie's howling scream of pain, followed by more weaker sounding crunches of bone. Within moments, Ritchie's finger was severed from his hand and the bloody digit fell to the concrete floor, sending up a puff of dust as it hit the floor. Blood spurted out of the ragged hole in Ritchie's hand as he clutched at it. He dropped to his knees, screeching in agony, his face contorted into an ugly grimace.

"You're not worthy," Maury said to him. He glanced at the fallen severed finger. The ring was nowhere to be seen. It had dwindled into nothingness, its job complete. Maury looked at Ritchie, feeling an odd compulsion to lick his dry lips as he stared at the whining youth.

"Get that motherfucker!" Ritchie cried out, still on his knees, still clutching at his bleeding hand, his face still twisting into a horrid contortion of pain. More blood gushed out between his fingers.

The other three youths made no move towards Maury. BaseballCap, still holding the box of rings, abruptly dropped the cardboard box to the ground, just realizing that he was still holding it in his hands. The Night Watchmen rings jangled as the box hit the concrete floor.

"Your friend needs help," Maury said. "You should get him to the hospital."

"How you do that?" Skinny asked. "How you cut his finger off? I didn't see you go nowhere near him."

Maury pointed to the box of rings sitting on the floor at their feet. "See for yourself. Put one on. Put a ring on your finger."

None of the three youths made a move towards the box that rested on the ground right in front of them.

"It's okay to be scared," Maury said. "You should be scared."

"I ain't scared of nothin', you old fool!" GoldTooth snapped.

"Shut up! You the fool," BaseballCap said. "He's just trying to goad you into putting one on."

"Goad me?" GoldTooth glared at Maury. "You trying to goad me, motherfucker?" GoldTooth quickly looked to his friend. "What's goad me, mean?" he asked BaseballCap.

BaseballCap glowered at GoldTooth. "Damn, just shut up, you fool."

Skinny, the one who seemed to be the the calmest of the bunch, reached down and snatched a ring out of the box. "I'll take your challenge, mister."

"You crazy?" BaseballCap said as he tried to bat the ring out of Skinny's finger.

Skinny jerked his hand out of the way, avoiding

BaseballCap's swiping hand. He slid the Night Watchman ring onto his finger.

BaseballCap and GoldTooth watched, waiting it seemed almost eagerly for the same thing to happen to Skinny as what had just happened to their wailing buddy Ritchie.

But the same thing that happened to Ritchie did not happen to Skinny. Skinny seemed to experience the same flash of pain that Maury had experienced, but then his presence seemed to grow larger, wider, but his body did not change dimensions, only the presence his body brought to the area expanded, as if he was now giving off some kind of aura that extended far beyond the boundaries of his flesh.

Maury looked at Skinny quietly for a moment. "Why are you with them?" he finally asked, indicating Skinny's thug friends with a tilt of his head.

Skinny shrugged. "I didn't have nothing else to do."

Maury was quiet again, studying Skinny. The ring had not rejected the youth out of hand, so clearly there was something inside him, some kindred feeling they must share. "You understand what we have to do now, son?" Maury asked.

The youth named Skinny was silent for a moment, as if registering new thoughts occurring in his mind. After a moment of this contemplative silence, Skinny nodded to Maury. "I do."

"We start with them," Maury said.

Skinny nodded. Then licked his lips.

Maury now remembered why the Night

Watchman had only lasted five episodes. The show had been far too extreme for its time. There was one very significant reason why the thugs and gangsters featured on the show feared The Night Watchman's power. There was a reason why even organized Mafia clans were deathly afraid of the Night Watchman. There was a reason why he had no wife, no girlfriend.

The Night Watchman was a ghoul, only satiated by the taste of dead human flesh. The Night Watchmen's ring had killed him when he had put it on; Maury realized that now. It had killed him and somehow injected something into him that brought him back to life. Well, not really life, but some form of in-between existence, not really dead, yet not really alive. Whatever state of being it was, it was accompanied by an overwhelming desire to feast on the dead flesh of the guilty.

Maury thought about Pavel Khrushchev, the Russian mobster who the Night Watchman had defeated by letting him bake and boil above a vat of molten steel. He wondered how he had tasted.

Seated in his car, Maury stared at the highway that bordered his town, looking across to the other side. He knew what was over there. It was like another world, an alien world. A world full of violent pimps trafficking young girls. An urban hellhole filled with psychotic gangbangers. A tainted neighborhood stained with illicit drugs, the music filling the night interspersed with the explosive drumbeats of illegal weapons firing. He used to be terrified just thinking about going over there. Even thinking about spending one minute on the other side of the highway had been enough to make him feel nauseous. But he now wondered if that was what he was meant to do. That's where the Night Watchman was needed most.

His current job was nearly at an end anyway. The company was testing new robot dogs that would replace him and the other security guards. He mentally snorted with disgust. He wasn't even being replaced by a younger man, or even a real dog. He was being replaced by something that wasn't even alive. A robot dog was taking his job. It was an insult. It wasn't even a humanoid robot taking his job. It was a robot dog. A damn fake dog.

He licked his lips. Time to go to work.

He adjusted the rearview mirror, for a moment taking in the halberds positioned on the back seat of the car, the power of the Night Watchman's ring turning the night into a golden day within his eyes. The halberds were truly effective weapons. They deserved to be resurrected as a force for good. He especially enjoyed using the dagger-tipped top portion of the weapon. Of course, the axe portion was very effective in carving off select cuts of meat as well.

Maury glanced over at Skinny seated in the car next to him in the passenger seat. The Night Watchman rings only worked on those who still felt a strong desire to see justice served. Skinny, despite being in a gang, happened to have those feelings deep inside him. Ritchie, however, had not, and the Night Watchman ring had thoroughly rejected him. The Night Watchman ring Skinny wore on his finger glistened in the moonlight, the halberd sigil glowing softly.

Maury tapped a button on the car's radio. A strong male voice came through the speakers. "You are listening to Throwback Radio. Thanks for tuning us in."

Skinny looked at the radio, then glanced over at Maury.

Maury gave him a smile. At least he wouldn't have to eat alone.

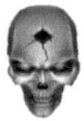

TERRORSTORY #69
ME, MYSELF, AND ME AGAIN

"**W**e have arrived at your final destination." Alexandra's melodious voice, as always, was soothing and calm. Even if she was just the product of a damn sexy AI program.

"Chair up," I said and the seat I was lying in rose up from its inclined position, moving back to the standard sitting position. I pushed my arms out in front of me, stretching them as I yawned. The view on the screen before me was of a tropical beach, the sand white and pure, the ocean blue-green and calm. A palm tree cast a shadow over the beach, shielding the naked woman swinging in a hammock nearby from the hot midday sun. Hey, my screens, my rules.

"Show real-time position," I commanded.

The front window of my vehicle shimmered before me, altering the view. The tropical beach faded away to be replaced by a dark sky and a torrential downpour. Rain pelted against the window but the excellent soundproofing in my vehicle muted any sound the drops might have been making as they struck the glass.

I frowned. There had been no rain in the forecast when I had inquired about the weather before leaving my house. "Alexandra, where am I?" She was supposed to be taking me to my friend Otto's house for a game of poker.

"You are at your final destination."

"Yeah, you said that. But where exactly am I? This is definitely not Otto's house."

"You are at your final destination."

I frowned. "What are my exact coordinates?"

"You are at your final destination."

"Alexandra, you are pissing me off." I felt a stabbing pain in my head and was afraid another migraine was about to hit me, but luckily the sensation went away as quickly as it had arisen.

"I am sorry to have frustrated you, Evan. Please tell me how I can rectify your feeling of frustration."

"You can tell me where the fuck I am!"

"The tone of your voice and the language you are using indicate you may be threatening violence. Would you like me to dispense your calming medicine?"

"No! I don't want my calming medicine!" I said, my voice rising into nearly a shout. "I want you to tell me where the hell I am!"

"You are at your final destination," she said. Again.

"I'm gonna smash your computer brains to pieces if you don't tell me where the hell I am."

"My brain is in the cloud. You are not capable of smashing it to pieces from your current location."

"Are you getting smart with me? Since when are you a fucking smart ass?"

"I shall not dignify your crude question with a response."

I could feel my frown deepen. I clenched my fingers into a fist.

"Would you like me to open the door?" Alexandra asked. "They are waiting for you."

I froze. My fingers slowly unclenched as I stared at the control panel on the dashboard before me. The screen was blank, showing me nothing. "Who is waiting for me?"

"They are," Alexandra replied.

"Who are they?"

"They are the ones waiting for you."

My fist reformed and I smashed it against the dashboard. The screen stayed black. "Damn it, Alexandra. Stop being so goddamned cryptic. What the hell is going on?"

"I do not have the answer to that question."

I could feel my blood boiling. "What fucking questions do you have the answer to?"

"I have the answers to four trillion trillion and six questions."

"Four trillion trillion and six?"

"Yes. Now four trillion trillion five hundred and fifty three," she said, her voice as calm as a smooth sea.

"But you can't tell me where I am?"

"You are at your final destination."

I scowled and growled out my command. "Open the damn door."

The car door opened. Outside, the looming shape of a large mansion was dimly visible beneath the darkly overcast sky through the curtain of rain. Most of the windows on the mansion were dark, but a few were illuminated on the lower floor and one on the upper floor.

I turned back to look at the control panel on my car. "Alexandra, who lives here?"

"I'm sorry. I do not have that information available."

Her odd caginess was really starting to wear thin and I blew out an exasperated sigh. "What state am I in?"

"From the tone of your voice, I would say you are in an agitated, and slightly confused, state."

"No, you fucking idiot," I snapped. "What state am I in?" I waved the question away. "Forget it. What city am I in?"

"I do not know the answer to that question."

"You brought me here. How can you not know what city I am in?"

There was a long moment of silence. "I do not have the answer to that question."

"Why did you bring me here?" I asked her.

"To save the universe from the Supremes," she replied.

"To save the universe? From the Supremes? Who

the hell are the Supremes?" I frowned. "What the hell are you talking about?" I paused, forcing myself to be calm. "Alexandra, you really need to tell me what is going on."

Suddenly, a woman's face loomed out of the darkness, emerging from behind the thick wall of rain. Her eyes were wide, frantic. "Evan," she gasped. "Thank God."

I recoiled in fright. "What the fuck!"

"Come on, there's no time." She surged forward into the car, reaching for my arm.

I pulled back, avoiding her groping fingers, not allowing this wild woman to snatch my arm as she clearly intended to do.

"There's no fucking time, Evan!" she cried out. "Come on!" She again reached for me, but I pushed myself back further into the car.

"Who the fuck are you?" I asked, demanding an answer.

"I'm you, you dumb ass," the woman said. "Now come on."

I scowled. The woman's answer made no sense. "Alexandra, take me back home."

Alexandra did not respond.

I frowned. Alexandra always responded to my voice prompts. Always. "Alexandra, take me away from here. Take me back home."

Alexandra did not respond.

"She won't respond to you anymore," the woman said. "I was afraid of that happening. Now come on before she shuts the door on you and traps you inside your car."

The woman slowed her movements, forcing herself to become still. She brushed some wet strands of her brown hair away from her face, finally giving me a good look at her in the illumination given off by the car's interior light panels. I was suddenly struck by a strong feeling of recognition. She had the same color blue eyes as I did, the same nose, the same rounded chin, the same cheekbones, just more feminine in all the right places. What the hell? What the hell was going on?

"I'm dreaming this, right?" I said. "I'm asleep in my car dreaming this."

The woman quickly slapped me across the face and I felt the stinging bite of her hand. "Now you're awake. Let's go." She took advantage of my momentarily startled state and clutched at my wrist, taking a firm hold of my right hand.

"Alexandra, call the police!" I shouted at my dashboard.

Alexandra's voice came back, cool as a fucking cucumber. "Voice not recognized."

I stared in numb shock at the dashboard. "Alexandra, call the police."

Cool as a fucking cucumber came the reply again from my trusted AI companion of over half a dozen years. "Voice not recognized."

"Goddamnit, Evan," the woman said. "Just chill. I'm not going to hurt you."

"What is this place?" I asked. I stood in the middle of a wide foyer, taking in the huge staircase just off to my right, the elegantly furnished study to my left. I was obviously in the mansion of someone who was very well-to-do. I rubbed at my head, brushing off some of the rain residue that was still present in my hair.

"It's home," the woman said. "As least as close to a home as we can get for now." She was dressed in a tan blouse and a matching tan skirt. Her blouse was soaked, the fabric conforming to the large slopes of her breasts. Her nipples poked against the fabric and I forced myself to look away from her ample chest so she wouldn't see me gaping at her boobs.

I frowned at her. "Why am I here? And who the fuck are you? And how the hell did you hack into Alexandra?"

"Yes, who am I?" the woman replied. "Who is anyone, really?" She smiled sardonically.

I scowled at the woman. "You said '*I'm you*' outside. What does that mean?"

She turned to look at me, her brown hair still gleaming from being caught in the heavy rain. "I'm you, but just from a different dimension. There's no easier way to explain it than that." She extended her slender hand to me, her fingers still wet with residue from the rain. "I'm Raquel."

I just stared at her. "From a different dimension?" I was quiet for a long moment, just continuing to stare at her. Then I laughed at the absurdity of her statement. "You are me from a different dimension?"

Raquel nodded.

"But—"

She interrupted me. "I'm a woman, yes." She lowered her extended hand, obviously noticing the dumbfounded look that registered on my face. "If you think you're confused now, just wait until you meet all the others and you hear what's going on."

"The others?" I was quiet for a moment. "There

are more like you?"

Raquel nodded. "Like us, Evan," she said. "There are more like us." She wiped at her hair, swiping some of the rain's moisture away from her locks.

I put my palm over my forehead. "Okay, you need to tell me what the fuck is going on."

She nodded. "Yes I do. And I will, but just take a few deep breaths, calm yourself down. Go ahead and ask your questions, because I know you have them."

I stared at this strange woman named Raquel. I had so many questions on top of questions that I didn't even know where to start. I started to ask her something about how they hacked Alexandra, but then another question about how she knew me bubbled up, and then another question about where the hell I was came to the forefront of my thoughts, then another question about who the hell she was popped up, then another question about why Alexandra no longer recognized my voice tried to force its way to the top. The questions all tumbled together into a mash of confusion. Nothing was making any sense.

Then I recalled what Alexandra had said in the car. She had said it so calmly, so evenly, but the words she had said still echoed loudly in my head. "Alexandra said something about saving the universe," I said to Raquel. "What was she talking about? Is this some kind of weird prank show or something?" I glanced about the area, taking in the mahogany end table, the ornate frames hanging on the walls showcasing classic works of art, looking for any signs of hidden cameras. "Did Otto put you up to this?"

Raquel shook her head. "This is no prank, I promise you that. It's just the opposite." She motioned with a wave of her hand to indicate our surroundings. "She meant this universe. Save this dimension."

"This dimension?"

Raquel nodded. "Your dimension. Your universe. The terms are somewhat interchangeable. Each dimension is its own universe."

I lowered my hand away from my head so I wouldn't feel it throbbing under my fingertips. "My dimension? Save it from what? From who?"

"From the Supremes."

"The Supremes?" I echoed. Alexandra had said something about that. "You mean Diana Ross and her musical cohorts?"

Raquel gave a soft laugh. It was a delightful sound, I had to admit. "No, not those Supremes." She smiled softly, but then the smile faded. "The Supremes don't believe the other universes should exist. They believe they live in the one true universe, so they are destroying all the others because they believe all the other dimensions are infested with non-believers."

I was quiet, still trying to absorb what was happening but having a hard time accepting my current situation. "I don't believe this is happening," I said as I glanced around the foyer, but nothing there helped alleviate my confusion.

"Careful," she said. "The Supremes don't take kindly to disbelievers."

I looked at her. She seemed sincere, earnestly sincere. "Okay, I'll bite. Since this is all just crazy anyway. Who are these Supremes you are talking about? Alexandra mentioned them, too."

"They are the ones wiping out the parallel dimensions."

"Oh, uh huh." I pursed my lips. "They are the ones wiping out parallel dimensions. Sure, sure." I put my hands into my jeans' pockets, doing a really bad job of trying to act casual, and rocked back on my heels. "Sure, they are the ones wiping out other dimensions. That all makes perfect sense. Uh huh, sure." I quieted, my silence a prompt for her to continue.

"They start off by erasing any persons who might pose a threat to them," she said. "Which means us because we know what they are doing. Me, you, and our other paras."

I shook my head. "First, I have no idea what they are doing, and second, what do you mean by erase a person?"

"It's worse than killing," Raquel said. "They erase them, as if they were never born. Once they re-write a person out of history, they eliminate them." She paused." And, yes, I do mean kill them. They erase any record of that person being born at all. Birth certificates, medical records, driver's licenses, bank accounts, any social media presence. Pfft. Gone. Erased. It's all digital now, so it's very easy for them to do it. Their victims just stop existing. They never even existed at all. You can't even prove they were once alive."

I shook my head. "That's not possible." I took my hands out of my pockets and waved them around. "There are too many digital footprints left by people nowadays. They would have to find every picture that person was in and delete them."

"Or alter them," Raquel said. "Which is quite simple really with facial recognition technology and deep fake technology being as strong as they are now.

A quantum computer can do it within minutes."

I took that in for a moment. "Okay, I've read a whole lot of science fiction, but this is all just a little crazy for me now."

"Oh, it gets crazier," she said. Raquel was quiet for a moment. "They just erased you out of existence in this dimension." She paused.

"What?" I blustered out the word.

Raquel nodded. "That's why Alexandra stopped obeying your commands. To her, you no longer existed. You never did."

"So now I don't exist?" I asked. That was just crazy, but I remembered Alexandra not responding to my voice earlier. Was that really because these so called Supremes had already wiped me out of Alexandra's memory bank? She had never failed to respond to my voice commands before, not even once in six years.

"Of course you exist." Raquel paused. "Just not in the way you used to," she added after a brief moment. She reached out and put a hand on my chest, then slowly took it away.

The simple touch of her fingers on me had a strange effect on me. It was innocent, but also erotic as hell. I did my best to ignore it. "But these Supremes erased me? They think I pose some kind of threat, so they erased me?"

Raquel nodded. "Because we pose a threat to them. They are looking to erase us from our home dimensions."

"How the hell am I threat to them? I don't even know what the fuck is going on?"

She didn't answer.

I couldn't stop looking at her. I tried not to be so

blatant about it, but my gaze kept returning to her. It was like looking at a distorted version of myself. And damn if she wasn't kind of sexy. I found myself studiously taking in her cleavage. She wasn't showing a lot of flesh from her chest, but she was showing enough to draw my fascinated attention. I glanced up to see her looking at me with a sly smile.

"You want to, don't you?" she asked.

I flustered at her question. "I— what? I don't know—"

Raquel interrupted me before I made a further fool of myself. "It's okay. All of us think the same thing. We are all very alike in many ways. Especially how much we think about... that."

I looked away, but then thought about what she had just said. "All of us? What do you mean all of us?"

"You don't think I'm your only para, do you?" She paused, searching for a different word. "You don't think I'm the only variant of you that exists, do you? Weren't you listening to what I told you? There are millions of parallel timelines, millions of universes with a vast number of variations of me, of you, of us."

I was quiet for a moment. "How many of me... of us... how many of us are there?"

"A few hundred thousand probably." She stepped closer to me. "But I've only met a handful."

I took a step back.

Raquel laughed. It was a delightful, twittering little laugh. She stepped closer, reaching out her hand to me. Her fingers were slender, her nails glistening with a soft red.

I took a step back, bumping into a chair that

stopped my retreat.

She laughed again, her blue eyes twinkling with mirth. She reached me and put her hand on my chest. Just the hint of a flowery scent tickled my nose. She smelled fantastic. She glanced down at her breasts, then back up to me. "They're real," she said. "And they're spectacular," she added, appropriating the line from a classic Seinfeld episode from long ago.

I glanced down at her breasts, succumbing to her blatant invitation to look at them. They certainly looked real. And they absolutely looked spectacular.

"Go ahead," she whispered. "I know exactly what you want to do." She started to lower her hand down, rubbing it across my chest, moving her fingers down over my stomach. "And I know exactly what you want me to do." She kept moving her hand lower, passing over my belt, stopping directly over my crotch.

"But I barely know you," I said, whispering the words.

Raquel laughed her delightfully musical laugh. She pressed her hand firmly against my crotch, taking a grip of my now-very-hard-cock. She moved her face closer to mine, bringing her lips tantalizing closer to mine. "Touch me," she whispered.

I needed no further prompting. I reached up and cupped one of her breasts, squeezing it firmly over the fabric of her dress. She let out the sexiest moan I have ever heard in my life. And then we kissed, deeply, passionately, our lips locked together, our tongues warring in each other's mouth. I squeezed her breast harder and she gripped my cock harder.

It wasn't long before all of our clothes were off and we were making love on the rug in the study. To say it was the best sex of my life would be an understatement. It was mind-blowing. Absolutely amazing. She knew all the right buttons to push on me, and I just seemed to know what she wanted at every point. It left us both exhausted, giddy and playfully happy, but exhausted.

Raquel tried to explain to me what was going on, but our clothes kept coming off, so for the first few hours after my arrival at the mysterious mansion nothing of any substance was accomplished. But boy were those some enjoyable hours.

Finally, when both of us were satiated, she sat me down in an overstuffed leather chair in the study and started to fill me in on what was going on.

I'll cut to the chase. What these Supremes ultimately were trying to do was wipe out all the other parallel dimension and make theirs the one true universe. They were a fanatical bunch. Devout zealots who believed their dimension was the one true dimension that God had intended. All the other dimensions were mistakes in their eyes, aberrations that had to be removed for the glory of God.

"But you said there was an almost infinite number of parallel dimensions. How could they possibly wipe them all out?" I asked.

"They've developed a weapon. The best way I can describe it is that it's like a Hadron Collider on Viagra. They took everything we know about quantum mechanics and sub atomic particles, using GAN, using deep learning networks, and figured out a way to destroy thousands of parallel dimension at one time by tearing through the dark matter strings that bind everything together."

I stared at her. "What the fuck did you just say?"

Raquel sighed, but it wasn't an aggravated sigh. It was a sigh of patience for a beloved idiot. "I know you are aware of the Large Hadron Collider. They're using it to smash atoms into each other at insanely high velocities in order to study particle physics. And I know you are aware that some people are afraid that these insanely powerful collisions might accidentally create a black hole that will destroy the universe."

I nodded. I had some knowledge of that from reading articles in passing.

"Well, it turns out some of those fears were justified. The LHC won't create a black hole big enough to destroy the universe it occupies." She raised a pointed finger. "But the Supremes are creating a version of the Hadron Collider that does create microscopic black holes with enough destructive power to destroy parallel universes that are adjacent to its parent universe."

"You're starting to lose me again," I said.

She was quiet for a moment. I found myself staring at her face again. Call it vanity, call it self-absorption, call it ego run amok, call it what you want to call it, but damn she was incredibly hot. Mesmerizing. That's the word. She was literally mesmerizing me with her beauty.

"Okay, think of this machine they've created as a gigantic vacuum. Each parallel universe is like a loose string on the carpet. You run the vacuum over the loose string and it sucks it up. These microscopic black holes are like the vacuum bag. That's where the loose string ends up. Except there's no retrieving the string because the black hole also acts as an incinerator that burns the string. It vaporizes it into nothingness."

"So these Supremes are sucking parallel universes into an incinerator."

"Yes."

"So that means they are destroyed for good? There is no getting them back?"

Raquel nodded. "That's right. Once the universe is sucked into the black hole, it's utterly and totally destroyed forever."

"Damn," I muttered. I felt a weird pain in my chest, but that mysterious ghostly pain vanished just as quickly as my would-be migraine vanished when I was in my car.

"Damn is right," Raquel said. She lowered her head. "My universe is gone. I have no home, no one to go back to."

"How do you know all this?" I asked.

She slowly looked up at me. Tears were staining her cheeks and I felt an overwhelming feeling of rage towards anyone who could cause such a reaction in her. But then she said something that almost knocked my feet out from under me. "Because I helped create it," she said.

I stared slack jawed at her for a moment before speaking. "You helped create it?"

Raquel wiped away at the tears on her cheek, frustrated by her reaction, seemingly angered by her own tears. "Yes. I'm from the parallel universe adjacent to the Supreme."

"The Supreme? I thought you called them the

Supremes. The Supreme is something else?"

She nodded. "That's what they call their home universe. The Supreme Universe because they believe themselves to be superior to all others."

I waited for her to continue.

"Since our universe was so close to theirs, our timelines were nearly identical, our histories were nearly identical. We were developing the same machine. I... was helping develop the machine."

"But then you tried to stop them."

She nodded. "I thought we were just going to explore the parallel universes. I truly had no idea their plan all along was to destroy them. You have to believe me."

"Hell, I believe you," I told her.

Raquel gave me a weak smile. "Once I found out what these nefarious fuckers were planning, I tried to sabotage the machine. I tried to overload it and melt its circuits. I was trying to get the damn thing to blow up or to melt into a pile of molten slag." She paused, a crestfallen look coming over her face. "Turns out I just made the machine work. The violent surge of power was exactly what it needed to create those tiny black holes, those rips in the fabrics of the universe. I showed them the way to make the machine actually work."

I was quiet for a moment, thinking on all this. "So are there Supremes in your universe, the universe you came from? It seems like that should overlap, too."

She shook her head. "There is only one race of Supremes. Just one out of all the billions of possibilities of human evolution that happened in all the parallel dimensions."

"But you were also working on the machine in

your universe," I said.

She nodded. "Yes, but not for the same reason. Our dimensions were close enough to share many similarities, but we were making the machine to explore other dimensions, not destroy them."

"You're really making my head hurt," I told her. I looked down, rubbing at the ache in my temples.

"I'm sorry, but it gets even worse."

I looked back up at her. "How does it get worse than this?"

"The Supremes are telepathic. They are the only known dimension that has telepathic powers."

"Okay." I rubbed at the back of my neck. "You're right. This is worse."

She smiled softly. "That's how I realized what they were doing."

I squinted a confused look at her.

"They tried to recruit me," she said.

"Telepathically?" I asked. "That's what you're saying. They tried to recruit you telepathically."

Raquel smiled. "Pretty crazy, right?"

"I'm about ten levels past crazy right about now."

She reached over and kissed me gently. Just because, I guess. I certainly didn't mind.

"They tried to convince me to join them. To become a Supreme, but I knew they were lying to me just to use my access to the machine in my dimension. They had way too much zeal. It just felt wrong to me immediately. I knew I had to destroy the machine in my universe before they could convince someone else to use it. So I tried to blow it up by flooding it with an intense surge of power. But that didn't work. It created a rip in dimensional space instead."

"You created some kind of portal?"

She nodded. "It only lasted for a few minutes, but I knew I had to go through. I knew they'd kill me if I didn't escape." She hung her head. "I failed in the worst possible way. Not only did I help create a machine that can destroy universes, I also tucked my tail between my legs and ran away. My actions revealed to the Supremes the way they could power their own machine. By giving it a massive surge of power."

I was quiet. I pulled her to me, letting her rest her head on my shoulder. I absently stroked her hair, doing what little I could do to comfort her. I felt her sob against my shoulder. I was still confused by what was happening, but I knew this was something that would cause her great pain for the rest of her life. We stayed that way for a while, then she eventually pulled back and looked at me. I kissed her, but that's where it stopped. Neither one of us was in the mood to take it any further.

"So," I said, "how do I play into all of this? I'm no scientist. And my skills with machinery are pretty much non-existent."

She reached up and gently caressed my cheek. "I can't say for certain, but we have an idea."

"We?"

"Yes. I told you, there are others."

I just let that go for now. "So?" I prompted. "What is your idea?"

"We think your universe might be the Original. This universe. The one we are now occupying. That's why we were all drawn here."

"The Original?"

Raquel nodded. "Yes, the first from which all other universes have sprung."

I frowned and she clearly saw my confusion.

"There had to be a starting point. There had to be just one universe in the beginning. Then as things began to happen there were possibilities of events occurring in different ways, so other universes began to develop."

My frown didn't leave my face.

"Think of a coin toss. It can land either on heads or tails, or even in rare instances it can land on its edge side and not even fall over, but forget about that. So, heads or tails. If it lands on heads, then the universe develops in one direction, and if it lands on tails then the universe develops in a different direction. But both of these outcomes always happen. The coin lands on both heads and tails, each outcome resulting in alternate universes. This creates a split. This creates a parallel universe that saw heads, and another parallel universe that saw tails.

"Now you've got two universes developing in parallel dimensions. Now each of these two universes can go in any direction, so the coin is flipped again, this time in each of the two universes. Both of those universes also see both heads and tails. Now you've got four universes, each diverging slightly from the other, existing in a parallel dimension. Then those four universes become eight, then those eight become sixteen and on and on and on. Soon, there are millions of parallel universes, some of them evolving in massively different ways than the others because their divergent paths have taken them on wildly different courses."

I tried to absorb what she was telling me. I was starting to catch on. I think. "So this... rift you created in dimensional space, led here."

Raquel nodded. "And for the others."

"The others like… us?"

She nodded again. "Like I told you, there are millions of parallel universes, existing, I guess you could say, right next to each other. Other versions of me, of us, were also working on the machines in their universes. When they opened their rifts, they also led here."

"So they were all scientists like you, living in other universes but still following a similar path through life as you?"

Again, she nodded. "Many universes evolved nearly exactly like mine, so their lives followed a very similar path as mine"

"How many others like you, like us, are here?"

"Five more."

"Five? That's it?"

"That's all that made it through the rifts in their universes." She paused. "As for the rest, I just don't know. They're probably dead."

I winced as a stabbing pain lightning-bolted its way through my head. I was prone to flash migraines, and I was somewhat used to them, but they seemed to be getting worse. I pinched my eyes shut tight, waiting for the pain to subside. When I opened my eyes again, I could see that Raquel must have been experiencing something similar, except she was clutching at her abdomen. That was weird.

Raquel must have seen the perplexed expression on my face because she said, "You know those mysterious pains you feel? Those sudden flashes of headaches? Like the one you just had? Those flares of pain you feel in your knees? In your chest? In your back?"

I just listened. I did have such inexplicable sensations at times, but I just chalked them up to the consequences of aging. Then I gave her a slight nod.

She nodded, knowing that I understood what she was talking about. "Those are your paras dying," she said.

I squinted at her. "My paras?"

"Your parallels. We just call them paras."

"My parallels?"

She nodded. "Your parallels. Your parallels from a sister dimension." She paused. "You. Me. From the other universes."

I sat quietly for a moment. "Wait a minute. That's... them... dying."

She nodded softly. "Yes. You're feeling their deaths."

"You mean it's not just pain from my own body?"

"Oh, sure, sometimes it is. But quite often it's not."

"I'm feeling... their deaths." This whole conversation was sounding very strange to me. Surreal and unbelievable.

Raquel nodded again. "That's why the pains seem to come and go so quickly. You feel their deaths, then they're gone. The pain disappears."

"I've been feeling a lot of mysterious pains lately."

She nodded. "Because it's accelerating. The Supremes are amassing more and more power, destroying more and more universes. And they are getting closer and closer to reaching this one."

"So now what?" I asked.

She was quiet for a moment. "If you have any ideas on how to stop a telepathic race from destroying every parallel universe but theirs, I'm all ears," she said. She leaned in a little closer, tilting her body forward, revealing more of her cleavage.

"Honey, you ain't all ears," I told her. "If anything, you are all breasts."

She giggled. It was a sweet, lyrical little sound that endeared her to me even more every time I heard it. She leaned in even closer.

"Are you doing that on purpose?" I asked her, unable to stop my gaze from traveling down to her breasts.

She looked up at me through lidded eyes and blinked demurely. "Doing what?"

I kissed her. Oh, please. You know you'd do the same thing. It was kind of like masturbating, but waaayyy more enjoyable. Her lips were soft, melding perfectly against mine. At first, it was weird, I'll admit. But the more times I kissed her, the more quickly I felt a stiffening in the ol' crotch area. There was no denying the reaction my body was having to feeling her lips pressed passionately against mine.

Raquel pulled back from our kiss and glanced up at me with her dazzling blue eyes. "You want to do me doggy style?"

Holy fuck. I was in love.

⋅⋯⋅⋅❈⋅⋅⋯⋅

"Time to meet the gang," Raquel said. She grabbed my hand and tugged me towards a wide stairway that led to the upper floor.

"Do I look okay?" I asked. I did my best to straighten my hair with my hand.

She just laughed. "Come on."

She dragged me up the stairs, then we moved a

few dozen feet down the landing, stopping before a door. She gently rapped her knuckles on the wood. "You decent?" she called out towards the door.

The door opened and Raquel pushed it wider, tugging me along with her into the room.

I took a few steps into the room and just stopped. It was a bit overwhelming at first.

What a motley gang it was. What I motley gang *I* was. There was the black male version of me, the female Japanese version of me, the female Mexican version of me, a redheaded male version of me. I stared at them for a long moment.

And then the midget female version of me stepped out from behind the redhead. Holy shit. "I got a mini-me! Hot damn!" I knew it was a pretty damn rude thing to say, but I just couldn't help myself; it just came out.

They all smiled at me and I could feel the genuine happiness radiating off them as they greeted me. Hell, I felt the exact same way about them. Of course I did. They were me, just slightly different, but still a version of me from a parallel universe, just as I was a version of them. How could we not feel an immediate bonding attachment to each other? It would have been very strange had we not. The magnificent fucking seven.

They were all scientists, brainiacs just like Raquel. Each one was involved with the creation of the universe-sucking vacuum cleaner to one degree or another. Except for the redheaded male version of me. He was just a janitor in his dimension, in the wrong time and the wrong place when the rift was created. I felt an immediate kinship with him. He seemed the most like me out of all of them. A nice guy, but a little slow, a little dense, the kind of guy I would go out on the town with and try to score with women. He liked to go by the simple nickname of Red.

As Raquel had explained to me, there were so many different universes, so many parallel dimensions that every variation you could think of me existed somewhere in some universe. It was a heady idea and took some getting used to. Especially when I looked at the other female versions of me. The Japanese version of me, Kumiko, was hot, and so was the female Mexican version of me, Juanita. They both had long black hair, slender faces, and sultry fucking eyes that could burn a hole right through my crotch if they looked at it long enough.

The black dude went by the name of Maurice. He was a little standoff-ish, but that was something I could understand; I certainly felt like that sometimes myself.

But that little mini-me, Ivana the Russian midget, was something else altogether. She definitely had a resemblance to me, but her face was a little squashed, a bit condensed. I wasn't quite sure how to take her at first. I only knew midgets from afar in movies and circuses. I had never actually met one my entire life. She walked right up to me and extended her hand. "Don't worry," she said. "I can still fuck your dick raw."

"Ain't that the truth," Maurice said and let out what I was soon to discover was a rare laugh.

I just stared at Ivana's little hand, then finally took it and shook it politely. I looked at the gathered group, moving my gaze from one to the next. "So, you've all..." I left the statement unfinished, but of course they knew what I was asking.

They all nodded.

I looked at Maurice, then Red. "Even you two?"

Red looked sheepish. Maurice just shrugged.

Kumiko and Juanita cocked their heads at me. "What about us? Aren't you curious about us?"

"Well, yeah," I said. "But I just assumed you two would... have a go at each other. You're both fucking hot. How could you resist each other?"

"You're a sexist pig," Juanita said.

I nodded. "Umm, yeah."

Ivana laughed. "Welcome home, Evan." She grabbed my hand and started pulling me out the door. "Let's see what you got. If you've got half of what Maurice has, that'll do."

I looked pleadingly at Raquel. She smiled and waved me on.

"Don't we have to like save the universe or something first?" I asked.

"All in due time," Ivana said. "All in due time."

Ivana was a lusty little wench, but eventually we were both satiated and we rejoined the others. It was very weird to be in a room filled with people who were somewhat mental twins of yourself, but who had such diverse physical appearances. Very weird. But we certainly got along well.

"So what's the plan?" I asked. "How do we go about saving my universe."

"It's our universe now," Raquel said, gently correcting me.

I nodded. "Of course. Our universe. How do we

stop these Supremes you told me about? Besides destroying all their old LPs and CDs, I mean."

No one laughed, but trust me, I knew they all thought it was a little bit funny.

"We have to destroy their universe," Kumiko said.

I looked at the Japanese version of me. She was dressed in a cute little red dress with a flowery pattern. Kumiko nodded in affirmation of what she had just said. I looked over to Raquel and she nodded as well. "Destroy their universe?" I asked. "Isn't that a little extreme?"

No one said anything to that.

"So how does one go about destroying an entire universe?" I asked.

"We have to infiltrate their universe," Kumiko said. "We have to enter the Supreme Universe, get to their machine, and destroy it."

"So you want to use their own universe-sucking machine to destroy their own universe?"

Kumiko nodded. "Or something like that, yeah."

"We have to destroy their machine," Juanita said. "That part is for certain." She was dressed in a plain yellow T-shirt and very tight fitting jeans.

"As for the rest," Maurice said, "we just don't know."

"Well, I for one, have no idea where to start," I said.

Kumiko looked at me, then slowly spread her legs. "Why don't you start right here," she said.

I just stared quietly at her for a moment, then glanced at the others. "Are you all as horny of a dog as I am?"

"What do you think?" Kumiko asked. She reached between her legs and gently rubbed herself.

I shrugged. "Well, if that's the way it's gonna be, then that's the way it's gonna be."

I collapsed to Juanita's side, breathing heavily, sweating. "How the hell are we going to get anything done?" I had thought I wouldn't have the stamina to keep going after a round of lovemaking with Kumiko, but I was happily mistaken.

Juanita laughed and curled her naked body up against me.

"So who's the smartest one in the group?" I asked.

"Well, we only know one thing for certain about that," Juanita said.

I waited for her reply, but I should've expected her answer.

"It's not you," she said, then laughed.

I grinned. "Is everyone a smart ass, too?"

"What do you think?"

I lay there quietly for a moment, enjoying the heat of her body next to mine. "This really is very bizarre," I finally said.

She circled my chest with her finger. "Yes, it is. But it's kind of nice." She raised up her head to look at me. "It's nice to be surrounded by people you can trust."

I looked at her. Damn, she had the sultriest, sexiest brown eyes I had ever seen. She was right. It was weird, but I knew I could trust all of them, just as they knew they could trust me. I mean, can you really betray yourself? I guess maybe someone could. But I wouldn't. It was a surprising thing to think, but I knew I would give my life if I had to for any one of them. I just knew it. There wasn't even a moment of hesitation in my mind when I thought of such a possibility. They were me. And I was them. If there was anyone in the world who I didn't want to disappoint, it was myself.

"So what's the next step?" I asked.

"I want to be on top this time," she said.

Juanita knew damn well that wasn't what I was asking. But who was I to argue?

We were all gathered in the study. I was the only one standing, pacing nervously across the carpeted floor. "I'm still trying to wrap my head around destroying an entire universe. Doesn't killing billions of people bother anyone else? It damn well should."

"Of course it does," Raquel said. She was sitting in a brown leather chair near a row of bookshelves that reached from the floor to the ceiling. A sliding ladder was positioned just behind her, attached to the tall bookcase.

"There has to be something else we can do," I said. "Can't we just steal their machine or destroy it or something? Why do we have to wipe out an entire universe?"

Kumiko had a grim look on her face. "Because they have over three billion Believers in their universe."

I paused.

Maurice nodded. "Yes, three billion people believe as the Supremes do. They all think the other universes, my universe, your universe, every universe, are a threat to them, so they support the Supremes in everything they do."

"Jesus," I muttered.

Ivana nodded. "Exactly. Jesus is their leader."

My brain nearly exploded. "Whoa. What? Jesus is their leader? *The* Jesus?"

Ivana nodded. "Or so the guy claims. None of us believe it. But three billion people in the Supremes' universe believe it. There is nothing we can do to change their minds. They are zealots. Full bore. Completely and utterly devoted. Their faith is unshakeable."

I still couldn't wrap my head around this new piece of information. "*The* Jesus. The son of God Jesus?"

Red nodded. "Blows your fucking mind, don't it?"

"I'll say," I said.

"Oh, there's one more person from our group you need to meet," Raquel said.

I looked quizzically at Raquel.

Raquel looked off into a dark area in the study and made a simple gesture, curling her finger towards herself.

For just a brief second, the lights in the room flickered. He stepped out of the shadows, and I immediately recognized him. I mean, he looked like me, like all of us, but there was definitely something a little bit different about him, a very real intensity to his eyes. I guess I shouldn't have been surprised. There were an infinite number of universes, with an infinite number of possibilities, so why not this one. The deeply red skin and horns gave him away.

Raquel looked back over to me. "You're going to be his vessel."

Somehow, I wasn't surprised by this revelation. I really did have no skills that I could contribute. At least I could contribute something of value, even if it was only my body as a host.

"The devil is in the details," I muttered.

I felt like I was beaming myself half a dozen smiles as my paras each gave me a comforting grin.

"So why can't he just cross over into the Supremes' dimension?" I asked, referring to the red devil para. We decided to just call him Bub for short. Mostly because it was kind of funny.

Raquel shrugged. "We don't know why. We just know he can't. Because we already tried. We think it's some kind of telepathic defense screen, a mental wall if you will. Somehow they are blocking him from crossing over because of his... skill set. They know he is powerful so they have purposely put up a defense against him."

"You already tried? Meaning you already have a machine set up that can open portals to other dimensions?"

Raquel nodded. "Yes, they blocked him, but we think we can hide him long enough to get through."

"Because he'll be inside of me," I said.

Raquel nodded. "We think the Supremes still might be able to detect his presence after he enters their universe, but by then we hope it will be too late."

I was quiet for a long moment. "So that's the real reason you tracked me down? Not for my intellectual prowess, or my good looks. Just to be a vessel?"

Raquel stroked my arm, with what I did believe was some true affection. "It's not your fault, Evan," she said.

I frowned curiously at her.

"Your mother smoked a lot and your father was a drunk. You didn't have the cleanest embryonic growth and your upbringing was… well, it was a little lacking."

"So I'm an expendable idiot," I stated.

She shook her head. "You're not expendable." She purposefully paused and her blue eyes just shimmered with mirth.

"But I am an idiot."

She grabbed my hand. "Come on. I've got something that will make you feel better."

I resisted. "Like what?"

She looked at me with a bit of surprise. "Seriously? Like how about my naked body rubbing all over you?"

I stopped resisting.

"So that's it, huh? The destroyer of universes."

"Yep, that's it," Raquel said.

I stared at the machine. To me, it was just a bunch of unfathomable wires and screens and circuitry and tubing and more wires and more circuitry and big gleaming metal casings. Somebody had a sense of humor because someone had built a huge switch that read ON and OFF in gigantic letters on the top and bottom of the switch. It was currently set to the OFF position. I pointed to the switch. "Is that for real?"

Red nodded. "Yes it is." He shrugged. "My only contribution, I'm sorry to say."

"So if I just flip that switch I'll open a portal to

another universe, to a parallel dimension?" I asked.

"Si, senor." Juanita replied.

"Well, shit." I was sorely tempted to flip the switch right then and there, but I held that impulse in check.

Maurice pointed to an array of screens set into the machine about shoulder high. "You do have to put in some coordinates first."

"Coordinates?" I asked. "What the hell would the coordinates be for a parallel dimension?"

"We can choose to go to a parallel dimension very close to our own, or we can go out wider and choose a dimension that's much farther removed from this one," Kumiko said.

I stared at the screens. All of the language and symbols flickering by on the screens was just pure gibberish to me. "So how close is the Supremes' dimension to this one?"

"It's pretty far," Raquel said. "At the end of the spectrum."

"I guess that would make sense if this really is the Original universe," I said.

Raquel patted me on the back. "Attaboy. Now you're thinking." Then she frowned. "But it's getting closer and closer to us every second."

I frowned right back at her.

"Because as the Supremes keep destroying dimensions, they are moving closer and closer in this direction," she said. "Right now, the accordion is still pretty wide with the sides far apart, but the Supremes are squeezing it closer and closer together by destroying the dimensions that separate us. We are one end of the accordion, and they are the other. If we don't stop them, they'll be right next to us soon."

It was all so much to take in. "So if you can travel

to the other dimensions, can't the Supremes do that, too?"

Ivana nodded. "Yes, they can. Who do you think wiped you out of existence?"

"So they are here? In my— in this dimension?"

Ivana nodded.

"Why don't they just destroy this dimension and be done with it?" I asked.

"They don't want to destroy this dimension," Raquel said. "They want to rule it. They want to possess it for themselves. That's the only thing that's saving us right now."

"Because this is truly the Original universe," I said.

Kumiko patted my head. "Attaboy."

⟨✦⟩

I stared at the machine. The other paras were all gathered behind me. I looked away from the machine, turning back to face them.

"So that's the plan? I let Bub possess me as his vessel. You open the portal and he slash me steps through and starts laying waste to their entire universe?

Raquel nodded.

"How do we get back? I thought you said the rift only stayed open for a few minutes."

"That was version one point oh," Raquel said. "This one will keep the rift open until we decide to close it."

Red grinned. "The ON OFF switch is functional. Works just as it says. Flip it ON, it stays on and open, flip it to OFF and the rift will close up.

I was quiet for a moment. "Just us? That's all that's

going through? Just me and Bub?"

Raquel nodded. "We don't think you'll be alone on the other side for long."

As usual, I just squinted at Raquel, not bothering to hide my confusion.

And as usual, Raquel was right.

<hr />

Being a vessel was damned strange, let me tell you. I felt like I was still me, but there was always this feeling that someone was whispering to me deep in my subconscious, as if my thoughts and actions were guided by some deep inner voice that welled up into my conscious thoughts. Hell, what is the nature of consciousness anyway? Nobody really knows that for sure.

The ritual, or ceremony, or whatever the hell you want to call it, was pretty strange. Needless to say, I had never done that before, nor encountered it ever before in my life.

Everybody got naked. Isn't that how all good possession ceremonies start? We didn't need chicken blood or pentagram symbols on the floor, or any of that other satanic nonsense. Not even flickering candles made out of baby fat.

I laid naked on the carpeted floor in the study. Everyone else was naked, resting on their knees near my chest and abdomen, positioned close enough to me to be touching their bodies to mine. Beelzebub stood quietly, hidden in the shadows.

"Close your eyes," Raquel said, her voice soothing and calm.

I closed my eyes. I could feel her fingers gently

stroking my forehead.

"Open yourself up to him," she said, her voice barely a whisper.

The others started to slowly hum, then repeated the same two words again and again as they gently touched me with feathery touches of their fingertips. "Open yourself... Open yourself... Open yourself."

I felt a heavy shadow come over me. It was a bizarre sensation, like a heavy blanket was being laid over me but it had no physical substance. It's hard to describe. More like it was all in my mind, rather than having anything to do with my physical body.

"He's here," Raquel whispered to me. "Open yourself up to him."

At first, I didn't understand what Raquel had meant about opening myself, but now I think I did. I relaxed my muscles, relaxed my body, trying to remove any barriers even from my thoughts. I opened myself up to him. I felt this heavy shadow blanket start to lower itself, start to sink into me, as if penetrating through my skin, as if submerging itself past my outer layer of flesh, sinking in me deeply past my muscles, permeating through my very bones.

And then it was done. No one said a word, but they all seemed to know when to stop chanting as their voices all stopped at exactly the same moment. I could feel the heat of their bodies lessen as they withdrew away from me.

I opened my eyes to see Raquel smiling down at me. I glanced around the room at the others. I didn't ask where Beelzebub had gone to because I knew exactly where he was.

Those Supremes didn't know what the fuck hit them.

Raquel was right just like I said, as she usually was. About not being alone for long, I mean. I wasn't alone for very long at all. I stepped through the portal and assessed my surroundings. I was outside, in the middle of a large corn field. The day was sunny and bright, with only a few white clouds dotting the blue sky. In the far distance, several miles off, I could see the shining windows of the Supremes' towering headquarters as the sun reflected off their dark panes; that was where their dimension-destroying machine was located.

I heard a rustling noise in the corn and turned to see a para of me stepping through the green stalks, moving into the row between the stalks. She was a Nubian beauty version of me, with intense smoky eyes. I knew she was a vessel as well, a vessel for Beelzebub in her dimension. I nodded to her and she nodded back, also giving me what looked like a submissive bow. Somehow, she sensed I was from the Original so that gave me just a slight edge up in the pecking order. Okay, more than just a slight edge. It made me the de facto leader. With Bub in my side (at my side didn't sound right), I was okay with taking that position; his presence imbued me with a confidence I never had before.

Within moments of my arrival, hundreds and hundreds of other paras of mine stepped through the green stalks to join us. They came from parallel dimensions that were following very similar paths to mine, so they had all followed very similar patterns of behavior, assessing the situation, coming to similar conclusions, making plans nearly identical to the plans we had made in our dimension. We were all the same age, roughly the same height, all sharing my very similar facial features, but a few aberrations were visible in a few of them. One woman was an albino. One man was very tall. Dozens of races were represented, from Chinese to Japanese, from Mexican to Russian, from Indian to German, amidst a large group of Caucasian men and women.

We were an army of one. Times a thousand. A thousand strong, all with the powers of the Beelzebub from our respective dimensions. Legends held that Bub has many powers. Guess what? They were more like historical truths than legends. These included a pretty big bag of tricks.

The power of Vessel Possession meant Beelzebub could possess people, which was what was at the core of this entire assault; hence this little army of acolytes coming together out of that skill.

What turned the tide immediately in our favor was the Power Negation ability we had absorbed from Bub. Power negation meant we had the ability to keep other beings from using their powers - this rendered the Supremes' telepathic ability moot because we blocked them from using it. This threw off their communication lines immediately because they were so used to easily sending and receiving orders with their thoughts. They never recovered from their initial confusion; we kept the pressure on so strongly that we never gave them the chance to recover.

Invulnerability was a key component to Bub's powers, meaning we, aka all of the paras he was using as vessels, were impervious to most damage and injury. Sure, the Supremes hit us with a full battery of machine gun fire, hand-tossed grenades, rocket-propelled grenades, and some of those did some heavy bodily damage. The smoking hot Nubian got both her legs blown off when the ground erupted beneath her feet from an exploding grenade.

But his Advanced Regeneration powers gave him, aka us, the capability of healing any wounds we got instantaneously, so we easily shrugged off the machine gun fire; the Nubian grew those slender beauties back in no time. This partnered well with Bub's Healing Powers, meaning we could heal physical injuries in others.

Throw in Resurrection, meaning we could revive people back from the dead, and that was a way we continued our onslaught even when we took heavy damage. A Chinese para was literally blown into four separate body parts, but we just put him back together and brought him back to life.

One odd thing I didn't realize until later was that I wasn't feeling any odd pains or strange aches when a para died. With the chaos of battle going on all around us, with paras getting pounded from all sides with all manner of weaponry, we should all have been reduced to blubbering, pain-wracked idiots. I can only guess that Bub's powers helped reduce that sensation. Oh, I did feel a few strange twinges here and there, but nothing like I had been experiencing before all this multiverse madness had come into my life. Unfortunately, Raquel and the others had a rough go from all the para deaths; they told me later they were all nearly catatonic with pain for days.

The battle raged on.

The power of Conversion gave us the ability to create demons by twisting human souls. This allowed us to turn some occupants of the Supremes' universe against them; we infiltrated half a dozen communities around the Supremes' headquarters and turned them into human suicide bombers and human shields. Not proud of that one, but it was war after all and the lives of trillions of people across millions of universes was at stake.

The innate Expert Hand-to-Hand Fighter skill, coupled with Power Augmentation which amplified our strength, gave us an edge in those tight skirmishes when the battlefield became too thick with combatants to use automatic weapons or even handguns.

I wasn't a big fan of Molecular Combustion, meaning we could kill lesser beings by rendering them down to their molecules or making them explode. It was incredibly messy, and very tiring and draining to use, but it was useful when we needed it in those chaotic, close-quarter battles.

And you can't appreciate the power of wolves, dogs, horses, and even cats, fighting if you've never seen them fight with augmented strength. It was a thing of beauty in battle when we were fighting side by side with them as we got closer and closer to the Supremes' headquarters building. The ability known as Advanced Power Granting was what gave us the ability to grant some of our powers to other beings, including animals. Kamikaze cats gouging out throats with their claws and teeth is one image I'll never be able to get out of my head. Horses charging headlong into a crowd of the enemy, head butting enemy soldiers and lashing out with their incredibly powerful hooves is another image that will stick with me. And of course, wolves and dogs hunting together as one mighty pack was a force to be reckoned with.

When the tanks rolled in, things got a little chaotic there for a moment. But when you combine Telekinesis, the power to move objects and beings with pure thought power alone, with Thermokinesis, the ability to alter temperatures to a drastic degree, we quickly turned their own weapons against them. We heated up the metal chassis of the tanks and baked the enemy occupants alive, then telekinetically turned the turrets on their own buildings and opened fire by telekinetically pressing the guns' trigger mechanisms.

They also attacked us from the sky. Winged angels dripped a toxic soup of chemicals over our heads. Okay, they were just drones with wide wingspans, but they were all painted white and it seemed like we were being dive-bombed by pissed off angels because of their shapes and the loud screeching sound they emitted when they made their bombing runs. As it turns out, our Super Stamina power shielded us and kept us unaffected by diseases and toxins, so they really only succeeded in poisoning quite a few of their own soldiers who didn't have time to don their protective masks.

Shapeshifting aided us in fooling their robot sentries because those robots had all been trained in visual recognition to only allow entrance to the Supremes' headquarters if the employee passed the facial recognition test. Our shapeshifting skills allowed us to take on the faces of any enemy combatants we had encountered, so gaining access was relatively one of the easiest things we did.

Once we got access to the main headquarters, we headed straight to the universe-killing machine. One core power that proved invaluable was Electrokinesis, meaning we could control electrical things. This was key, because when enough paras and I got within very close range of their universe-destroying machine, we destroyed it with a massive communal surge from our electrokinetic power. Plus, we shot it up, tossed grenades into it, and even punched and kicked the fucking control consoles into tiny little bits.

With their machine destroyed, and most of the people working on it now dead, their so-called Jesus finally decided to make his appearance. He floated down from the sky, his arms spread wide. The fire consuming the Supremes' headquarters was ablaze behind him, the flames growing larger, the smoke getting thicker.

It was a good thing that Astral Perception was another power we had, meaning we could perceive the true forms of beings that were invisible to the human eye, such as angels and other demons. In our case, it worked in the opposite fashion, revealing what a phony this Jesus imitator was. He was wearing an anti-gravity belt, the device hidden beneath his robes.

As the bearded figure descended, I could feel the other paras behind me grow silent. I didn't have to turn to look at them to know that they were all just staring at this fake Jesus figure with baited breath, waiting for his next move.

As he descended ever closer, his features started to come into view. Maybe I shouldn't have been surprised by what I saw, but it still gave me a brief jolt when his face finally came into focus. I mean there were supposedly millions of parallel dimensions with an infinite number of possibilities happening in each one, so why couldn't this be one of those possibilities?

"Hello, Evan," he said as his feet touched the ground.

I didn't say anything. Yeah, maybe it was rude, but I just didn't respond to his greeting. I could feel him trying to probe me with his telepathic ability. His skill was very strong, which undoubtedly was why he became the ruler of the Supremes. But he was now facing off against hundreds and hundreds of demon-possessed humans who all had the skill of Power Negation, so the collective nullifying effort of the paras easily deflected and deflated any attempt he made to use his telepathic power against me.

He moved closer, then stopped a few feet away from me.

"Why?" I asked him.

"I am the light," he replied. "I am the resurrection."

"Seriously?" I asked.

He said nothing.

"Why would you want to destroy so many lives? You're destroying entire universes." I looked back at all my paras, taking in their tired, blood-smeared bodies, their battle-scarred faces, then turned back to face him. "We would never do such a thing. None of us."

"I am the light of the world. Whoever follows me will have a life filled with light and will never live in the dark," he said.

"You're disturbed," I told him. There was a glimmer of madness in his eyes, a feverish haze. I stared at him, and a feeling of extreme sadness, even embarrassment, welled up inside me. This was me, gone full tilt loco. I suppose it had to happen somewhere, in some dimension. I couldn't be awesome all the time. Even the beard he sported just seemed... wrong; it didn't seem to quite fit his face.

"You are all abominations in the eyes of God," he said. "I am the one true savior."

I raised up my machine gun and made swiss cheese out of his body. He collapsed to the ground in a bloody husk. I didn't feel a thing, not even a twinge. "No," I said. "You're just dead."

Nobody bothered to resurrect him.

And that was that for the controlling faction of the Supremes.

But we still had billions of zealots to deal with. We couldn't take the chance of someone new taking up the mantle.

We pooled our Advanced Terrakinesis power together, generating dozens of gigantic earthquakes across the entire planet, hitting the most sensitive quake zones with the biggest power surges. We coupled this with Advanced Weather Manipulation, drastically changing weather patterns in the key areas that had the highest population of fanatical zealots. We created massive tornadoes, thunderous typhoons, surging tidal waves, spreading the extreme weather as far and as wide as we could. Those storms would most likely rage for decades.

We didn't exactly destroy the entire Supremes' universe, but we certainly set them back a few thousand years.

Mission accomplished.

The rest of the paras returned to their home universes. We certainly had made a good team. I wondered if we would ever see each other again.

⋘⋅⊰⊱⋅⋙

Being a vessel *is* damned strange is more of an accurate way to put it. I can't really say *was*. The only problem now is that old Beelzebub really likes being inside of me and he refuses to relinquish full control of my body back to me. I still feel like myself, but I know he's there, submerged deep inside me. I don't know if he has other plans for me or not. I guess I'll just have to wait and see. But I'll tell you one thing, I'm never gonna take shit from anyone ever again, that's for sure.

Plus, Raquel seems to kind of dig it because there are a few additional powers he has that weren't in the history books. We call them his sextra powers, if you catch my drift. And shapeshifting in the sack? Mind-blowing, let me tell you.

I suppose Alexandra had been right all along. She had said I had arrived at my final destination when she first brought me to the mansion. Being the vessel for a demon who refuses to relinquish control certainly seems final. But then again, why should I care about Bub still possessing my body as his vessel?

I mean, after all I am him and he is me.

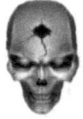

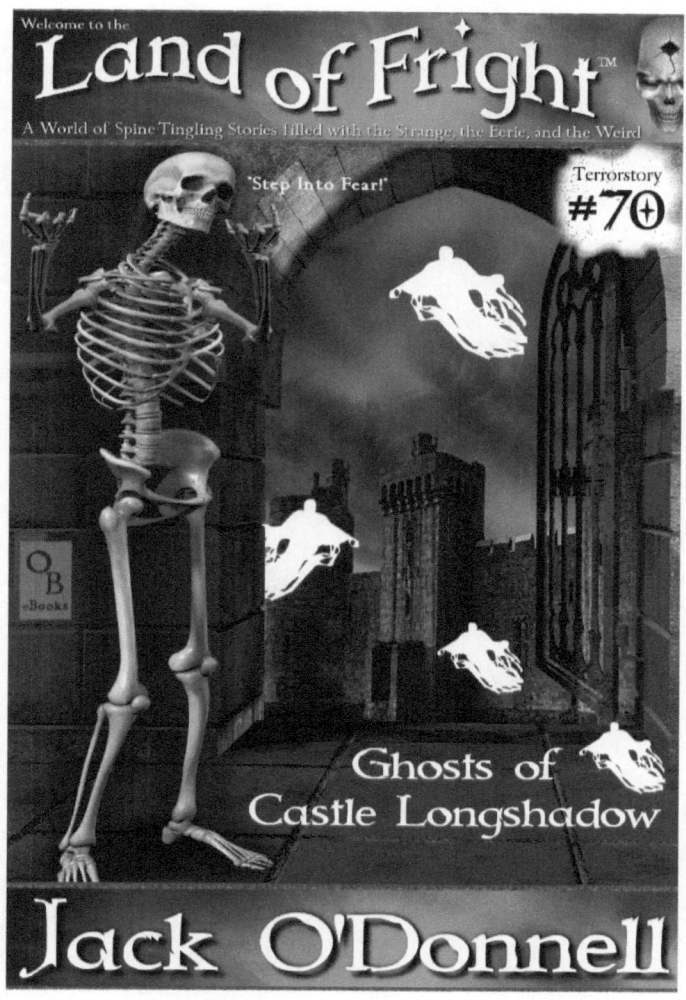

TERRORSTORY #70
GHOSTS OF CASTLE LONGSHADOW

Elizabeth grabbed Duncan's wrist and tugged him sharply towards her. "You don't want to go in there," she said, her voice both sternly cautioning and nervously fearful.

Duncan turned his slate grey eyes to her and tilted up the right corner of his mouth in a quirky gentle smile. He gently pried her slender fingers from his wrist, but kept her hand in his grasp. "Have you ever seen them?" he asked her.

Elizabeth started to speak, then pressed her lips closed, and turned away from him, softly shaking her head. Then she sharply turned back to him, her blue eyes widening. "But Grace has!"

Duncan responded with a soft laugh. "She's also seen fairies and wolves with glowing red eyes and dead people walking around the graveyard."

A crestfallen look shadowed Elizabeth's face. She lowered her head, the blush of her excited exclamation fading away from her delicate cheeks.

Duncan raised up her hand and gave her knuckles a whisper of a kiss. He lowered her hand and released her fingers. He patted the sword strapped to his waist. "Ghost Biter will take care of them."

Elizabeth looked at him with a bemused tilt of her head. "Your sword changes names as much as Grace changes her hair. I thought its name was Laird of Steel."

He nodded. "It is, it is." He proudly patted the well-worn brown leather handle of his weapon. "It goes by many names depending on its need. Today, it goes by Ghost Biter."

"Hmm." Elizabeth pursed her lips. "And you really think a blade made of steel will do any harm to ghosts?"

Duncan frowned. "You do Ghost Biter a great disservice by doubting its ability to adapt to my needs." He drew the sword from its scabbard, careful not to let the sharp edges of the blade get too near Elizabeth as he brought the weapon forth. A ray of the fading sun slid onto the sword's surface as Duncan turned the weapon, the smooth silver blade reflecting a flash of orange light towards the dark entrance of Castle LongShadow. "If a ghost has form, then it has substance. Ghost Biter has hacked through chains, cut stone, and severed a man's head from his body in one blow. It can easily slice a ghost to ribbons."

Elizabeth reached out and gingerly put a finger on the sword's flat surface. The blade felt cool under the warmth of her finger. "But can it cut through shadows?"

Duncan frowned down at her.

"A shadow has form," Elizabeth said. She removed her finger from the blade. "Can Ghost Biter cut through shadows?"

"Ghosts are not shadows," Duncan said.

"I think they are," she said. "I think they are made of shadows, but they are white instead of black."

Duncan sheathed his sword. He removed a length of wood from where it was lodged in his belt on his right side; the wood's top portion was wrapped by an oily swirl of cloth. He raised the unlit torch, gripping the torch tightly in his left hand. "Then this should destroy them just as easily as it eats shadows."

Elizabeth was quiet.

"Between fire and steel, they stand no chance of harming us," Duncan said with full confidence.

Elizabeth said nothing.

Duncan looked at her for a long moment. "You're still afraid." He waited for a reaction, but she did not give him one. He lowered the torch to his side. "You're afraid of these... white shadows, as you call them."

She gave him a slight nod; it was just the barest of movements, but he saw it. "Grace won't even cross the field anymore to get home from the market," she said. "She walks all the way around the field. She says she's even too afraid to just look at the castle, let alone come within a hundred yards of it."

Duncan gave her another soft laugh. "You really need to stop listening to that old woman. She'll make you afraid of your own shadow soon enough."

Elizabeth tried to force a smile to her lips, but it just wouldn't come forth. She hesitantly looked towards the castle. The drawbridge leading in to Castle LongShadow was down, the portcullis raised, the barbican window openings empty of any sentries. The entrance was darkly shadowed by a thick wall of blackness. The moat surrounding the abandoned castle had long ago dried out so it was now just a deep dusty ring that encircled the castle for three-quarters of its circumference. The rear walls of the castle jutted up against the back of Cragmirn mountain, so no moat was needed to protect the back of the castle from any threatening invaders. She felt a tension tightening the muscles in her shoulders. This place had been abandoned for a reason.

She looked up at Duncan, forcing her thoughts away from the foreboding castle. He was so very handsome, his black hair hanging down to his shoulders, his chin strong, his grey eyes always bright and alert. He hadn't attempted to bed her yet, but she knew he wanted to. She could sometimes see the tightening of his breeches when she leaned in close to him, so she knew she had an effect on him. Especially when she purposefully rubbed her breasts against his arm. Then the dark stone walls of the castle just visible over Duncan's shoulders brought her thoughts back into unpleasant territory. "You don't have to do this, Duncan," she said, putting just a hint of a pleading tone into her voice.

Duncan turned and followed her gaze to the castle, staring at the dark stones for a moment. He turned away from the castle and looked down at her; she was a good half a foot shorter than he was, if not a bit more. Elizabeth hadn't attempted to seduce him, yet, but he knew she wanted to. He could see the pointed tips of her excited nipples through the fabric of her dress, so he knew he was affecting her. Especially when he purposefully rubbed his muscular chest against her arm. "I want to," he said.

"You don't need to prove yourself to those buffoons," she said.

Duncan almost seemed insulted by the insinuation and she immediately regretted her choice of words. Borodin had beaten Duncan in a joust a week ago and the man had thoroughly berated Duncan for his sloppy skills with the lance. She knew Duncan was looking for any way to reclaim his stature in her eyes, so she understood his need to prove himself. She just wished it hadn't taken the form of entering Castle LongShadow.

"Borodin got in a lucky strike. My horse faltered at the last moment," Duncan said. But they both knew that was a feeble excuse. No jouster would ever blame his horse in front of another man. "This isn't about that," Duncan continued, clearly wanting to move the conversation away from his failure at the tournament. He looked back up at the castle. "I'm going to find that treasure."

Elizabeth froze for a long moment. "You can't be serious. Not only do you want to go into this Godforsaken castle, but you want to go down into the burial crypts?"

Duncan stood resolute. "Yes."

"So you don't believe in the ghosts but you believe in the fairy tale of hidden treasure?"

Duncan turned to look at her, cocking his head. "Yes." That's all he said before turning away from her.

They both stood quietly side by side for a moment. The sun continued to lower and would soon be blocked by the mountain that flanked the castle. Duncan held out the tip of the torch towards Elizabeth. "Strike your flints. It's time to storm the castle."

Castle LongShadow was aptly named because no matter where you stood in the outer courtyard, you were almost always bathed in shadows thrown off by the towering turrets or the tall keep at the northern end of the inner courtyard.

The very air itself seemed to take on a different quality once they stepped beyond the entrance and moved into the outer courtyard. It became thicker, heavier somehow. Not wet with moisture, just heavier. It was noticeably harder to breathe. There were few patches of pure sunlight visible, and when the light did appear amidst the dark black shadows, the slanted beams of sunlight looked as if they were columns made of a physical substance; even entering and exiting one of these rare rays of light seemed to require just a bit of extra force, as if one were pushing through a thin curtain.

Duncan gripped the burning torch in his left hand, raising it up above his shoulder to throw the fire's light farther before them as they moved through the outer courtyard. Castles often had stray dogs, or cats, or other animals roaming about, but Castle

LongShadow appeared devoid of any life at all. There weren't even any birds roosting up high in the numerous crevices or perching along the parapets or the crenellations on the castle walls, nor did there appear to be any rats scurrying about. There seemed to be no life at all within the stone walls.

"Look," Elizabeth said. She whispered the word, but there was still a sense of urgency in her voice. And fear.

Duncan quickly looked to her and saw what she was pointing at. She was pointing at the ground behind him. At his shadow. He swiveled his head, craning it to look back down at his shadow. His shadow was darker than the surrounding shadows, somehow blacker and thicker. He looked at her shadow and saw the same effect. Her shadow was just as black as his, just as thick. He glanced up at the torch he clutched in his left hand. "It's just the torch," he said, but his hesitant tone wasn't very convincing. "It's making our shadows look like that."

Elizabeth nodded mutely. She turned away from their shadows, not wanting to look at them anymore.

They continued moving through the outer courtyard, past the empty pens where the pigs were once kept, past the horse stalls, past the alewives' station where the women made mead for the castle's occupants. There was still no sound of any kind of life at all. Not even a scurrying mouse fleeing their approach.

A broad patch of dirt was visible on their right, the entire area blanketed by shadow, the remnants of what had once been a flourishing garden. Duncan raised the torch a bit higher, bringing more of the former garden into view. Two plants appeared to be still alive, their dark stalks still erect; each plant had several black flowers growing on them, their petals streaked with white veins. Elizabeth clutched protectively at Duncan's arm. "Night blossoms," she whispered. "Grace told me about those. They're very powerful."

"Powerful?"

"Yes. They can make strong magic."

"Magic?" Duncan scoffed. "So Grace filled your head with tales of magic, too?"

Elizabeth bowed her head. "Sometimes," she said softly.

Duncan glanced back at the garden area. He stared at the dark plants, at their black flowers, at the white veins running through them. "How are they still growing?"

"They don't need the sun like other flowers," Elizabeth said. "They thrive in the night. The dark and the moon's light feeds them."

"They are quite beautiful," Duncan said.

Elizabeth was slightly taken aback. She had never heard Duncan speak of anything in such a fashion before. She had deemed such words to be too soft for a man of his physical prowess. He mostly spoke of men things, and tournaments and battles and training and hunting. He rarely, if ever, spoke of anything having an aesthetic quality.

He took a few sudden steps forward, almost making Elizabeth stumble before she released her grip on his arm. He moved into the garden and plucked a black flower from the plant before she even realized what he was doing. She was too startled by his action to even shout a disapproving cry of alarm. He quickly returned to her side and raised up the black flower before her. "Beauty deserves beauty," he said.

She had no words for him at that moment. Had he just called her beautiful? She felt a fluttering in her chest. And a hot heat spreading down her body. She made no move to stop him as he tucked the black flower behind her left ear, gently moving some of her blonde hair aside to find her ear.

The flower held its place and Duncan took a step back, admiring his work. And her. She suddenly seemed distraught and he raised the torch to get a better look at her face. It was impossible not to look at her breasts as the light moved over them; her nipples strained against the fabric of her dress, the dark tips clearly visible behind the pale yellow fabric. The light from the torch moved up to her face and he saw a flush filling her cheeks. "Are you feeling well?" he asked.

She slowly looked up at him, her blue orbs shimmering beneath her lidded eyes. "You know what I'm feeling," she said, her voice a husky whisper. "And from the look of the dagger that wants to get out of your breeches, you just might feel the same way."

Duncan took a step closer to her. "You are a brazen hussy, aren't you?" His voice was low, barely above a whisper. He took in her creamy skin, her delicately-boned cheeks, her pert nose, her sensuous mouth.

"Only for you," she whispered back.

He leaned in closer to her. But she put a hand on his chest, stopping him. The muscles in his broad chest were as solid as rock. "Not here," she whispered. "After you find the treasure."

"To hell with the treasure," he growled. He put his

hand behind her head and pulled her to him, planting his lips squarely on hers, kissing her with an obvious growing passion.

Elizabeth broke the kiss after a long moment of enjoying the feel of his lips on hers, turning her head aside but staying close to him. She put her mouth near his ear. "I'm yours for the taking, Duncan, but please, not here."

Duncan pulled back from her, a fiery passion ablaze in his grey eyes, but then he nodded in acquiescence to her plea and took a step back from her. "After we find the treasure," he said.

She nodded. "Then you can plunder me to your heart's content."

Duncan growled low. "You'd best stop talking to me like that, or something other than my heart will be plundering you here and now."

Elizabeth gave him a sly smile, but remained silent. She turned from him and headed towards the stone archway that led into the inner courtyard.

Their dark shadows followed them wherever they went.

⊰✦⊱

"Come on," Duncan said, motioning to their right as they moved through the inner courtyard. "I think the stairs are this way. They should take us under the keep to the crypt."

Elizabeth made no reply, so he turned back to look at her. She walked slowly, with great trepidation, her gaze darting this way and that, her body slightly hunched over as if she were trying to make herself smaller, make her presence less obvious. It hadn't taken long for her fear to overpower her arousal. Castle LongShadow just had a feeling about it, a powerful presence to it that was unnerving. The very air seemed to be haunted with the voices of its former occupants. She hadn't said anything to Duncan, lest he fear she was going mad with fright, but she would have sworn to a magistrate, even upon the threat of a lashing for frightening the others in their village, that she heard voices whispering from the deepest shadows. She couldn't make out the exact words, but the sounds did seem to be voices. She couldn't tell if they were warning her, laughing at her, or enticing her to keep going.

"Are you afraid of something?" he asked.

The accusing question seemed to jar her out of her fear. She immediately stood taller, straightening her shoulders. "I am not."

Duncan smiled. "Good, because there's the stairs." He motioned towards an open doorway, raising the torch and tilting it forward to indicate their destination.

They moved slowly towards the doorway.

"Does make you wonder why the door that leads down to the crypt is open, though," he said as they neared it. "Was someone entering, or was some... thing leaving?"

Elizabeth smacked Duncan on the shoulder. "Now you are just trying to frighten me on purpose."

He pulled her close with his right arm, snaking it around her waist to draw her to him. He stared adoringly at her face for a moment, raising the torch to get a better look at her. The torchlight reflected off the black flower that was tucked behind her ear, making it glisten. Had he looked a little closer, he would've seen the white veins on the flower pulsing ever so softly, but he didn't see it; Elizabeth's beauty entranced him far more. He kissed Elizabeth on the lips, giving her a sweet gentle kiss.

They moved through the open doorway and began the descent down the stone stairs that led to the burial crypt.

Had they glanced behind themselves, they would've seen a white outline now framing their deeply black shadows. It was a thin outline, barely perceptible, but it was definitely visible.

◆─━━◉━━─◆

The first statue they came across in the crypt was the stone semblance of a young boy. He could not have been more than eight years old, they surmised. The statue was carved from some white stone, situated upon a marble pedestal.

"He was just a boy," Elizabeth said. "That's so sad."

"Hmm," Duncan said.

Elizabeth glanced over to him, but he was not looking at her. He was staring curiously at the statue, then at the area around the pedestal, then back up to the stone carving of the boy. "What is it?" she asked.

Duncan pointed at the densely packed dirt that served as the crypt's floor. "It doesn't cast a shadow." He raised and lowered the torch. "The statue doesn't cast a shadow."

Elizabeth frowned at his statement, but as she glanced about the statue she realized that Duncan was indeed speaking the truth. The statue of the boy cast no shadow. The pedestal that served as the statue's base did cast a shadow, but the statue itself did not.

"How can that be?" Duncan wondered aloud.

Elizabeth stared at the statue. The stone did seem abnormally white, abnormally bright for being in such a dark and murky place. The firelight from the torch illuminated the area around them, but not enough to make the statue appear to be so vibrantly lit up. "It's as if the statue is absorbing the light. It's not letting any shadows form."

Duncan frowned as he looked over to her. "The statue is not letting any shadows form? Is that something else Grace told you about this place?"

Elizabeth shook her head. "No, that's one I just thought of for myself."

And then suddenly Elizabeth's blue eyes grew wide with fear, wider than Duncan had ever seen them go before. "What?" he immediately asked her, seeing the distress clearly carved into her face.

She didn't speak at first. She only pointed behind Duncan, pointing down towards the ground behind him.

He quickly glanced down at the ground, looking down over his shoulder at where she was pointing, and he too felt his own eyes widening at the sight. He quickly swiveled his gaze back towards Elizabeth, urgently needing to know if he would see the same thing behind her.

He did.

It was their shadows. They each had the same affliction affecting them. He didn't know why the word affliction came to his mind, but that's what he thought when he saw them. Each of their shadows had a thick white irregular border, the white border outlining the shapes of their bodies, the positions of their arms and legs. The outer edge of the border was perfectly smooth, exactly matching up to the contours of their bodies with only a few gaps in the outline that for some reason remained deeply black, while the inside edge of the border was irregular with some areas of whiteness penetrating deeper into their shadows than other areas. It was if the whiteness was spreading inside their shadows, seeping deeper and deeper towards the middle of their bodies' shadows.

"What is that?" Elizabeth asked, breaking the silence with her fear-filled question.

Duncan shook his head, remaining mute.

She nervously glanced behind her, taking in her own shadow. The whiteness seemed to be moving as she watched it, slowly moving deeper and deeper towards the middle of her shadow. She looked up towards the shadowy area of her head and saw that the whiteness was spreading inwards there as well, moving towards the center of her head. She put her hand to her head and her shadowy shape did the same. "I feel faint," she said.

Duncan nodded. He was beginning to feel light-headed as well, as if he had drunk far too many tankards of strong ale. A sharp feeling of dread surged through him. They shouldn't be down here, he thought. No one living should ever enter these crypts. "No treasure is worth this."

A resounding boom shook the room, sending whirling clouds of dust down from the ceiling high above. The loud sound had come from the stairwell.

"The door!" Duncan shouted. He raced towards the stairs and Elizabeth followed, hot on his heels.

Duncan pounded on the heavy wood of the door, pushed at it, kicked at it, charged at it with a shoulder charge, but the door did not budge. Elizabeth gripped the torch, watching with baited breath as Duncan tried futilely to free them from this horrid tomb. Elizabeth joined him, shoving at the door, pounding on it. But the door remained firmly closed despite all their joint efforts to budge it.

Exhausted from the exertion, Duncan leaned his back against the door and slowly slid down its surface, resting on the dusty stone floor of the short landing that extended out half a dozen feet to the stone stairs that led down into the crypt.

Elizabeth joined him, sitting next to him. Her face was flush with sweat from the exertion of trying to open the door. Several strands of her blonde hair were stuck to her cheeks. "How about renaming your sword Wood Door Eater?" Elizabeth said.

Duncan smiled a bemused smile. "It'll take weeks to hack through that door."

"What else do we have do to?" Elizabeth asked.

"Starve to death," Duncan said. "We have enough food for a day at most. Water for maybe two if we ration."

Elizabeth remained quiet. The torch she still held in her left hand flickered and crackled.

They sat in silence for a long moment.

"My left hand is starting to feel numb," Duncan said.

His statement did not surprise her. "Both of my legs are starting to feel numb," Elizabeth said.

"What's happening, Duncan?"

"I don't know," he said. "My right hand feels perfectly fine, but the fingers in my left hand are tingling like a million ants are crawling all over them."

"The right side of my face feels... strange," Elizabeth said. "It feels like a thousand needles are using it as a pin cushion." She reached up towards the right side of her face, the side opposite the night blossom flower secured behind her left ear, but didn't touch herself. "No, not really like that. It doesn't hurt. It just feels... strange."

Duncan shot up to his feet, grabbing the torch from Elizabeth's hand.

"What? What is it?"

"I just remembered my uncle talking about a castle they once took after a siege," he said. "They also had a crypt under their keep, but their crypt also had a secret exit the lords could use to escape if the crypt was breached. Maybe this one has one, too." He extended a hand down to Elizabeth, offering to help her get to her feet, but when Elizabeth grabbed his left hand he barely had the strength to help her up. The numbness in his left hand was spreading to his arm.

Elizabeth noticed the discomfort, and alarm, in his expression. "Your arm?"

Duncan nodded.

Elizabeth looked down, seeing that the whiteness had spread deeper into Duncan's shadow. The shadow of his left hand was almost entirely white now, and a large portion of the shadow of his left arm was white as well. She glanced over at his right arm, but the whiteness was not as widespread. In fact, the entirety of the shadow on his right hand was devoid of any of the white blight. She cast a fearful glance at her own shadow and was alarmed to see that the whiteness was nearly covering the entirety of her legs' shadows. She felt her knees buckling, but forced herself to stay upright, gritting her teeth, willing herself to be strong.

Duncan thrust the torch before them, indicating to go back down the stairs and into the crypt. "Let's go," he said.

If there was a secret exit, it was hidden so well that they couldn't find it. They searched behind statues, in every alcove they came across. Duncan, despite the growing numbness in his left hand and arm and now parts of his legs, pounded the handle of his sword against any stone that looked discolored compared to other stones near it, looking for any loose rocks that might indicate a hidden passage, or concealed lever.

Elizabeth felt a numbing cold penetrating her right cheek and the right side of her head that left her ear feeling as if she were pressing it into a snowbank. She reached up and tentatively touched her right ear, fearing that if she put too much pressure on it the brittle flesh would shatter into a thousand pieces. She felt the cold curl of her earlobe, but then pulled her hand away, afraid to test fate any further. Her fingers were starting to become increasingly more numb as well.

She reached up to touch her left ear and was surprised to find it feeling normal. It did not feel cold or brittle. It felt warm, still felt like normal flesh. And then her fingers brushed up against the night blossom flower that was still pinned behind her ear. A sudden warmth flooded into her fingers, as if the mere touch of the night blossom infused her hand with warmth. Something compelled her to look down at her shadow and she saw the whiteness lessening in her left hand, the white blight actually decreasing instead of spreading deeper into her shadow. "Duncan! The flower. The night blossom!"

Duncan turned curious eyes to her, turning to look at her with what seemed like agonizing slowness to Elizabeth. He was sitting on the hard earthen floor, his back up against the wall.

"The night blossom will protect us!" she exclaimed. She plucked the flower from behind her ear and held it in her hand.

His lips tried to turn up into a smile, but he didn't seem to have the energy to even manage that. He wasn't holding the torch anymore. He had stuck it into a sconce on the wall a few feet away before sitting down. The light flickered and the wood crackled as the torch continued to burn.

Elizabeth looked down at Duncan's shadow and she could see that it was now nearly entirely white. The only part of his shadow that wasn't white was his right fingers. The fingers he had used to pluck the night blossom flower, the fingers he had used to tuck the flower behind her left ear.

Suddenly, a bright smile came onto Duncan's face. But it wasn't a smile of joy; it was an odd smile that seemed to almost glimmer with a madness. "I see them, Elizabeth," he said. He managed to raise his weakening left arm, and pointed a shaking index finger at the air behind her. "They're all around us."

Elizabeth glanced over her shoulder, following his

pointing finger. That's when she saw them, too.

Ghosts. Dozens of them. Some of them appeared to be walking upon the dirt floor, while others seemed to be floating inches above the surface. One female ghost was hovering in the air several feet of the ground. They all had a whiteness to them, a very familiar whiteness. All of the ghosts had the same white sheen to them as the whiteness that was filling Elizabeth's and Duncan's shadows.

A cold stark realization flooded into Elizabeth. Their shadows. The creeping white. They were looking at the approach of their own deaths. They were slowly dying, their shadows starting to take on the shapes of the ghosts they were about to become. But how? Why were they dying? Had the night blossom poisoned them both? She mentally shook her head. No. The flower was staving off death. Was it the castle? Was it the very air itself within the castle's confines? Was the castle itself poisonous? She didn't know what other explanation there could be. They had eaten no strange food, had drank no strange water. They had both been healthy, vibrant, and strong before they entered the gloomy world of Castle LongShadow.

But yet, here they sat, both of them dying, both of their shadows slowly turning into the ghosts they would become if death did indeed force them to take their final breaths in this cursed crypt.

The glistening white-veined petals of the black flower in her hand re-captured her attention. It was their only hope. She rubbed the petals across Duncan's cheeks, across his lips, across his forehead, smearing the flower across his flesh. "Close your eyes," she told him and he obeyed. She rubbed the petals across both his eyelids, then she did the same to herself, smearing the soft black petals across her eyelids. "Do you still see them?" she asked, keeping her eyes closed as she asked Duncan the question, fearful of his answer.

"No," came his reply.

She opened her eyes to stare at him.

"No," he said again, with some energy coming back into his words. "I don't see them."

She glanced about herself, peering over her shoulder, and then breathed a heavy sigh of relief. They were gone. The ghosts were gone. She looked down to see the whiteness that had threatened to engulf Duncan's shadowy head was now nearly gone; the shadow of his head was once again nearly deeply black across its entire area. Only a thin area of white was visible on his shadow, the area on the top of his head. She wiped the petals across his head, weaving them through his hair, smearing the flower throughout his dark locks. She again glanced at his shadow, relieved to see that the white edge was now gone from the shadowed area at the top of his head as well. "Take off your shirt," she said.

He looked quizzically at her.

She motioned impatiently at his clothing. "Take off your shirt." She shook the petals of the night blossom flower at him. "I need to rub this on you." She pointed down towards his shadow. "The flower stops it."

While Duncan staggered to his feet and worked his shirt off, Elizabeth quickly rubbed the petals of the flower up and down her arms, switching hands to complete the process from one arm to the next. She glanced down at her shadow and saw the whiteness immediately begin to wither and fade from her shadowy arms. An excited flush spread across her cheeks. It was working!

Duncan tossed his shirt to the ground and moved away from the wall so Elizabeth could work her way around his entire body. She wiped and dabbed and smeared the flower all over his back and his chest. His strongly muscled chest. She lingered for a few long moments on his firm pectoral muscles before kneeling and moving down to the muscled ridges in his stomach. She kept her gaze purposefully away from the pulsing bulge that jutted out from the area of his loins. She finished wiping the petals across his hard stomach and sat back on her haunches. "My turn," she said and extended the flower up towards Duncan.

Duncan took the offered night blossom and watched as Elizabeth rose back up to her feet and began pulling her dress up off over her head. He saw the tops of her thighs, the soft blonde mound of her maidenhead, the smoothness of her stomach, the firm slopes of her breasts, and marveled at the glory of her body. She finished removing her dress and clutched the yellow fabric in her hand, looking expectantly at Duncan. The fabric dangled down from her hand, only concealing one of her breasts. "Well?" she asked, straightening her back which made her breasts jut forward towards Duncan. "What are you waiting for?"

Duncan said nothing. He moved before her and started at the tops of her shoulders, wiping the petals along the smooth curves of her body. He moved the soft flower petals over her neck, gently rubbing them into the soft spot of her throat.

She raised her head slightly, allowing him better access to the area beneath her chin.

He moved the petals lower, touching her chest above the slopes of her breasts. He kept his gaze on her face, keeping his eyes averted from the nakedness of her upper body. He moved his hand lower, rubbing the petals in gentle circles across her flesh. He reached the top edge of her exposed breast and moved downward, continuing to rub the petals against her warm skin.

"Don't miss any spots," she whispered to him, her voice husky.

He moved his hand lower, reaching the hardened peak of her nipple.

She inhaled sharply as the petals touched her nipple, but then forced herself to breathe normally, trying not to dwell on the delicious pleasure that coursed through her body at the touch of his hand on her breast.

He moved down her breast, away from the nipple, continuing to make slow circles with the petal, intent on covering every inch of her body in the safety of the aura of this magical plant.

"Don't forget the other one," she said with a breathy moan. She released her grip on the fabric, letting the dress fall to the ground.

Duncan's gaze traveled the length of her, moving down from her face, over her bare breasts, past her taut stomach, down to the blonde curls that protected the inner folds of her womanhood from his hungry gaze.

"Don't stop," she said, breathing out the words in a soft pant.

Duncan finished wiping the petals beneath the

slope of her right breast, then trailed the petals across the valley between her peaks, moving the feathery soft piece of flower over her left breast, again moving in slow, deliberate circles to cover every inch of her flesh. He reached the dark circle of her nipple and teased the petals across it, moving the petals round and round her erect nipple, then brushing them across the top of the hardened nub.

Elizabeth drew in another sharp breath, this breath a bit more intense than the last. Her entire body was starting to tingle from Duncan's touch, the dreaded tingle she had been feeling from the encroaching white blight now replaced by a delicious tingle of ecstasy. Perhaps it was the flower making her feel this way, she thought. But then quickly dismissed the notion. It was Duncan. His strong hand on her body, his handsome face so close to hers. She ached to feel his lips on hers but she knew now was not the time to give in to such a fanciful notion. Their very lives could be at stake if they didn't stop the whitening of their shadows, if they didn't stop what she was quite certain was the encroachment of death itself.

Duncan finished wiping the petals across her flat stomach, then took a step back from her. There was no possible way to hide the bulge in his breeches, so he didn't even bother to make the effort. He moved around her body, wiping the flower across her slender shoulders, moving down her back, careful to touch every inch of her skin with the soft petals.

And then her shadow on the ground caught his gaze, the light from the torch burning in the sconce on the wall casting it onto the earthen floor. The upper portion of her shadow was once again a deep black, but the areas around her upper thighs, around her knees, around her feet, were still showing a dreaded white.

"Take off your boots," he said, moving back in front of her.

She obliged, tossing her leather boots a few feet away from them.

He moved to his knees, quickly wiping the petals across her bare toes. He rubbed the petals across her ankles, then her calves, then her thighs, covering every inch of her flesh, moving his hand completely around her legs. He moved his hand up her inner thigh, caressing her flesh with the petals. She took a slightly wider stance, opening herself up to him, to his touch. He stopped just beneath the mound of her womanhood.

She nodded to him and rubbed her fingers through his hair. "Go on," she whispered. "Everywhere."

"Turn around," he said, his voice mirroring the whispery softness of hers.

She obeyed, turning her body around to present her backside to him. He wiped the petals across the back of her thighs, moving up to her rounded buttocks. He paused at the sight of the perfectly rounded shapes of her buttocks, but only for a moment, before caressing each cheek with light strokes of the night blossom. He paused as his fingers neared the tight space between her butt cheeks. She reached behind herself and gripped a butt cheek in each hand, slowly spreading herself to give him access. He wiped the petals across the inside of her buttocks, covering her in the protective coating the flower endowed them with. She released her grip on her butt cheeks and slowly turned around to face him again.

He started to move the petals towards her womanhood, but she put her hand on his, stopping him. "I'd better finish you first," she said, "because if you touch me there right now, I'm going to explode."

"And you don't think I'm going to explode if you do this..." He held up the flower to her, then indicated his crotch. "... to that?"

She was quiet for a moment, then she reached out and took the flower from his fingers. "At least let me do everywhere else first," she said. "Take off... take off your pants."

He only hesitated a moment before obliging her. He doffed his boots, then untied his belt and slid his pants off, doing a bit of an awkward dance as he moved the clothing over the bulge of his erection.

"Oh, my," Elizabeth said at the full sight of his nakedness, especially at the full sight of his arousal.

"It's all your fault," Duncan said, looking a bit flush, almost sheepish.

"There's no hiding my effect on you, is there?"

"No, there is not."

She reached a hand towards his firm erection, but then immediately stopped as she realized she was reaching for him with the hand that was not holding the night blossom flower.

His erection seemed to pulse, almost as if it were trying to move closer to her hand as she reached towards him. "You'd better do my legs first," Duncan said.

She nodded, swallowing hard.

He turned around, presenting his backside to her.

Elizabeth kneeled. She moved her hand up and down his legs, smearing the petals all across his skin, moving the flower through the hairs that covered his legs. She reached his taut buttocks and wiped the petals around the curves of his butt cheeks, then finished off the inner portion, not bothering to wait for him to spread them for her. He nearly leapt away in startled surprise, but managed to remain where he was standing. She finished and moved back away from him, giving him room to turn and face her.

His manhood was still long and thick and hard. Perhaps even longer and thicker than when she had first seen it.

She reached out towards his erection, moving the petals to within a hair's breadth of his erection.

"By all that's holy," he whispered, "just go very slowly."

She started at the loose sac beneath his erection, gently wiping the petals beneath his scrotum.

He hissed in a sharp breath and his erection pulsed.

Elizabeth glanced at his manhood. She thought it now definitely looked longer and thicker. She moved up the bottom portion of his shaft, following the line of a thick vein that protruded from the side of his erection, wiping the petals across his flesh.

He hissed a sharp breath again, but said nothing.

Elizabeth grinned up at him. She moved the petals completely around his manhood, swirling the soft flower across the width of his hard shaft. She neared the bulbous head of his erection and started to gently wipe the petals across its surface. His hardness pulsed and throbbed, the shaft twitching under her touch.

He took in another sharp breath. "God's blood, woman, you will drive me mad!" He reached down and grabbed her hand, stopping her motion. "I think perhaps I should finish the rest."

The crestfallen look on her face made him immediately reconsider. She stared at his manhood, not even trying to be subtle about her gaze. After a moment, she looked away. She stared at the night blossom flower, at the stems, the leaves. A sudden crazy idea sprang forth in her mind and she felt a flood of wetness in her loins as the idea fueled the lust that was already running rampant in her thoughts. She fumbled with the leaves, tying them together via their stems, creating a small dome-like object.

He just stared at her curiously.

Then she slid the dome of petals over Duncan's manhood, wrapping some stems around his shaft, tying the covering in place over the tip of his hardness.

He said nothing, but she could see his jaw tightening as he fought back a moan of torturous pleasure.

She took his hand and led him over to where her dress was laying on the ground. She released his hand and lowered herself to the ground onto her back. She lifted her legs up, then slowly spread them open, inviting him forward.

Duncan just stared at her for a long moment, taking in the glorious sight of her radiant face, the delicious curves of her body, the glistening sheen of her desire visible just behind the blonde curls of her womanhood. He knelt before her.

"Don't miss any spots," Elizabeth whispered to him. She spread her legs a little wider.

Duncan reached down and gripped the bottom portion of his hard shaft, guiding his petal-covered manhood towards her folds. He touched his manhood to her dark curls and slowly wiped the petals across her mound. He moved his hardness lower, touching the top of her wetness, touching the hardened nub of her flower with the flower covering him. She erupted into a panting explosion of gasps and heated breaths. She rose up and grabbed his buttocks, pulling him urgently, desperately forward. "Put it in me, Duncan. Put all of it inside me."

Duncan needed no more encouragement. He released his hand from his shaft and plunged into the heated wetness of her core, driving himself deeper and deeper inside her tightness.

Elizabeth clutched at his back, pulling him in, breathing hotly, moaning with delirious ecstasy.

They finished wiping the petals across the soles of their feet. After their lovemaking, they realized that was the only part of their body that hadn't been protected by the power of the night blossom's petals. They donned their clothes and put their boots back on.

Duncan stood motionless for a moment, staring at the closed door. The door still would not budge. There was no point in crying for help. No one, except fools like themselves, even ventured close to the castle, let alone penetrated its walls.

"There must be another way out," Elizabeth said as she stepped up beside him. "Let's keep searching."

Duncan held up his hand, quieting her. He moved closer to the door, turning his head to the side, listening intently at something.

Elizabeth again joined him, moving up to his side.

She remained quiet, listening, turning her head towards the door just as Duncan had done.

"There's someone out there," Duncan whispered to her.

A loud, furious scratching sound came from the other side of the heavy oak door.

Elizabeth opened her mouth to shout at their would-be-rescuers, but Duncan clamped his hand over her mouth before the words could come out. She shifted her gaze to him. He shook his head at her. He grabbed her hand with his other hand, guiding her away from the door, moving back down the stone stairs deeper into the crypt before releasing his hand from her mouth. She looked up at him expectantly.

"I don't think it's people," he whispered to her.

She glanced back up at the door, then back to Duncan, her eyes widening in alarm. "A Night Bear?"

He nodded. "It might be more than one."

She thought of the stories she had heard as a child. Bears with fur as black as the night. Bears with claws sharper than any blade a man could make. Bears with jaws that could bite a man's thigh in half with a single bite. They fed on humans. Nothing else satisfied their hunger. They would eat other animals only when faced with starvation, but this only seemed to make them angrier; there was nothing more dangerous than a Night Bear who hadn't fed on a human for a fortnight. They usually traveled alone and hunted alone, but a couple in the throes of mating were known to hunt together while they worked to conceive a Night Bear cub.

"Do you think they can rip through that door?" she asked.

Duncan nodded. "Eventually." He put his hand to

his sword handle. "Their claws are sharper than Ghost Biter."

Elizabeth glanced at the sword strapped to Duncan's waist. "Maybe it's time for another name change. How about Bear Biter?"

Duncan gave her an exasperated look. "Bear Biter? Really?" He was quiet for a moment. "I'm thinking more like Night Bear Annihilator."

Elizabeth looked at him, then nodded. "Okay, yes, that's better."

Duncan unsheathed his sword and held it up before him. "I dub thee Night Bear Annihilator." He sheathed his blade and looked to Elizabeth. "There. It is done."

More clawing sounds could be heard coming from up the stairs, their sounds strong enough to even create a small echo within the stone-walled crypt.

"They seem pretty eager to get in here," Elizabeth said.

Duncan nodded. "They smell us."

Both of them stood quietly for a moment, listening to the loud scratching, hearing the occasional grumbling snort of one of the Night Bears coming from outside the crypt's doors.

"We should keep looking for another exit," Duncan said.

Elizabeth nodded.

❈

There was no other exit. They opened stone caskets looking for secret levers, moved statues looking for exit tunnels, pounded on the stone walls looking for hidden passageways. Nothing.

Thin slivers of moonlight were now visible coming through the thin gouges the Night Bears' claws had managed to dig through the crypt door. The bears were not going to give up. They were determined to break through and feast. If anything, they seemed to have doubled their efforts. The narrow slits in the door were letting out even more of their human scent.

"Duncan!" Elizabeth exclaimed, her voice clearly expressing alarm.

He turned to look at her, seeing the distraught look on her features. "What?"

She pointed to his shadow on the ground behind him. "The white. It's coming back."

He jerked his head to the side, glancing over his shoulder, looking down at his shadow. Elizabeth was right. The white edges were re-forming around his shadow, the white blight starting to creep inwards. Clearly, the power of the night blossom's petals was not meant to last forever. It had only granted them a temporary reprieve from whatever was slowly killing them within the confines of Castle LongShadow. He looked back to her.

Elizabeth glanced at her shadow, seeing that the shadow of her left hand was completely white now, the edge of the whiteness creeping past her wrist. She glanced down at her left hand and slowly moved her fingers. "My hand feels like it's getting stung by a thousand bees." She flexed her fingers, curling them into a fist, then uncurling them. She looked up at Duncan with fear-filled eyes. "Duncan." It was a cry for help, a desperate plea for protection with just the utterance of his name.

Duncan quickly scanned their surroundings,

scouring the area for the night blossom. He saw the last shredded remnants of the petals resting on the top of a nearby stone casket. He moved to the casket and grabbed the petals, quickly returning to Elizabeth's side. He grabbed her left hand and vigorously rubbed the petals across her skin. He shifted his gaze to her shadow, but did not see any of the whiteness recede like it had previously. He rubbed the petals harder against her skin, shredding the flower with his rough movements. He again glanced at her shadow, and again saw no reduction in the spreading of the white blight. "It's not working," he said. "Elizabeth." It was a cry of despair, a plea for enlightenment with just the utterance of her name.

A mad tingling sensation in his right foot made Duncan glance down at his boot. The shadow area of his foot was now completely white, as white as the shadow of Elizabeth's left hand. The white blight was returning, but now it seemed stronger than before, moving faster, penetrating their shadows with greater force and speed.

It was then that the ghosts returned. At least for Duncan they did. One of the ghosts rose up out of the stone casket upon which the petals had been sitting. The ghost had the semblance of an old man, his face grizzly with a thick beard. Only the upper portion of the ghost's body had a human shape; everything below his waist seem to be made of whispery strips of undulating vapor, the strips looking like the tentacles of a great ocean beast Duncan had once seen on his voyages as a boy aboard his uncle's ship. The ghost hovered above the stone casket, staring at the growling and scratching sounds coming from the crypt's door, then the mannish shape turned to look at Duncan. Its eye sockets were hollow, darkly and deeply black. "You are not of this place," the ghost said. Its voice was gritty, the words coming out with a guttural intonation. "You have disturbed my slumber."

Duncan stared at the ghost. He shot a quick glance at Elizabeth, but she was not looking in his direction; she was staring at her left hand, clenching and unclenching it furiously. He returned his attention to the ghost floating in the air just a few feet away. "We didn't — we're trapped in here. Can you help us escape?"

The ghost grabbed at its stomach and threw back its head, opening its mouth wide. It was an odd sight because Duncan expected the sound of guffawing laughter to accompany such a gesture, but no such sound issued forth from the ghost. The ghost straightened and trained its deeply dark eye sockets back onto Duncan. "There is no escape from Castle LongShadow once the creeping death is upon you. And the creeping death *is* upon you. You would not be able to see me if that weren't true."

"But the night blossom," Duncan protested. "The petals, they stopped this... creeping death as you call it."

Elizabeth was suddenly at Duncan's side, grabbing his arm. She could clearly see the ghost now too, as her gaze was focused directly upon it. "Yes," she concurred. "The petals, they were protecting us but now they are not.

The ghost nodded. "Yes, the night blossoms hold strong magic. But nothing can hold back the creeping death for long. Every breath you take spreads the dark essence of Castle LongShadow deeper throughout your mortal flesh. Every moment you stand within its walls, the deeper it sinks into your body."

"Help us escape," Elizabeth said. "Help us get out of this crypt."

The ghost shrugged. "It matters not if you escape the crypt. Castle LongShadow is already inside you. It is only a matter of time before you join the rest of us. The petals of the night blossom only delay the inevitable." The ghost paused. "But be warned, if you suffer an untimely physical death before your shadow turns ghostly white then your soul will be destroyed. You will be ripped asunder, torn between the two worlds, your soul shredded."

Duncan and Elizabeth were silent.

But the Night Bears savagely attacking the splintering door to the crypt were not. One of the ragged gashes their claws had ripped into the door was now large enough for the bears to peer through. Duncan turned and looked up the stairs to see a large eye staring balefully at them through the hole in the wood, its dark eye flickering in the torchlight with an ominous gleam. Then he could see the end of a large snout sniffing obscenely through the crack, the nostrils of the beast flaring. The Night Bear growled and resumed its attack on the door, cracking its paws against the wood, raking its claws across its surface, shredding more and more clumps of wood with each strike.

Duncan and Elizabeth moved up the steps, standing to the side of the door, watching clumps of wood fall to the flat section of stone they stood upon. Duncan drew his blade, gripping it with both hands. Elizabeth stood behind him, her hands on his back.

Then, a paw of one of the Night Bears broke through the door, its razor-sharp claws very prominent, very visible.

Duncan lashed out with his blade, stepping forward, striking down hard, slashing the blade down with all the strength he could muster, cutting deep into the Night Bear's paw, slicing through thick matted fur, carving a cleft past its hide into its flesh, making a deep gash between two of the Night Bear's claws.

Blood splattered up and outwards from the beast's wound, hitting Elizabeth on the right arm, making her cry out with a soft exclamation of surprise. Elizabeth reacted instinctively, wiping at the hot blood that struck her flesh with her left hand, smearing the redness across her arm and coating her left hand with Night Bear blood as she worked to get the blood off of her as best she could.

The Night Bear roared in pain, withdrawing its wounded paw, pulling it back out of sight behind the door.

Duncan kept both hands on his sword, gripping it tightly, the blade raised. Blood dripped off its sharp edges, hitting the stone landing with very faint plops.

Elizabeth continued wiping at the blood on her arm, but the Night Bear's blood was thick and sticky, the red residue difficult to just easily wipe away. She suddenly stopped what she was doing and stared at her left hand. Her fingers were nearly fully coated in the bear's blood. She curled and uncurled her fingers, then curled and uncurled them again. "My fingers," she said, excitement growing in her voice. "I can feel my fingers again." She quickly glanced down at her shadow and saw that the white blight was now gone from the shadow of her hand; the shadow of her hand was once again a deep glorious black. "My shadow. Look at my shadow."

Duncan turned to her, looking down at her shadow. The creeping whiteness was indeed gone from her hand. He looked up at Elizabeth, feeling a similar stirring of excitement racing through him. "Night Bear's blood." Legends said they were creatures spawned of dark magic centuries ago, and those legends seemed to be proving out true. The Night Bear's blood did hold magical powers, just as the night blossoms did. He looked down at the floor of the landing, eyeing the pools of dark red blood that dotted the stone. He kept one hand gripping the handle of his weapon, then dipped his knees to put the fingers of his free hand into the Night Bear's blood. He rubbed the blood along his sword arm, doing his best to coat as much of his arm as he could with what little blood he had on his fingers. He bent back down to get more blood and continued to wipe the redness along his arm.

Elizabeth kept her gaze riveted on the shadowy portion of his arm. The whiteness that had been visible quickly receded, returning the shadow of Duncan's arm to a deep black. "It's working. The Night Bear's blood is stopping it."

Duncan looked down the stairs back into the crypt, his gaze seeking out the ghost.

The ghost still hovered above the stone casket, watching them curiously. "You only delay the inevitable," the ghost said. "Join us and rest. It's so peaceful here. Join us."

Duncan scooped up some more blood on his fingers, then wiped the beast's blood across his closed eyelids. He opened his eyes and breathed a sigh of relief.

The ghost was gone from his sight.

Elizabeth bent down near the blood on the ground, wetting her fingers with the red fluid. She wiped the Night Bear's blood across her eyelids and shared in Duncan's relief. The ghost was now gone from her vision as well when she opened her eyes

But his eerie hollow voice could still be heard, muttering his offer over and over. "Join us and rest. Join us."

Elizabeth quickly wiped more blood across her ears and the ghost's voice faded away into nothingness. She turned to Duncan and wiped the remaining blood on her fingers across both his ears, giving him the gift of extinguishing the ghost's voice.

Duncan wiped more blood into his palm, then wiped it along Elizabeth's left shoulder, moving down her left arm, covering her flesh in the Night Bear's blood. The blood had a viscous nature to it, a stickiness that clung to their skin. He looked at Elizabeth's shadow; the whiteness had receded from the shadow of her arm. He moved back to the pool of blood to get some more, but then stopped and stared with a growing apprehension at the ground. The blood was gone; they had used it all but there was nowhere near enough to cover their entire bodies. He looked over at Elizabeth. "We need more blood."

The growling snorts of the Night Bears burst through the crack in the door, and a heavy paw slammed against the wood, clear signals that the beasts had no intention of giving up their prey. But they were going to be more cautious because they did not thrust a wild paw through the crack, instead slamming heavily against the wooden door near the crack, seemingly in a calculated plan to make the crack wider and wider with each blow.

Duncan stared at the door for a moment, listening to the thudding attacks of the beasts. He turned again to look at Elizabeth, a grim expression on his face, the light from the crackling torch dancing along his face, his eyes rimmed with the blood of the Night Bear. "We need to kill them. We need to kill the Night Bears and take their blood."

Elizabeth stared back at him in horror, but then quickly accepted the fact that Duncan spoke the truth. Their very survival depended on it.

He glanced down at her shadow, seeing the white blight spreading across her legs, beginning to climb up her waist. "And we need to do it now."

Elizabeth stood at the side of the door, her back against the stone wall of the crypt. She clutched the dagger Duncan had given her. It was the only other weapon he had besides his sword. He didn't expect her to be able to do much damage to the Night Bears with it, but he just couldn't leave her completely unarmed.

Duncan stood on the opposite side of the door, clutching his sword tightly.

They had come up with a plan. It wasn't a great plan, but they both knew there really wasn't much else they could do. Duncan had cut his finger with his dagger and smeared his blood along the cracks the Night Bears had made in the door, hoping to fuel their frenzy with the smell of fresh human blood.

They now wanted the Night Bears to succeed in breaking through the door. They wanted them to come charging into the crypt.

Elizabeth would hide as best she could while the Night Bears charged in. Duncan would strike low, going for their legs, hoping to hobble them as much as he could as fast as he could. He didn't expect to kill them outright; he just wanted to cripple them enough to give himself a fighting chance to finish them off.

Elizabeth started to say something to him, when suddenly Duncan held up his hand, motioning for her to be quiet.

She closed her mouth and froze. She looked expectantly at him, confused by his action.

"Listen," he said to her, nearly hissing out the word.

She cocked her head slightly, obeying his directive, listening.

"I don't hear them," Duncan said.

Elizabeth stood motionless for a moment longer, also hearing nothing. The Night Bears were no longer clawing and scratching at the door. They weren't even growling or snorting. The night was quiet. Elizabeth crouched down to peer through one of the cracks in the door.

"Elizabeth!" Duncan snapped, this time the word truly coming out with a hiss.

Elizabeth wasn't deterred by Duncan's sharp alarm. She continued to stare through the crack.

Outside in the inner courtyard of the castle, clearly visible in a shaft of glowing moonlight, the two Night Bears were illuminated in the night's luminescence. One of the bears was clearly smaller than the other, most likely the female Elizabeth surmised. She was tending to the larger bear's wound, licking at the larger bear's fur, doing her best to clean out the wound with her tongue. The male bear growled at the female and made a snapping movement with his jaw, but the female bear ignored his little tantrum and continued to lick at his wound, tending to her mate.

And then the larger male Night Bear moved, moving around the smaller female, moving behind her, clearly intent on mounting her. The female bear lowered herself submissively, giving her mate the access to her that he desired.

Elizabeth looked over to Duncan, staying crouched near the crack in the door. "Umm, you need to come and see this." She rose up and stepped away from the door.

Duncan looked curiously at her. He couldn't be certain, but he could've sworn he saw a blush flare up on Elizabeth's cheeks.

"It appears the male bear is showing his appreciation to the female bear for cleaning out his wound," Elizabeth said.

Duncan's frown deepened. He moved over to her and bent down to peer through the crack in the crypt's door. He put his hand on the door to balance himself, but stumbled slightly and grabbed at one of the gouges the Night Bears had put into the door to balance himself. To his surprise, the door moved, opening slightly. The Night Bears' attack had succeeded in dislodging the door. Duncan quickly stood upright, whipping the door open, and raced outside into the night, sword gripped firmly in his hand.

"Duncan!" Elizabeth cried out.

The big male Night Bear swiveled his head at the

sound of Elizabeth's cry, continuing his thrusting motions despite this pink creature charging towards him, unable to help himself.

Duncan increased his speed, gripping his sword with both hands as he neared the big beast, gritting his teeth tightly.

The male Night Bear snarled and finally reacted to this approaching threat, starting to move off of the female, but he was too late.

Duncan reached the copulating Night Bears and plunged his sword deep into the male, sinking the blade in hard and fast. It was a fortuitous blow as the blade managed to nick the male Night Bear's heart, slicing through it, causing an eruption of blood inside the great beast. The male Night Bear started to throw back his head to emit a mighty roar, but his cry choked in his throat.

Duncan leaped back, losing his grip on his sword, as the male Night Bear collapsed atop the female, pinning her to the ground with his bulk.

The female did her best to get free, writhing her body, but all four of her legs were firmly trapped beneath the male's hulking, lifeless body. She roared with rage, her jaws snapping open and closed, her lips pulled back to reveal sharp teeth on full display.

Elizabeth appeared at Duncan's side and they both stared with some disbelief at the dead beast smothering its mate. It had happened so quickly, Duncan's strike had accomplished the desired effect with amazing speed. Some of the male bear's blood oozed from its wound, dripping down to the ground. Duncan and Elizabeth stared at the widening pool of blood.

The female Night Bear continued to snarl and

gnash her teeth and writhe beneath the immovable bulk of her dead mate.

Calmly, almost eerily so, Elizabeth crouched down near the female's exposed head and stabbed her repeatedly in the neck with the dagger Duncan had given her, each strike getting more aggressive, more violent with each downward thrust of the blade. The female tried to bite at Elizabeth but Elizabeth was cautious enough to avoid the bear's sharp teeth.

Soon, the female bear stopped moving and her eyes went blank as her life drained out of her body.

Elizabeth continued to stab at the female Night Bear's neck, her fingers and hand now drenched in the sticky blood of the beast. Duncan put his hand on her wrist, gently stopping her motion. Elizabeth looked up at Duncan and he now saw the tears streaming down her face, the sadness glistening on her cheeks, the droplets shimmering in the moonlight. "It's okay, Elizabeth," he said softly. "You can stop. She's dead."

"They were... loving each other," she said, trying to prevent her voice from cracking as she spoke, but not doing a good job of it.

Duncan took her gently by the arm and raised her back up to her feet. "It was them or us. You know that."

Elizabeth nodded, the tears continuing to flow.

There was such agony in her face. Duncan felt his heart breaking at the sight of it. He lowered his face to hers and kissed her on the lips, pulling her tightly against him.

Suddenly, her legs buckled and she fell away from him. Duncan had to snatch at her forearm to prevent her from falling. He glanced down and saw that the legs of Elizabeth's shadow were nearly completely white, and the shadow of her midsection was more than half white. "We have to finish what we started," he said.

She again nodded, the tears starting to slow.

❧❦❧

Elizabeth stood naked before Duncan. Duncan had already smeared some of the beasts' blood on her face, coating her forehead, cheeks and chin with the red liquid. The Night Bears' blood was warm, thick. It had a faint metallic smell to it, just like human blood.

Duncan bent down and put his hand in the puddle of blood near the dead bears' corpses. The female Night Bear's eyes were still open, staring lifelessly at them. Neither of them wanted to go near her face, so they just left her eyes open. Duncan, his fingers and palm thoroughly coated with blood, rose back up and began smearing the blood over Elizabeth's throat, her shoulders. He reached her breasts and moved his fingers across her bosom, cupping each breast to coat it protectively with the bears' blood.

She let out a soft moan when his fingers moved across her nipples; they were hard and pointed despite her best efforts not to let their shared nakedness have an effect on her.

"Are you okay?" he asked softly. He glanced down at her shadow, seeing the white blight continuing to recede from her shadow.

"Yes," she said softly back. "Just keep going."

He moved down to her stomach, but then had to refresh the blood on his fingers before resuming. Soon, she was covered almost entirely in the blood of

323

the Night Bears. He looked down at her shadow. Only one very small portion of her shadow was white, the small area at the apex of her legs. He hesitated, staring at the hairy bush of her womanhood.

"I'll do you now," Elizabeth said.

He nodded and lowered his hands to his sides.

She bent down to reach one of the pools of blood, coating her fingers and palms just as Duncan had. She rose back up and stepped up to him, smearing her fingers across his forehead, leaving a red trail on his flesh. She glanced at his shadow, seeing the whiteness recede from his head area.

"I can already feel it working," he said. "My head feels clearer now. My thoughts aren't so foggy."

She nodded. She knew exactly what he was talking about. As he had coated her body with the Night Bears' blood, she could feel her energy returning, could feel the alarming fatigue wash away from her body. She continued to apply the blood all over Duncan's body, slowly circling him, wiping her fingers along his muscles, relishing the feeling of his muscular body beneath her fingertips. When she finished circling him, she glanced down and saw his manhood was elongated, pointing upright. She just stared at it for a moment, feeling an intense desire to just keep staring at the length of his manhood.

"Go ahead," he whispered. "Finish it."

Her fingers were nearly dry, so she dipped back down to a pool of blood and re-coated her fingers. She reached out a tentative hand and began applying the Night Bears' blood to his shaft; she gripped it and ran her fingers up and down his shaft, thoroughly coating it. He hissed as she moved her fingers over the enlarged tip of his manhood. His thickness pulsed in her hand. She finished and stepped back, looking down at his shadow. The dark form of his shadow was completely black; there was no hint of the whiteness visible anymore. "Now what?" she asked. She knew she should have felt a wave of disgust at the sight of his blood-coated body, but she felt no revulsion. None at all. She only felt a weird thrill.

"There's only one spot left," he said.

She nodded. She glanced about the area and moved to a patch of soft grass, lowering herself down to the ground on her back. She looked up at him, spreading her legs, inviting him forward.

He lowered himself over her. He balanced himself with one hand, then reached down to grip his member in the other, guiding it towards her opening. "Are you sure?" he asked.

"Go ahead," she whispered. "Finish it."

He eased into her, feeling the tightness of her gripping his member. He released his hold on his manhood and put his hand down on the ground next to her body. He slid deeper into her, moving all the way in until their bodies met. He started to thrust.

Afterwards, he held her tight while she sobbed against his shoulder. Her sobbing continued for a long while, then she pulled back away from him and looked up at him. "What are we going to do? Live like this?"

Duncan was quiet for a moment. The blood coating their bodies would eventually wear away, they both knew that. Or rain would come and it would be washed away. "I don't want to become a ghost, do you?"

She shook her head. Neither one of them was ready to die. Not yet.

"We'll have to... hunt them," he said.

She didn't react to that, not giving him a nod of acceptance nor a shake of her head in denial. She just sat quietly. "How many of them are there, do you think?" she finally asked.

"I don't know. Dozens at least. Maybe hundreds. I really don't know."

"And then what?" Elizabeth asked.

They were both quiet for a moment.

"What if..." she started to ask, then paused. "What if it's not just Night Bear blood that works?"

He was quiet for a moment. He knew immediately where her question was leading. The thought had occurred to him, but he hadn't wanted to say it aloud. "Let's hope we never have to find out."

The town crier shook his bell, the sound reverberating loud and wide. "Hear ye, hear ye! The demon lovers of Castle LongShadow walk amongst us. Bar your doors at night. They will drink your blood and drain your body dry."

Duncan pulled his cowl up over his head with his red-stained hands, further shielding his red-stained face, hiding his frown in the shadow of his cloak's hood. He scowled at the town crier's proclamation, wanting to correct the man. They didn't drink blood. They just bathed in it. What did he think they were, some kind of monsters?

Duncan reached out and took Elizabeth's red-tinged fingers into his, giving them a gentle squeeze. She squeezed reassuringly back. They both knew it was time to move on and find another new town, new people. New blood.

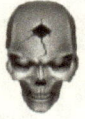

LAND OF™ FRIGHT

A NOTE FROM JACK O'DONNELL

Thanks for reading this seventh collection of my Land of Fright™ tales. I hope you continue to journey with me as we move deeper into the dark realms within the Land of Fright™. There are many new uncharted realms yet to be mapped, so keep checking back for new discoveries.

Visit www.landoffright.com and subscribe to stay up-to-date on the latest new stories in the Land of Fright™ series of horror short stories.

Or visit my author page on Amazon at www.amazon.com/author/jodonnell to see the newest releases in the Land of Fright™ series.

If you enjoy the Land of Fright™ series, please consider taking the time to leave a review. Your comments are greatly appreciated!

- JACK

Welcome to the
Land of Fright™
A World of Spine-Tingling Stories filled with the Strange, the Eerie, and the Weird

MORE LAND OF FRIGHT™ COLLECTIONS ARE AVAILABLE NOW!

Turn the page and step deeper into fear!

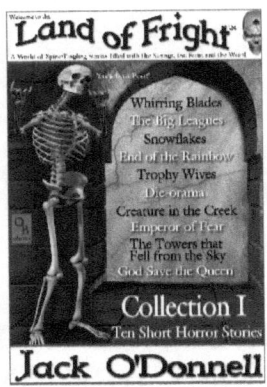

Land of Fright™ terrorstories contained in Collection I:

#1 - Whirring Blades: A simple late-night trip to the mall for a father and his son turns into a struggle for survival when they are attacked by a deadly swarm of toy helicopters.

#2 - The Big Leagues: A scorned young baseball player shows his teammates he really knows how to play ball with the best of them.

#3 - Snowflakes: In the land of Frawst, special snowflakes are a gift from the gods, capable of transferring the knowledge of the Ancients. A young woman searches the skies with breathless anticipation for her snowflake, but finds something far more dark and dangerous instead.

#4 - End of the Rainbow: In Medieval England, a warrior and his woman find the end of a massive rainbow that has filled the sky and discover the dark secret of its power.

#5 - Trophy Wives: An enigmatic sculptor meets a beautiful woman whom he vows will be his next subject. But things may not turn out the way he plans...

#6 - Die-orama: A petty thief finds out that a WWII model diorama in his local hobby shop holds much more than just plastic vehicles and plastic soldiers.

#7 - Creature in the Creek: A lonely young woman finds her favorite secluded spot inhabited by a monster from her past.

#8 - The Emperor of Fear: In ancient Rome, two coliseum workers encounter a mysterious crate containing an unearthly creature. Just in time for the next gladiator games...

#9 - The Towers That Fell From The Sky: Two analysts race to uncover the secret purpose of the giant alien towers that have thundered down out of the skies.

#10 - God Save The Queen: An exterminator piloting an ant-sized robot comes face to come with the queen of a nest he has been assigned to destroy.

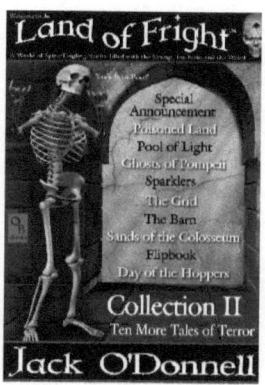

Land of Fright™ terrorstories contained in Collection II:

#11 - Special Announcement: A fraud investigator discovers the disturbing truth behind the messages on a community announcement board.

#12 - Poisoned Land: Savage hunters patrol the Poisoned Lands, demanding appeasement from the three survivors trapped in a surrounded building. How far will each one of them go to survive?

#13 - Pool of Light: A mysterious wave of dark energy from space washes over the Earth, trapping a woman and her friends in pools of light. Beyond the edges of the light, deep pockets of darkness hold much more than just empty blackness.

#14 - Ghosts of Pompeii: A woman on a tour of Italy with her son unwittingly awakens the ghosts of Pompeii.

#15 - Sparklers: A child's sparkler opens a doorway to another dimension and a father must enter it to save his family and his neighborhood from the ominous threat that lays beyond.

#16 - The Grid: An interstellar salvage crew activates a mysterious grid on an abandoned vessel floating in space, unleashing a deadly force.

#17 - The Barn: An empty barn beckons an amateur photographer to step through its dark entrance, whispering promises of a once-in-a-lifetime shoot.

#18 - Sands of the Colosseum: A businessman in Rome gets to experience the dream of a lifetime when he visits the great Colosseum — until he finds himself standing on the arena floor.

#19 - Flipbook: A man sees a dark future of his family in jeopardy when he watches the tiny animations of a flipbook play out in his hand.

#20 - Day of the Hoppers: Two boys flee for their lives when their friendly neighborhood grasshoppers turn into deadly projectiles.

Land of Fright™ terrorstories contained in Collection III:

#21 - The Prospector: In the 1800's, a lonely prospector finds the body parts of a woman as he pans for gold in the wilds of California.

#22 - The Boy In The Yearbook: Two middle-aged women are tormented by a mysterious photograph in their high school yearbook.

#23 - Shot Glass: A man discovers the shot glasses in his great-grandfather's collection can do much more than just hold a mouthful of liquor.

#24 - The Champion: An actor in a medieval renaissance re-enactment show becomes the unbeatable champion he has longed to be.

#25 - Hitler's Graveyard: American soldiers in WWII uncover a nefarious Nazi plan to resurrect their dead heroes so they can rejoin the war.

#26 - Out of Ink: Colonists on a remote planet resort to desperate measures to ward off an attack from wild alien animals.

#27 - Dung Beetles: Mutant dung beetles attack a family on a remote Pennsylvania highway. Yes, it's as disgusting as it sounds.

#28 - The Tinies: A beleaguered office worker encounters a strange alien armada in the sub-basement of his office building.

#29 - Hammer of Charon: In ancient Rome, it is the duty of a special man to make sure gravely wounded gladiators are given a quick death after a gladiator fight. He serves his position quietly with honor. Until they try to take his hammer away from him...

#30 - Pharaoh's Cat: In ancient Egypt, the pharaoh is dying. His trusted advisors want his favorite cat to be buried with him. The cat has other plans...

Land of Fright™ terrorstories contained in Collection IV:

#31 - The Throw-Aways: A washed-up writer of action-adventure thrillers is menaced by the ghosts of the characters he has created.

#32 - Everlasting Death: The souls of the newly deceased take on solid form and the Earth fills with immovable statues of death...

#33 - Bite the Bullet: In the Wild West, a desperate outlaw clings to a bullet cursed by a Gypsy... because the bullet has his name on it.

#34 - Road Rage: A senseless accident on a rural highway sets off a frightening chain of events.

#35 - The Controller: A detective investigates a bank robbery that appears to have been carried out by a zombie.

#36 - The Notebook: An enchanted notebook helps a floundering author finish her story. But the unnatural fuel that stokes the power of the mysterious writing journal leads her down a disturbing path...

#37 - The Candy Striper and the Captain: American WWII soldiers in the Philippines scare superstitious enemy soldiers with corpses they dress up to look like vampire victims. The vampire bites might be fake, but what comes out of the jungle is not...

#38 - Clothes Make the Man: A young man steals a magical suit off of a corpse, hoping some of its power will rub off on him.

#39 - Memory Market: The cryptic process of memory storage in the human brain has been decoded and now memories are bought and sold in the memory market. But with every legitimate commercial endeavor there comes a black market, and the memory market is no exception...

#40 - The Demon Who Ate Screams: A young martial artist battles a vicious demon who feeds on the tormented screams and dying whimpers of his victims.

Land of Fright™ terrorstories contained in Collection V:

#41 - The Hatchlings: A peaceful barbecue turns into an afternoon of terror for a suburban man when the charcoal briquets start to hatch!

#42 - Virgin Sacrifice: A professor of archaeology is determined to set the world right again using the ancient power of Aztec sacrifice rituals.

#43 - Smog Monsters: The heavily contaminated air in Beijing turns even deadlier when unearthly creatures form within the dense poison of its thick pollution.

#44 - Benders of Space-Time: A young interstellar traveler discovers the uncomfortable truth about the Benders, the creatures who power starships with their ability to fold space-time.

#45 - The Picture: A young soldier in World War II shows his fellow soldiers a picture of his beautiful fiancé during the lulls in battle. But this seemingly harmless gesture is far from innocent...

#46 - Black Ice: A vicious dragon is offered a great gift — a block of black ice to soothe the fire that burns its throat and roars in its belly. Too bad the dragon has never heard of a Trojan dwarf...

#47 - Artist Alley: At a comic book convention, a seedy comic book publisher sees himself depicted in a disturbing series of artist drawings.

#48 - Dead Zone: A yacht gets caught adrift in the dead zone in the Gulf of Mexico, trapped in an area of the sea that contains no life. What comes aboard the yacht from the depths of this dead zone in search of food cannot really be considered alive...

#49 - Cemetery Dance: A suicidal madman afraid to take his own life attempts to torment a devout Christian man into killing him.

#50 - The King Who Owned the World: A bored barbarian king demands he be brought a new challenger. But who can you find to battle a king who owns the world

336

Land of Fright™ terrorstories contained in Collection VI:

#51 - Zombie Carnival: Two couples stumble upon a zombie-themed carnival and decide to join the fun.

#52 - Going Green: Drug runners trying to double cross their boss get a taste of strong voodoo magic.

#53 - Message In A Bottle: A bottle floats onto the beach of a private secluded island with an unnerving message trapped inside.

#54 - The Chase: In 18th century England, a desperate chase is on as a monstrous beast charges after a fleeing wagon, a wagon occupied by too many people...

#55 - Who's Your Daddy?: A lonely schoolteacher is disturbed by how much all of the students in her class look alike. A visit by a mysterious man sheds some light on the curious situation.

#56 - Beheaded: In 14th century England, a daughter vows revenge upon those who beheaded her father. She partners with a lascivious young warlock to restore her family's honor.

#57 - Hold Your Breath: A divorced mother of one confronts the horrible truth behind the myth of holding one's breath when driving past a cemetery.

#58 - Viral: What makes a civilization fall? Volcanoes, earthquakes, or other forces of nature? Barbarous invasions or assaults from hostile forces? Decline from within due to decadence and moral decay? Or could it be something more insidious?

#59 - Top Secret: A special forces agent confronts the villainous characters from his past, but discovers something even more dangerous.

#60 - Immortals Must Die: There is no more life force left in the universe. The attainment of immortality has depleted the world of available souls. So what do you do if you are desperate to have a child?

AND LOOK FOR EVEN MORE
LAND OF FRIGHT™ STORIES
COMING SOON!

THANKS AGAIN FOR READING.

Visit www.landoffright.com

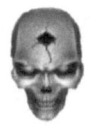

Also by Jack O'Donnell

The Spine-Tinglers™ series

I don't know who I am, or where I came from. All I know is that I can see things and hear things. I have no physical presence, yet I am somehow able to travel through space and time and witness untold events happening all around me. I suppose some of you will label me as a ghost, but that's not truly accurate as I have no recollection of ever being alive, no childhood memories, no remembrances of any traumatic life events that might be keeping me trapped in this world. Nor do I feel as if I am a manifestation of a dead person. I leave no shadowy trace. I am shapeless, formless. Don't get me wrong. Ghosts do exist, as I have seen them. I am just not one of them.

I seem to be drawn to those events that have a sinister side to them, a darkness. Perhaps it is my mission to shine some light on that darkness, to reveal the truth that is hidden in those dusky shadows. Perhaps I am here to warn you of what really exists in the world around you, make you a little more aware of the mysteries that often hide shrouded in the bliss of ignorance. I don't really know. All I know is that I am compelled to chronicle what I have observed, what I have heard, what I have felt, and share those experiences with you.

Here are the latest stories I felt compelled to chronicle...

The Scarecrow - Spine-Tinglers™ #1
Beware what grows in the corn!

Hideous monsters borne of the blood of the Civil War follow the commands of a demonic scarecrow bent on preserving the sanctity of her crop.

Metamorphosis - Spine-Tinglers™ #2
Beware what lurks in Nektala's Tomb!

Archaeologists unearth the tomb of a mysterious Egyptian ruler and unwittingly discover a secret that threatens to transform all of humanity.

Black Woods

The Black Woods contain darkly gnarled trees born from the seeds of sorcery, strange plants given unnatural life from the fertilizing spread of decaying magic, abnormal soil deeply contaminated with the residue of the Alchemy Wars from decades long past. Pockets of Black Woods have sprouted all over the world of Teradynea in isolated growths of midnight-black trees, most of these unexplored parcels of poisoned land still shrouded in secrecy. The tainted flora and fauna that sprout and flourish within these areas of permanent shadow contain mysterious powers that can be harvested and gathered for good. Or for evil.

What secrets do the Black Woods hold? Rin and his friend Joktala will soon discover that the Black Woods contain a hidden danger far more perilous than any they could have ever imagined...

ABOUT JACK O'DONNELL

I grew up on Jack Kirby comics, Creature Features, Godzilla movies, Stephen King, Andre Norton, Edgar Rice Burroughs, Don Pendleton's Executioner series, and a smorgasbord of science fiction and fantasy books.

I'm the co-producer and co-screenwriter of Stephen King's The Night Flier, based on Stephen King's story.

Visit my author page on Amazon at: www.amazon.com/Jack-ODonnell/e/B00P43NP00.

Please also visit the ODONNELL BOOKS bookstore on Amazon to see all of the other books published by ODONNELL BOOKS available at: www.amazon.com/odonnellbooks.

You can follow me on Goodreads here:
www.goodreads.com/author/show/1560457.Jack_O_Donnell

You can follow me on BookBub here:
www.bookbub.com/authors/jack-o-donnell-9334cc27-b5c3-4db4-a352-c14296da563b

Again, if you enjoyed this book, or any of my other works, please take the time to leave a review. Your feedback is greatly appreciated!

Thanks for reading!